The
INCORRIGIBLE CHILDREN
of
ASHTON PLACE

Book 5: *The* UNMAPPED SEA

Also by Maryrose Wood

THE INCORRIGIBLE CHILDREN OF ASHTON PLACE

The
UNMAPPED
SEA

by MARYROSE WOOD

illustrated by ELIZA WHEELER

BALZER + BRAY
An Imprint of HarperCollins*Publishers*

Balzer + Bray is an imprint of HarperCollins Publishers.

The Incorrigible Children of Ashton Place Book 5: The Unmapped Sea
Text copyright © 2015 by Maryrose Wood
Illustrations copyright © 2015 by Eliza Wheeler

ISBN 978-0-06-211041-1

Typography by Sarah Hoy
15 16 17 18 19   CG/RRDH   10 9 8 7 6 5 4 3 2 1

First Edition

For Donna Bray,
the incorrigibly devoted editor of these books

THE FIRST CHAPTER

The family tree in winter.

"IT IS NOT INFLUENZA. NOR is it dropsy, nor the vapors." The doctor gave Lady Constance Ashton a sour look. "And it is certainly not the chicken pox. Thank goodness! A disgusting illness, in my opinion. All that itching and scratching."

His full name was Dr. Charles Veltschmerz. He was a morose and irritable man, not at all the sort of person one would expect to spend his days caring for the sick. His gruff speech and lack of sympathy made his patients feel far worse than they did before; consequently, they put on brave faces and made heroic efforts to rise from their sickbeds, so as to never have to see the unpleasant doctor again. Naturally, these miraculous cures were attributed to the skill of Dr. Veltschmerz. His reputation grew until he was considered the finest physician in the county.

Barring unexpected illness, we too are unlikely to have a second encounter with Dr. Veltschmerz. In fact, we will do our best to avoid it, and the less said about him, the better. We need not reveal his favorite food (bread pudding) or his preferred style of dancing (oddly enough, the polka, a surprisingly cheerful step for a man so grim). The secret nickname he gave his most beloved childhood toy is completely irrelevant to our tale. (Honey Hee-Haw, the stuffed donkey, was little Charlie's bosom companion for more years than he would care to admit, and even accompanied him to medical school, a fact that has not been publicly disclosed until now.)

No; none of these details about Dr. Veltschmerz are remotely worth mentioning, and you should erase them from your minds at once. What is important is that *weltschmerz* is an actual word whose meaning all well-educated people ought to know. (As the polyglots among you are doubtless already aware, the German *weltschmerz* is pronounced "Veltschmerz," and it means—but more on that topic later. Lady Constance has yet to hear her diagnosis, and patience was never one of her virtues.)

A pathetic cry rose from the fainting couch in the front parlor of Ashton Place. Dr. Veltschmerz frowned and arranged his stethoscope around his neck. "Lady Ashton, need I remind you? You are with child. An intruder grows within your womb, and it cares not one whit about your discomfort. The monster is far too busy kicking its tiny, vicious feet and pummeling away with those miniature yet brutal fists. With your permission . . ." He pressed the stethoscope to the lady's heart and listened. "Mother's heartbeat, strong as an ox. Your indigestion, fatigue, backache, and other miseries are all because of this curséd parasite of a baby."

"I could hardly feel worse if I had eaten an ox." Lady Constance leaned back on the couch with operatic weariness. "I am hungry all the time, yet taking a single bite is enough to make me seasick. How much longer am I expected to bear this horrible ordeal?"

"Until spring, when the baby comes. Then you'll have new and worse ordeals to complain about!" Dr. Veltschmerz spoke in a jolly tone, as if he were pleased by this fact.

"Spring? But it is only January!" Lady Constance

"Ten moons!" Lady Constance began to weep,
and count, but mostly weep.

tried to sit up and failed, until Mrs. Clarke, the head housekeeper of Ashton Place, gave a helpful boost from behind. "Dr. Veltschmerz, I insist that you—*ugh!*—do something."

At this the doctor laughed—imagine, a doctor laughing at his own patient! "Get used to suffering, that's my advice. Human babies take ten moons to grow properly, and this one will be no exception."

"Ten moons!" Lady Constance began to weep, and count, but mostly weep. "Moon, moon, moon, moon, moon . . ."

Mrs. Clarke dabbed away the lady's tears with a clean pocket handkerchief, an item that no well-brought-up person ought ever be without. "There, there, my lady," the kind housekeeper said, with a warning look to the doctor. "Many a woman's been with child before, else none of us would have been born to grow up and complain about our aches and pains, would we? They all managed it somehow, and you will, too, and a sweet little baby makes it all worthwhile in the end. I'm sure that's what the doctor meant to say."

Dr. Veltschmerz checked his watch. "I will waste no more time at Ashton Place. The lady is perfectly well, and my job is to treat the sick." To Mrs. Clarke he added, "Your mistress is strong of constitution but weak of spirit. Tell her to buck up and stop complaining. No need to call me again until the baby comes."

Mrs. Clarke opened her mouth to speak, but closed it again at once. For her (or anyone else) to tell Lady Constance Ashton to "buck up and stop complaining" was not likely to be well received, and she was only the head housekeeper, after all.

"Very good, sir," she mumbled, and went to get his coat and hat from the closet.

"O, endless moons of misery!" Lady Constance cried. "Has the medical profession come to this? Will no one help me? Woe, woe, and more woe! I am alone, adrift, abandoned in my hour of need! I hope you are writing all this down, Miss Lumley. Otherwise, no one is likely to believe my tale of abuse. The horror! The cruelty! The injustice!"

And so you see: Miss Penelope Lumley was also present during this unhappy scene. Miss Lumley was the governess at Ashton Place. Her job was to care for the three wards of Lord Fredrick Ashton, otherwise known as the Incorrigible children. However, because of her exceptionally neat handwriting, she had been summoned from the nursery the moment the doctor arrived and told to copy down whatever instructions he might give for the care of Lady Constance. So far she had not written anything but *strong as an ox.* Near these words she had doodled a four-legged creature that looked rather more like an elk than an ox, but as she had no model to draw from, it was the best she could manage.

She had also doodled ten moons in various phases: full, waning, waxing, gibbous, crescent, and so on. The new moon was hardest to draw, since it cannot be seen, but she got around that by drawing an empty box and writing a caption beneath it that read *new moon (invisible).*

"As you wish, my lady," she answered, and hastily wrote *Dr. V says stop complaining, worse ordeals in store.* Penelope enjoyed both writing and doodling as a rule, but she was not pleased to be stuck in the parlor taking notes. For one thing, it meant that the Incorrigible children were upstairs in the nursery with no one to supervise them but their pet squirrel, Nutsawoo. There was no question that the squirrel was alert; most squirrels are so perpetually nervous that they notice threats both real and imaginary, and sometimes bolt for no reason at all. However, the bushy-tailed rodent did not possess much in the way of judgment, and was therefore not an ideal babysitter.

Penelope doodled an unhappy face inside one of

her full moons. "As a proud graduate of the Swanburne Academy for Poor Bright Females, I know that a bit of pluck, optimism, and good common sense are more than enough to manage most situations perfectly well," she thought. Now the moon looked strikingly like Dr. Veltschmerz, especially once she added a frown and two gloomy, down-slanting eyebrows. "Yet I do sometimes wish that storybook magic were real. Why, if I had a magic lamp with one of those wish-giving genies inside, I would use one entire wish just to get rid of this depressing doctor! Why on earth would a person like him enter the medical profession to begin with? Instead he ought to have become . . ."

But kindhearted as she was, Penelope could not think of a position in which being grouchy and unfeeling were actual job qualifications. (Here Penelope's youth and inexperience were in evidence. Hard-hearted people may be no fun to sit next to at parties, but they are just as entitled to earn a living as the rest of us. Fortunately—for them, at least—the need for insurance adjusters, tax collectors, theater critics, and the like continues unchecked to this very day.)

"The insensitivity! The lack of human compassion!" Even in her weak condition, Lady Constance somehow found the strength to express her feelings at high volume. "The misfortune! The misery! The . . . whatever is worse than misery!"

Dr. Veltschmerz latched up his medical bag and retrieved his hat from the waiting hands of Mrs. Clarke. "Lady Ashton, your caterwauling pains my ears. I shall have to call for my own services soon if you do not gain control of yourself! Of course, there is one thing that might improve your health, if not your disposition, but it would be a considerable expense," he said, as an afterthought. "I will talk it over with your husband, if he is at home."

At the word "expense," Lady Constance brightened. "Oh, please do! Fredrick will agree to any expense for my sake, of that I am sure."

"Poor fellow!" was all that the disagreeable doctor said, and took his leave.

THE MOMENT DR. VELTSCHMERZ WAS gone, Lady Constance sat up on the sofa and cheerfully demanded luncheon. Despite the lady's complaints, Penelope thought she looked quite well. Her cheeks were plump and pink, her complexion glowed, and her middle— well, it was not quite as round as it would be, come springtime. But she was halfway into her pregnancy, and somehow the fullness of her face and figure made

9

her seem less like a doll-like, spoiled young lady of great wealth and little sense, but someone rather more sturdy and robust.

Penelope found it a marked improvement. She only wished the lady's flights of dramatic behavior would alter to match her new, more earthbound physique. But poor Lady Constance was so used to making a fuss, it seemed she could hardly bring herself to stop, even when things were going her way.

"It is a reminder that one ought to choose one's actions carefully, for any sort of behavior can turn into a habit if one repeats it often enough," Penelope thought. "As Agatha Swanburne once said, 'It is harder to break one bad habit than it is to forge ten good ones.' That is a lesson worth sharing with the children—if ever I make my escape from this room, that is!" (Agatha Swanburne was the founder of the Swanburne Academy. Her countless pithy sayings were at the heart of Penelope's education there, but one need not be poor, bright, or female to benefit from the wise lady's advice.

Mrs. Clarke rang the bell to summon food, but Lady Constance could not wait. She declared herself to be "absolutely ravenous" and gestured for Margaret to approach. Margaret was a high-strung girl with a high-pitched voice; even kind doctors made her nervous, and Dr. Veltschmerz had rendered her mute with fear. Now he was gone, but the young housemaid's hands still trembled. She held a silver tray that bore a plate of thin, plain wafers and several boxes of chocolates.

Obediently she stepped nearer, so that Lady Constance might examine the contents of the tray. After a moment's consideration, the lady swept the food into her lap and gobbled as she spoke. "I wonder what the doctor will have Fredrick buy for me? I am sure it will do me a world of good. A lavish purchase is bound to improve any situation, in my experience. But Mrs. Clarke, what did Dr. Veltschmerz mean when he said 'new and worse ordeals' were in store for me? Surely he was joking!"

Mrs. Clarke blushed, which was not something she often did. "I believe he was referring to when the baby comes, my lady," she said cautiously. "The birth of a child often has some . . . discomfort . . . involved."

With a fistful of chocolates melting in one hand, Lady Constance used the other to stuff her mouth with wafers. "Nonsense—pardon my crumbs. What could be uncomfortable about a baby? They are small and soft, like pillows, and if I tire of holding it, I will simply give it to Margaret to carry."

Mrs. Clarke folded her arms across her mighty

bosom. "My lady, you do know how the baby is born, do you not?"

Lady Constance's mouth was so full she could barely speak. "Why, that is the doctor's business! I am sure it is none of my concern."

"Dearie me! It's not quite as simple as all that." Mrs. Clarke glanced at Margaret, who had only narrowly avoided dropping her tray. "Well! We'll have to have a bit of a talk about it . . . later."

"But I wish to know *now*. Truthfully, Mrs. Clarke— and don't think I don't see you there, too, Margaret, your eyes round as crumpets!—the looks on both of your faces make me uneasy! You must tell me every- thing there is to know about having babies this second, or I shall be even more upset than I already am. And surely that would not be good for the child." Her head whipped in Penelope's direction. "Miss Lumley, the doctor is gone. There is no need for you to continue writing down my every word. Unless *you* would like to explain his meaning?"

Penelope covered the page with her arm so that no one could see her pictures of Moon-Faced Veltschmerz, as she had just named him in a caption. (It was rude to write such a thing, and perhaps she ought not to have done so, but it must be said that her penmanship was beyond reproach.) "Mrs. Clarke is a woman of great maturity and experience, my lady. I am quite sure it is best if she were the one to illuminate the subject for you." She stood and bobbed a quick curtsy. "With your permission, I will leave you to discuss the matter in private."

Mrs. Clarke gave her a wild, pleading look, but Penelope was already at the door. She knew quite well how babies got out of their mothers, for she had assisted the Swanburne veterinarian at the birthing of lambs and calves since she was a little girl. Still, she hardly felt it was her place to discuss the matter with Lady Constance. That kind of information was best learned from a grown-up and thoroughly trustworthy person, and Mrs. Clarke was nothing if not that.

"NUTSAWOO, HOLD STILL!" CASSIOPEIA INCORRIGIBLE, the youngest of the three Incorrigible children, was in the midst of painting a portrait, and she was having a devil of a time getting her subject to pose properly. "No twitching, no nibbling, no scampering, please!"

The nursery smelled like oil paint, turpentine, and ponies (this last aroma was due to the horsehair paintbrushes the children used). All three young artists stood before their easels. All three had been attempting to paint the same model, which is to say, Nutsawoo. All three had remarked, ruefully and more than once, that they now understood why there are so few portraits of squirrels hanging in the great museums of the world, for the job of an artist's model is to hold still, and this is something the average squirrel finds exceedingly difficult to do. Even as Cassiopeia scolded him, the restless rodent dashed to the window, which was closed against the frigid winter air. He wrung his paws pleadingly to be let out, while those nervous, beady eyes gazed with longing at the snow-covered elm branches just outside.

It is a common misconception that squirrels hibernate during the winter. They do not, but there is little for them to do in the cold weather, and so they stay in their treetop homes, cuddled up with their squirrel friends for warmth and living on the nuts and seeds they so frantically hoarded in the warmer months. Only a highly unusual squirrel, half tamed with cooing words, gentle head scratches, and the frequent offering of treats, could be persuaded to leave a cozy wintertime nest and come skittering indoors through a nursery window to pose for a portrait in oils. Nutsawoo was just such a creature, but he was still a squirrel, and his walnut-sized brain had no room for patience, never mind an appreciation for art.

This was no reflection on the talent or dedication of the artists, of course. The children liked to look at art, and they liked making paintings. They had become quite skilled at it, too, for Penelope considered art an essential part of their education, as it had been of hers. (Some of you may already be familiar with the excellent paper she once wrote on Ominous Landscapes for her art history class at Swanburne. Less successful was her attempt to re-create the pottery of ancient Greece. Making pottery is a messy business, involving buckets of muddy clay, rapidly spinning wheels, and special ovens called kilns that bake at fiendishly hot temperatures. As befalls many beginning potters, Penelope's first effort was lumpy and off-center, and developed a large crack while in the kiln. However, as Agatha Swanburne once said, "To do something familiar and succeed is no surprise. But to try something new and fail—why, that is the start of an adventure!")

In just this bold and Swanburnian spirit, each of the three children had resolved to paint Nutsawoo's portrait in a different style. Alexander, the eldest, had taken a classical approach, and depicted Nutsawoo draped in a toga, as people wore in the long-ago days of the Roman Empire. That proud fuzzy head gazed out upon a view of the Colosseum, a wreath of bay laurel perched on teeny-tiny ears. Long, thoughtfully splayed whiskers gave the twitchy creature a philosophical expression; one upraised paw held a gilded acorn. The acorn, Alexander explained, was symbolic. His siblings nodded sagely at that.

Beowulf, a few years younger and possessed of a true artistic temperament, chose a more experimental style. His portrait was made of countless small dabs of color— not plain russet browns and grays, but bright, unmixed tints never before seen on any squirrel in the whole long history of squirrels. Up close, one only saw the dots, but as the viewer stepped back, the image of the squirrel came thrillingly into view. (Beowulf had no way of knowing this, of course, but some decades later this exact style would be taken up by a small but influential group of painters, mostly in France. They were called the Pointillists, and their dot-filled paintings hang in museums to this very day. Bear in mind that one does not have to be a Pointillist, or even French, to make attractive pictures out of colored dots. If paint is scarce, small, brightly colored candies will do in a pinch, assuming one has the discipline not to devour one's work while creating it. Art is a perfectly nutritious thing to consume, but candy is best eaten in moderation.)

As the youngest Incorrigible, Cassiopeia may have known less about art than her brothers, but she knew what she liked, and what she liked was excitement and adventure, and a touch of spookiness, too. She had placed a large and fierce-looking Nutsawoo in what could only be called an Ominous Landscape—a murky grotto festooned with moss, with half-hidden figures lurking in the shadows and storm clouds swirling through a gunmetal sky. Nutsawoo stood in the middle, barrel-chested, with bulging biceps and fat squirrel cheeks pulled back in a toothy snarl, and all around him was fog and mist and yellow glints of danger, like eyes peeking out of the unseen cave depths.

The real Nutsawoo was unimpressed with these imaginative portrayals. The squirrel wanted out, and the moment Cassiopeia cracked open the window he bolted through, bouncing his way to the ground on snow-laden branches that spilled their frozen burdens in his wake. Hunks of wet snow thudded silently into the snowbanks below, and the reluctant model's tiny paw prints soon disappeared in the blowing drifts.

"WELL, THAT WAS QUITE AN adventure!" Penelope burst into the nursery breathless, for she had bounded up the two flights of stairs from the parlor just as Nutsawoo was bouncing his way down the elm branches. "The doctor was the most unpleasant man you could imagine. And poor Lady Constance! To think that she will soon be having a baby of her very own, and yet seems to have no idea whatsoever—" She stopped, for she did not wish to make the children overly curious about Lady Constance's personal affairs. "Never mind all that. How are the portraits coming along?"

Alas, the painters were in a funk. The loss of their model had made their creative energies pull up short, like a pony shying from a jump, and now three potential masterpieces lay unfinished. Even if Nutsawoo came back, it would be of no use, for the mad rush of inspiration had fizzled. The usually energetic children lay draped over the furniture, limp as empty coats.

Penelope sniffed. "It smells like painting in here, at least. Surely you have made some progress?"

The Incorrigibles heaved long, morose sighs and shook their heads. They were stuck, sunk in a quicksand of gloom. Optimism had become its opposite. The very notion that art mattered, or that squirrels mattered, seemed laughable.

In short, they had *weltschmerz*.

"Eureka!" you may well cry. "So that is what *weltschmerz* means! Why, it is nothing more than the grumpy feeling one gets when a pleasant task is interrupted." If only it were so simple. *Weltschmerz* is not the frustration and despair of dropping an ice-cream cone to the hot August sidewalk after taking but a single lick. Nor is it the pang of disappointment one feels after tearing open an attractively wrapped present, only to find it is something hideous: a sweater so itchy it might as well have been knitted from poison ivy, for example, or one of those dreadful "educational" toys that teach only how difficult it is to properly insert batteries. The fact that one must still write a courteous thank-you note despite the wretchedness of the gift only makes the suffering worse, but that, too, is not *weltschmerz*.

Snow globes that slip and shatter, best friends who move to faraway towns, birthday parties missed because of an ill-timed case of pinkeye—such misfortunes, difficulties, and losses are part of life. This is why sensible people always carry a clean pocket handkerchief: One never knows when a few well-earned tears may need to be shed. But *weltschmerz* is another kind of misery altogether. To the *weltschmerz* stricken, disappointment itself seems a disappointment. They care nothing for snow globes or parties. They are too busy bemoaning the difficulty of making good art in an imperfect world, and are often found writing melancholy poetry to mourn the tragedy of it all.

(Interestingly, the French also have a word that means a painfully bad mood. They call it *ennui. Ennui* means you have grown weary of the world. How someone could grow weary of living in France is another question altogether; the cheese is beyond compare and so are the sweets, especially those involving *chocolat*–but that topic, like so many others, is best saved for later.)

"You must have done something while I was downstairs," Penelope said, mystified by the children's behavior. "May I look?"

The trio of artists groaned and slumped, and gestured wanly in the direction of their easels. Penelope examined the paintings, one by one.

"These are marvelous, and so different from one another!" she exclaimed. "They simply need to be finished. If you have run out of pep, you can easily complete them tomorrow. There is no need to be discouraged. Rome was not built in a day, you know," she added, for Alexander's painting had put her in mind of this old but still true saying.

Beowulf, ever the most sensitive of the three, slid bonelessly to the floor. He landed with a thud, and lay there helpless as a sack of flour.

"No finishing," he moaned. "No squirrel! And thus, no art."

"Nutsawoo ran away," Alexander explained. "Now we have no model."

"And no hope!" Cassiopeia pressed her hands to her temples and let her eyes roll up in their sockets. It was quite a dramatic gesture, worthy of a stage performance on the West End.

"Being an artists' model is no job for the twitchy. But surely you know what a squirrel looks like by now," Penelope reasoned. "They are all more or less alike, save the color."

Whether a squirrel would agree that squirrels were all more or less alike was a topic for debate, but there was no opportunity to discuss it just then, for a strange noise pierced the air. It was not a howling sound, exactly, but certainly howling-like: a high-pitched wail of shock and dismay.

"Lord Fredrick?" the children asked, then frowned, for it did not sound like him. Nor did they need an almanac to tell them the moon was not full. The waning crescent was clearly visible out the nursery window, perched like a rocking horse on the bare branches of the elm.

"I fear it is Lady Constance." Her way blocked by

the easels, Penelope climbed over the armchair so she might listen at the door. "Remember, children. We do not discuss Lord Fredrick's howling with anyone. It is a private matter, and we are obliged to respect that." (As only a very few people knew, Lord Fredrick's urge to howl during the full moon was the result of a curse placed on his family several generations before, when his great-grandfather, the admiral, was shipwreck'd on a cannibal-infested island named Ahwoo-Ahwoo . . . well, it is a long story, as you might imagine.)

"Oh, woe! Ohhhhh, oh, woe!" Again the tragic sound came. Penelope flinched. If Lady Constance felt in need of a more in-depth biology lesson after her conversation with Mrs. Clarke, Penelope would be the logical person to provide it, given that she was the only professional educator in the household. Once more she pressed her ear to the door. To her great relief, she heard no one approach.

"Does Lady howl, too?" Cassiopeia asked with hope. The Incorrigibles were expert howlers themselves, although not because of a curse. They came by it quite naturally, for the three siblings had been raised by wolves, until the day Lord Fredrick had found them running wild in the vast forests of Ashton Place. Thanks to their own efforts, and the skill and patience of their governess, they had since learned to temper their canine ways. However, small, tasty-looking animals did sometimes set them off, especially if it was near suppertime, and little wolfish *ahwoos* continued to pepper their speech. To be frank, they also liked talking that way, as most children would, and saw no urgent reason to stop.

"Maybe Mrs. Clarke will howl next?" Beowulf impishly proposed.

"Or Margaret?" Cassiopeia attempted a high, squeaky howl of the sort Margaret would be likely to emit. Even Penelope had to chuckle at that.

"Or Cook." Alexander attempted a full-bodied sort of howl that seemed just right for Cook.

"Or Jasper!" Jasper was a young manservant in the house, and a special friend of Margaret's. His howls, as performed by Beowulf, were quite manly and romantic, and made a comical duet with the squeaky Margaret howls that Cassiopeia offered in return.

"Or Old Timothy." Alexander imitated the enigmatic coachman's rolling, bow-legged walk. All three children tried to howl in the way they imagined the strange old fellow might, low and gruff and full of mystery.

Cassiopeia was so full of mirth she could barely

speak. "Or . . . or . . . or Lum*ahwooooo!*"

That did it. The mere thought of their governess howling made the children helpless with laughter. All three were soon reaching for their pocket handkerchiefs, as tears of merriment streamed down their cheeks.

Penelope held back a smile. "Lady Constance does not howl, at least that I know of. However, I believe she may just have had . . . well, let us call it a rude awakening. . . ."

But the dream of a happily howling household had caused Beowulf to have an epiphany of his own. "Let us paint family portraits—of everyone!" he suggested, and the sheer perfection of this idea was enough to send the children racing back to their easels. The Nutsawoo portraits were laid carefully to the side, to be finished at a future date. Fresh canvases were found. Beowulf chewed thoughtfully on the end of his paintbrush, always a sign that his muse was speaking to him.

"So many family portraits to paint," he murmured. "Nutsawoo and Lady Constance . . ."

"Lord Fredrick and Mrs. Clarke," Alexander agreed.

"Margaret . . . Jasper . . . Old Timothy . . . Simawoo . . ." This last was their nickname for Simon Harley-Dickinson, an especially well-liked friend of theirs and, more to the point, of Penelope's.

"Mama Woof and the other woofs." These were the wolves that had tended the children during their early years in the forest. They were very large, very fierce, and frankly, very unusual wolves.

"Bertha the ostrich!" Bertha had been left at Ashton Place by a visitor. Although not as clever as Nutsawoo, the tall, flightless, yet astonishingly speedy bird was a favorite of the children's, who liked to go on wild ostrich rides when Bertha was in the mood to race.

"Surely not all of these people—and wolves, and rodents, and birds, and what have you—belong in a gallery of family portraits," Penelope protested. "We shall soon run out of walls to hang them!" But then she stopped herself. "Yet it is better to have too many relatives than too few," she murmured, too low and too sad for anyone but herself to hear.

The list grew and grew: Miss Charlotte Mortimer, the headmistress of the Swanburne Academy. Madame Ionesco, a soothsayer who, in addition to being able to see Beyond the Veil, also baked tasty Gypsy cakes, which the children liked very much. They even thought of Lord Fredrick's mother, the Widow Ashton, who had been kind to them the one time she had visited Ashton Place.

Now that the children's good cheer had been restored, obstacles melted like snow in springtime, and everything seemed possible. But as you may have noticed, their unshakable conviction that nearly everyone they had ever met deserved a spot on the Incorrigible family tree had cast a shadow of gloom over their governess, who even now was reaching for her own pocket handkerchief. It was not *weltschmerz*, exactly, for she was sad for a particular reason, which was this: For as long as she could remember, her own family tree had been as bare as the elm that even now stood cold and leafless outside the nursery window.

She had parents, of course. If not (as Mrs. Clarke had earlier observed), Penelope could never have been born to grow up to miss them so. Now, at the ripe old age of sixteen, she asked herself daily: What had become of the Long-Lost Lumleys after they dropped her off at the Swanburne Academy, so many years ago? And why had they stayed absent and silent for so long? And what about the Incorrigible children's missing parents, and the strange curse upon the Ashtons, the roots of which were somehow buried in that family's genealogy? (This she had learned from Edward Ashton himself, and a most unpleasant man he was—but more about him later.)

"One could plant a whole forest of mystery out of all these family trees, for there are question marks hanging on every branch," she thought. "If only finding one's true family was as simple as painting pictures and hanging them on the walls!"

To the Incorrigibles, of course, it was. They were still calling out names as they retied their smocks around their waists and readied themselves to paint.

"Agatha Swanburne!"

"Queen Victoria!" The children had never met either of these ladies in person, as Agatha Swanburne was long dead and Queen Victoria was busy being queen of the realm, but that hardly seemed to matter.

"Don't forget Incorrigibles!" Beowulf said. The thought of painting one another amused them greatly, and they struck many hilarious poses.

"Incorrigibles—and Lumawoo, too," Cassiopeia added.

"Lumawoo! Lumawoo!" her brothers agreed. "First we paint Lumawoo."

Laughing and determined, they led their governess to where the light seemed best. They debated about how she should pose, and what style of painting would suit her. In the end, they decided to show her in the nursery, in the comfortable chair where she often sat to read poems and stories to them. On the wall behind her, they would add the portrait of Agatha Swanburne that hung in Miss Mortimer's office at the Swanburne Academy for Poor Bright Females. This way, they reasoned, they would make a painting of a portrait and a portrait of a painting, all at the same time.

The portrait could not pose for them, of course, but the children remembered its subject well: a young Agatha wearing an impish, amused expression, with eyes as sea green as Cassiopeia's, and smooth, vividly auburn-colored hair. It was a striking shade, quite like that of the children's hair, and Penelope's, too, as it so happened.

Obediently, the young governess posed with her favorite book of poetry in her lap, one hand resting on the cover. "'I wander through the meadows green/ Made happy by the verdant scene,'" she recited softly. These were the first lines of "Wanderlust," her favorite of the poems. Miss Mortimer had given her the book as a gift, many years earlier. It was a collection of melancholy German poetry in translation, and Penelope had read it cover to cover more times than she could count.

Perhaps it was the poem that soothed her lonely heart, or the thought of her kind headmistress, or the good cheer of the Incorrigibles as they dipped their pony-scented paintbrushes into the paint, but her gloom left her all at once, like a flock of sparrows taking flight. Now she too found herself with an impish smile playing on her lips.

She turned her face toward the window, to better catch the light. "The Long-Lost Lumleys are bound to turn up someday," she thought, "and as for the other mysteries, I am quite sure they can be solved as well, with a bit of effort and pluck."

Naturally she thought so; after all, she was a Swanburne girl, through and through. Yet as Agatha Swanburne herself once cautioned, "Things are rarely as complicated, or as simple, as they seem."

The Second Chapter

*There is an unfortunate
misunderstanding.*

The unpleasant doctor's recommendation to improve Lady Constance's health was not revealed right away—at least, not to her. It so happened that one of the household butlers had delivered a fresh box of cigars to Lord Fredrick's study at the very moment that Dr. Veltschmerz had come by to discuss the matter, and had thus overheard their entire conversation.

If only the butler had gone more often to the theater! If he had, he would have known that eavesdropping leads only to humiliating discoveries and unfortunate misunderstandings (comedies), or people being run through with swords while cowering behind the drapes (tragedies). But the poor fellow had not had that luxury, and now he wasted no time in telling the other butlers all that he thought he had learned. They in turn told the housemaids, who told the scullery maids, who told the stable boys, and on it went. Soon the whole estate was in a hushed frenzy of anticipation.

"The sea!" the staff whispered eagerly among themselves. "The doctor says Lady Constance must travel to the sea! I wonder which of us will be lucky enough to go?"

It was terribly exciting, for a trip to the sea in January could mean only one thing: a luxurious ocean voyage of some sort, most likely to southern Europe, but someplace warm and lovely in any case. Some of the servants hoped for the French seaside, and argued the merits of various resorts they had seen on picture postcards or heard about from their fellow servants at other estates. The weather in Deauville would be cool in January, but there was always Biarritz, near sunny Spain. And Nice would be divine, nestled on the curving coast of the blue-green Mediterranean Sea.

Others preferred the Italian Riviera, although

whether the seafood was better in San Remo or Portofino was a matter of opinion. And if the goal was to bring Lady Constance to the water, why not a more exotic destination? A cruise down the Nile was all the rage among the adventurous English of Miss Lumley's day. Great wooden sailing ships called *dahabiyyas* were devoted to this very purpose, taking wealthy travelers for a pleasant sail south from the pyramids of Cairo to the great temples and tombs of Luxor, then back again.

But as is nearly always the case with gossip, the true facts were quickly overrun by the made-up ones until it was impossible to tell them apart. It took three days for the ship of rumor to circumnavigate its way back to Lord Fredrick, when the tailor politely inquired if his lordship would prefer his new bathing costume to have navy-blue stripes, or black.

"Italy? The Riviera? Poppycock!" Lord Fredrick exclaimed, once he was made to understand why a new bathing costume had been ordered. "England is an island nation, what? Perfectly good beaches all around. So what if it's January? Brisk temperatures and the invigorating salt air! That's what the doctor says Constance needs, and by gum, that is what she shall have. Blast, I hope she doesn't think we're going abroad. Someone needs to set her straight at once, or I'll never hear the end of it." Then he rang for Mrs. Clarke.

Alas, Lady Constance did think they were going abroad. In fact, she was already practicing her socially useful Italian phrases, for the rumors of a balmy holiday on the Italian Riviera had reached her ears too, and she was more excited about it than anyone.

"Buongiorno, Signora Clarke," she chirped when the housekeeper finally worked up the courage to come to her dressing chamber and deliver Lord Fredrick's message. *"Dove si trova il Colosseo?"* ("Good morning, Mrs. Clarke. Where will I find the Colosseum?")

"Charmed, I'm sure, my lady," Mrs. Clarke replied, with an anxious curtsy. "I have a message for you from His Lordship." The whole way there, she had practiced saying, "There's been an unfortunate misunderstanding," as Lord Fredrick had instructed, but now that the time had finally come to speak, the words got all jumbled from nerves. "There's been a fortnight of mist on the landing," she announced, staring straight ahead.

Lady Constance frowned. "A fortnight of mist? How odd. As for Fredrick's message, don't tell me, please! Let it be a surprise, or let it seem like one, at least. For I already know he is planning a trip to Italy. My seamstress let it slip when she came to let out the waist of my skirts." She held up a hand, as if trying to hail a hansom cab. "Wait! I believe I just said something amusing. 'She let out the secret as she was letting out the skirts.' Is that what they call a pun?"

"You'd have to ask Miss Lumley about that." Mrs. Clarke swallowed hard. "About the, uh, mist on the landing—"

"Open a window, Mrs. Clarke! That is what I would do, if I were shrouded in mist. Honestly, sometimes I feel I have more common sense than all the rest of you put together. Except Fredrick, of course. What a darling husband he is, to plan a secret holiday in *bella Italia*! I would like nothing better than to kiss him on the nose in thanks, as if he were a precious pet poodle. But I will not spoil his surprise. When Fredrick finally decides to tell me about the trip, I promise I shall play the part of shock and delight with all the conviction of an actress on the West End."

"I'm afraid that's just it, my lady. We're not going to Italy." Mrs. Clarke wrung her hands, fidgety as a squirrel. "His Lordship bids me tell you we're to holiday at a beach in England. It'll be too cold for swimming, or sunbathing, or sandcastles, or much of anything, I suppose, but the doctor says it's for your health, and the baby's, too."

There is a very old saying, older than the Roman Colosseum, that states: "Don't kill the messenger who brings bad news." Nowadays it may seem obvious that messengers ought not to be blamed for the news they bear. Think how difficult it would be to run an efficient postal service if the mail carriers had to flee angry mobs every time the headlines reported something unfortunate: THE RICH GROW LESS RICH, THE POOR GROW POORER STILL, for example. Or CAKE DECLARED EXTINCT: LAST KNOWN SLICE EATEN BY MISTAKE (BIRTH-DAY BOY TO BLAME).

Yet in the heat of strong emotion, even obvious truths are forgotten, and that is why no one likes to be the bearer of bad news. It is why Penelope did not care to discuss the pain of childbirth with Lady Constance. It is why Lord Fredrick did not come in person to tell his wife that they would be vacationing at a freezing English beach rather than a sunny Italian resort. And it is why poor Mrs. Clarke was now nearly faint with worry, for this was the second time in a week that she had been forced to deliver bad news to her mistress. If it happened again, the poor woman feared, her job might be at risk.

Lady Constance gazed at her blankly for a full half

minute. Then she began to laugh.

"An English beach in January? Hilarious! Mrs. Clarke, you cannot fool me. Obviously my husband has discovered that his surprise reached my ears by mistake. Now he has sent you to tell me this ridiculous story to keep me 'off the scent,' as the gentlemen of the hunt would say. But I am not so easily bamboozled! No intelligent person would plan a beach vacation in the off-season. Not a soul of interest would be there. There would be no one to meet for luncheon, or with whom to go shopping. It would be absurd to take such a dull and unpleasant holiday. Clearly we are bound for *bella Italia*. How sweet that Fredrick would go to such pains to keep it a secret, and how clever of me to catch on to his tricks! My, you look so nervous all at once! Fear not, Mrs. Clarke. I promise, I will pretend that I believe you, so as to play along with Fredrick's scheme!"

LADY CONSTANCE HAD IT ALL wrong, of course, but there was nothing Mrs. Clarke could say to convince her otherwise. Eventually the good housekeeper gave up trying and took refuge in her small office near the kitchen. "Poor Lady Constance! And her poor husband, and poor everyone," she fretted to Margaret, who had brought a warm footbath and a glass of blackberry cordial to settle the older lady's nerves. "It'll be a dangerous state of affairs, once she discovers the truth. I hope I'm nowhere near when that rude awakening comes."

Meanwhile, disappointment swept through the estate faster than an epidemic of chicken pox. "An English beach in January? Just our luck," grumbled the servants as they went about their chores. Those who had previously begged to join the Ashtons on holiday now volunteered to stay home and polish the silver. The entire household felt cheated, as if a sun-soaked adventure in foreign lands had been snatched unfairly from them. (That they would grieve so bitterly over the loss of a trip that never existed in the first place only goes to show how much people like to look forward to pleasant things. As Agatha Swanburne once said, "Getting one's hopes up is easy; getting them down again often requires a ladder.")

Only in the nursery did this farcical mix-up escape attention. The Incorrigibles were too young and too busy painting to care about grown-up gossip. As for their governess, her full attention was on the hard work of holding still, for once more she had been asked to pose for a portrait.

"No fidgeting and no frowning," Beowulf scolded.

"Keep your eyes big and round. Rounder, please! Try to look silly."

His instruction was not so odd as it sounded, for at the moment Penelope was pretending to be Lady Constance, whom the children rightly assumed would never agree to pose for an Incorrigible family portrait. Still, they wanted to include her, and so they had artfully wrapped Penelope in bedsheets to approximate a flouncy gown. A hand mirror and a box of chocolates lay on the table next to her, and a skein of yellow woolen yarn was draped over her head, to stand in for Lady Constance's long, butterscotch-colored hair.

"Holding still is more difficult than it looks." Penelope took the opportunity to scratch her head, for the woolen yarn made her scalp itch. "For once I am beginning to feel real sympathy for Nutsawoo. Shall we break for tea? Biscuits, anyone?"

"Later," the artists mumbled, and went on with their painting. They found their task so interesting that they could have worked through luncheon and dinner and scarcely noted the hours whizzing by. Yet for Penelope, who was hot and uncomfortable, time had slowed to the pace of Honey Hee-Haw, the stuffed donkey, which is to say it scarcely moved at all. "How could the day pass so quickly for some and yet so slowly for others,

"Shall we break for tea? Biscuits, anyone?"

all in the same room?" she thought. "If I were a scientist, I would surely investigate this, for it appears that even such a seemingly fixed idea as time is not fixed at all, but relative. A Theory of Relativity might explain it all quite nicely. . . ."

But there was neither time nor space to devise a Theory of Relativity just then. A familiar voice rang high and piercing from the hallway. "Halloo, children! Halloo, Miss Lumley! It's Margaret. I'd knock but my hands are full. May I come in?"

"Oh, yes, please!" Penelope called eagerly, for the itching had become unbearable and one foot was beginning to cramp. Margaret swung into the room with a basket of freshly laundered clothes cradled in her arms.

"Playing dress-up, I see. Why, you look just like painters in those fancy smocks." She set the basket down. "And Miss Lumley is dressed as Little Bo Peep! That's the sweetest thing I ever did see. I love a good nursery rhyme, myself." She placed a hand on her heart and recited, in her adorable mouse squeak of a voice:

"Little Bo Peep has lost her sheep,
And can't tell where to find them.

Leave them alone, and they'll come home.
And bring their tails behind them."

"We are not dressed as painters. We *are* painters," Cassiopeia corrected, polite but firm.

Penelope stood up, grateful to stretch her legs. "But I am not Little Bo Peep, although I suppose there is a resemblance. Thank you for bringing up the clean laundry, Margaret. Children, if you please—" But the Incorrigibles had already taken off their paint-splattered smocks and begun to fold and put away all the clothes. Being the wards of one of the richest men in England was no excuse not to do household chores, and the children had been taught to be helpful at all times. Penelope had made sure of that.

"You're quite welcome. 'Twas my pleasure to get away from all the hullabaloo downstairs." Margaret gave a sidelong wink at the children. "Besides, a letter's come for you, Miss Lumley, and I do know how you like a good letter. I wonder who it's from?" She handed Penelope an envelope. Puzzled and excited, Penelope tore it open.

Dear Penelope,
How goes the war? That's just a figure of speech,

of course. Being a bard, I'm partial to them! I hope no one's at war at Ashton Place, unless it's little Nutsy-woo, at war with the acorns of the world. The poor nuts don't stand a chance against that chubby-cheeked menace.

Simon Harley-Dickinson! It had been two months since she and her playwright friend had last seen each other, and the arrival of his occasional letters made any day feel like a holiday. She read on.

Good news from London! The tale of my true-life adventures aboard a pirate ship has attracted the interest of some West End producers. One small problem: They won't let me use the word "pirate" anywhere in the play. They fear it'll remind people of Pirates on Holiday, *and what a flop that was, as I'm sure you recall.*

Indeed, *Pirates on Holiday* was a perfectly dreadful operetta whose opening night had ended in near calamity for Penelope and the Incorrigibles, and even worse reviews for the show. Still, it had been her first time at a West End performance, and Penelope had fond memories of the evening's glamour and excitement.

The costumes, in particular, were quite convincing; anyone would have taken the actors for real pirates, at least until they had begun to sing all those complicated lyrics in close harmony. (As everyone knows, real pirates prefer to sing boisterous sea chanteys loudly and off-key, while keeping their voices limber with frequent sips of rum.)

The letter continued:

> *To write a pirate tale without mentioning pirates has put my poetic license to the test. I'm scribbling 'round the clock! But I did squeeze in a trip to Brighton to see Great-Uncle Pudge.*

Great-Uncle Pudge! At last Penelope's eyes grew as big and round as Beowulf had requested, so much so that the boy dashed to his sketchbook to draw some quick studies. In addition to being Simon's great-uncle, old Pudge was the last living crew member of Admiral Percival Racine Ashton's ill-fated voyage to Ahwoo-Ahwoo. Pudge's shipboard diary was the only written account of what had taken place on that mysterious isle, so many years ago: *An Encounter with the Man-Eating Savages of Ahwoo-Ahwoo, as Told by the Cabin Boy and Sole Survivor of a Gruesomely Failed Seafaring*

Expedition Through Parts Unknown: Absolutely Not to Be Read by Children Under Any Circumstances, and That Means You, it was called.

Against great odds, Penelope and Simon had gotten hold of the diary and discovered how to decipher its pages, for clever young Pudge had written it in invisible ink. Unhappily for them, the book had been stolen away before they could read it and learn the secrets of the Ashton curse. Worse, it had been stolen by Edward Ashton, Lord Fredrick's father, who (despite what everyone believed) was not even remotely dead.

> *Wish we could get Pudge to tell us what happened on Ahwoo-Ahwoo! I hate thinking Edward Ashton knows something we don't.*

That, of course, was the difficulty, for Pudge had sworn an oath of secrecy and would discuss the events of that dreadful trip with no one but the admiral himself. Unfortunately, the admiral was long dead.

"Who sent the letter?" asked Alexander. Margaret had just taught the children how to make sock balls. They had filled a whole laundry basket with them, and now they were tossing them back and forth.

"Simon," Penelope said softly, touching one fond fingertip to the envelope. "Simon Harley-Dickinson." There was no return address given, for Simon had lost the lease on his tiny garret apartment in London while at sea with the pirates and now lived, as he liked to say, out of his suitcase and off of his wits.

If only she knew where to send a reply! She longed to tell him her own news: that despite Edward Ashton's resolve to use the secrets within the stolen diary to rid his family of the Ashton curse once and for all, it seemed his plan had failed. During the last full moon (during which Lord Fredrick was nowhere to be found), the wild, relentless howling that echoed across the estate had grown so frightening that local farmers armed themselves with muskets and slept by their henhouses and sheep pens.

"Simawoo, harr!" The children swaggered about and made pirate noises, for they liked the clever young bard. Penelope was once again lost in the letter.

Speaking of Not-So-Dead Edward, here's the big news: I ran into Madame Ionesco in London. She was reading coffee grounds in a tea shop, or tea leaves in a coffee shop, can't remember which. Hope you don't mind, but I told her about Pudge's diary, and all that ominous bunkum Edward Ashton said about family trees split in two and so on. Well, the soothsayer went pale as the full moon and fainted dead away. For a minute I'd thought she'd taken a jaunt Beyond the Veil herself! When she woke up, she asked for a hot meal and told me to give you a message. I'll write it the way she said it, so as not to lose any of the spooky nuance.

"This curse is not so simple as it looks. The wolf babies are in danger. Time is running out. But to break a curse is no joke. Tell your redheaded friend— a curse is like a contract. It's all in the wording. She must find out the exact words of the curse. Then, maybe I can help. Also, tell her my services will not come cheap."

I'll say they don't—it cost me a chicken dinner just to get that much out of her. Say, is your hair really red? You'd think I'd have noticed that by now! My head's in the clouds. The price of genius, I suppose.

Smooth sailing till we meet again,
Simon

As sock balls flew thick and fast overhead, Penelope tried to connect the dots. "'This curse is not so simple as it looks' . . . that is a nice use of iambic pentameter, at least. The 'wolf babies' in danger . . . by that she means the Incorrigibles. I shall have to be even more watchful than usual. And 'time is running out' . . . hmm! That does sound ominous."

Still, that Madame Ionesco might be able to undo the curse was cause for optimism, in Penelope's view. Many things were, of course. Swanburne girls were taught to look on the bright side of things, so much so that they were often in real danger of optoomuchism, a word that means precisely what it looks like it means.

But how to discover the exact wording of the curse? Edward Ashton had run off with Pudge's diary. Pudge was in the Home for Ancient Mariners in Brighton and would only talk to a long-dead admiral. "Blast!" she said aloud in frustration.

Margaret had been ducking sock balls and prattling away this whole time. "'Blast?' You sound like Lord Fredrick! Anyway, as I just said, Her Ladyship has me running errands faster than Bertha the ostrich galloping at full speed. You'd think we were going to the moon, instead of Brighton."

The letter Penelope had just read nearly slipped

from her hands. "Did you say Brighton?"

"Haven't you been listening? I just told the whole story! The doctor says Lady Constance must take the sea air for her health, and he knew a hotel that would take us in the off-season, and now we're all going to shiver ourselves to pieces in Brighton."

A poorly aimed sock ball hit Penelope square in the forehead, but she scarcely noticed. "Brighton, England?" she asked, disbelieving.

Margaret sat down, dreamy eyed, and folded her long legs beneath her on the armchair. "Yes, Brighton. It's a shame, really. I've always longed to stroll the pier and the sea walk, and watch all the bathers in their finery, and perhaps get a glimpse of Her Majesty Queen Victoria, taking the air at her summer palace, but in wintertime there'll be none of that. That awful doctor! Why couldn't he have ordered a trip to a nice cozy spa, with hot mineral springs to soak in and a gift shop for buying picture postcards? By the time we come home from Brighton I'll be an absolute wreck!"

Wreck . . . shipwreck . . . Ahwoo-Ahwoo! "Be on guard against hyperbole, Margaret," she said quickly, for a plan was already unfolding in her mind. "There is no need to exaggerate. I daresay the weather in Brighton will be no worse than it is here at Ashton Place. It is not as if you are traveling to the Arctic, as so many brave explorers do. Or even to wildest Canada, among those fascinating Eskimaux and their snow huts and sled dogs."

At the mention of sled dogs, the children dropped their socks and galloped in circles 'round the nursery. "Mush, mush!" they cried to egg themselves on, although, like most children, they hardly needed encouragement to run around making noise.

Margaret stretched lazily; it was rare she got to sit down. "You're right, Miss Lumley. I oughtn't complain. It's just that at the beach you expect it to be warm and sunny, which makes it seem all the colder when it's not." She cocked her head to the side. "But I suppose the ocean is just as vast in January as it is in July, and the horizon just as far. That'll be something wonderful to see! And what will you and the children do while we're away? It'll be nice and quiet around here, I suppose." Even as she said it, she looked doubtful; between alternating cries of "Harr, mateys!" and "Mush, mush!" the Incorrigible pirate sled dogs were making a fearsome amount of noise.

"Oh, we will keep busy with this and that," Penelope replied evasively. "Letters to write, bookshelves to tidy. The children are painting family portraits, too—"

Like a pat of butter tossed in a hot skillet, Margaret's cheerful expression melted all at once. "The poor loves! Painting family portraits, and them with no family but one another, *tsk, tsk!*"

"On the contrary, they have a great many people to paint. Even you, Margaret." Penelope spoke briskly, for she was not in the habit of feeling sorry for the children, who never felt sorry for themselves. "In fact, I was posing for them when you came in."

"As Little Bo Peep? My heart aches to hear it! Taking characters from nursery rhymes and pretending they're family, since they've no real family of their own." Margaret's lip trembled as if she might cry. "So brave these children are, and so lively in spite of their hardships."

The children were lively to be sure, but at present their only hardship had to do with the difficulty of building an igloo out of sock balls. Their sled-dog game had given them the idea to build an entire Eskimaux village out of the materials at hand. Alas, sock balls have a tendency to roll, and this was just as true in Miss Lumley's day as it is in our own. A proper igloo ought to be made of snow, the children wistfully agreed. With deep longing they looked out the nursery window at the powdery white fields below.

Reluctantly, Margaret rose from the chair. "I'd best get back downstairs before I'm missed. I wish you all *arrivederci!*" The way she said it sounded like the peeping of newborn chicks. "That's what Lady Constance says. *Arrivederci!* Soon there'll be a new baby in the house, won't that be exciting? I wonder what they'll name the wee thing."

Empty laundry basket tucked under one long arm, Margaret took a hop, then a skip, and whirled out of the nursery. She really was a charming sort of girl. She walked as if dancing, spoke as if squealing with delight, and sounded merry even when she had cause for complaint. No wonder Jasper was so keen on her.

The children begged to go outside and build igloos, after which they intended to carve some canoes suitable for paddling through Arctic seas, but a look from Penelope reminded them that they ought to tidy up their painting project before starting something new. As they did so, she too gazed with longing out the window.

"So the Ashtons are going to Brighton, and all because of that clever Dr. Veltschmerz," she murmured. "Clever, clever Dr. Veltschmerz! For I believe a winter beach holiday is just what the doctor ordered. . . ."

A FEW HOURS AND SEVERAL lopsided igloos later, Miss Penelope Lumley, having changed out of her boots and wet things and dressed in fresh, dry clothes, stood at the door of her least favorite room in Ashton Place. It was Lord Fredrick's private study, which housed his large and varied collection of taxidermy, as well as the family portraits of his accurséd ancestors. First, his father, Edward Ashton. Then his grandfather, the Honorable Pax Ashton, a judge known more for his cruelty than his sense of fairness. And finally, his great-grandfather, Admiral Percival Racine Ashton, whose misadventure on Ahwoo-Ahwoo had somehow caused the curse in the first place. But had it happened? And why?

"Well, I shall soon get to the bottom of all that," Penelope thought determinedly. "I need only discover the exact words of the curse, and Madame Ionesco will do the rest. Why Edward Ashton has made such a fuss about it all these years is beyond me. It is simply a job for a Swanburne girl, I suppose."

As you can see, Penelope's optoomuchstic thinking was in full flower. She tugged at her sleeves and smoothed her hair, which had been freshly rewound into an authoritative bun. She was no stranger to the art of making persuasive speeches, and she had carefully planned what she would say to Lord Fredrick. "A trip to Brighton offers a cornucopia of educational opportunities, as follows," she practiced under her breath, and raised her hand to knock. "One, observation of the tides. Two, identification of seashells. Three, in-depth study of the properties of sand . . ."

The door flew open before her hand could strike. "Mrs. Clarke!" Lord Fredrick bellowed over her head. "Timothy! I need Miss Lumley, right away. Someone fetch the governess, please."

"I am right here, my lord," she said with a gulp.

Lord Fredrick's eyesight was poor, and it took him a moment of swiveling his head this way and that before he got Penelope firmly in view. "What? Blast! Who's there—why, it's you! How did you know I was about to send for you? That's odd. Never mind, though. We have business to discuss, come in, come in."

He patted the pocket of his jacket anxiously as he waved her inside. "Good, it's still there. Blasted almanac! I've been up since dawn looking for it. Wanted to check the dates of the full you-know-what."

"Moon?" she suggested, trying to be helpful. He cringed.

"Yes, moon! Finally found it on the shelf right there, near that dead duck. How it got there I've no clue, but I don't want it to fly away again. The book, not the duck." He moved to light a cigar, then stopped. "Bit early in the day for a cigar, I suppose. Sit down, if you please. Would you like coffee? I'll ring for some." He swiped at the bell pull that hung near the door, but missed.

"No, thank you, my lord." Penelope was more of a tea drinker, personally. And why on earth would Lord Fredrick send for her? The sheer unexpectedness of it threatened to knock what she had planned to say about learning the difference between gulls and terns right out of her head. "If I may inquire—what sort of business . . . ?"

He snorted. "Baby business! That's what sort of business. Do you know, I'm going to be a father before long?"

"I did know that, sir." Her heart sank. Surely Lord Fredrick was not also in need of a lesson about how babies are born? Hesitantly she added, "My sincere congratulations to you and Lady Ashton."

Too restless to sit, he paced the length of the study. "Congratulations, ha! I wish I felt that way. You've never been a father, I take it? No, of course not. Believe me, it's quite an odd feeling. And the baby's not even here yet." The servants still told the story of how Lord Fredrick had reacted when he learned that his wife was expecting. "Expecting what?" he had exclaimed, dumbfounded. "A baby? Nonsense. Surely there's been some mistake." He prowled the halls for hours, one floor after another. Then he locked himself in his study until cigar smoke drifted like fog through the crack beneath the door.

Whether he had since warmed up to the idea of fatherhood no one knew, but since emerging from his study that day, he had been kinder to and more patient with Lady Constance than he had ever been before. One might even say he doted on her, in his fashion. He spent far less time at his gentlemen's club, and was more willing to endure his wife's meandering streams of conversation, although he still had little to say in answer but "Harrumph!" "Blast!" and "Imagine that!" Luckily, Lady Constance was more of a talker than a listener and rarely paused for breath, so Lord Fredrick's conversational skills were more than sufficient.

He perched on the arm of his chair. "A baby, a baby, a baby. Blast! A man gets married, and this is what happens. I suppose I was a fool to think it could be avoided forever." He sprang up and gestured with his unlit cigar. "I've made my peace with howling during the full moons—but no child of mine ought to go through it." He stopped and fixed her with his blurry gaze. "I won't have it. I simply will not. Miss Lumley, you've got to do something."

"Me?" Penelope was amazed.

"Yes, you. Who else? You and the wolf children and Old Timothy are the only ones who know about my howling fits. And Mother, too, of course, but she's still traipsing around Europe, playing croquet and waiting for my dead father to turn up again. Highly unlikely, I'd say! Poor fellow, what a way to go. Drowned in a tar pit, and while on holiday, too. Gooey, gooey, gooey." He lost himself in the sad memory for a brief interlude, then shook it off. "It's plain as day, Miss Lumley. You're an educated person, and you've experience with wolfy matters. No, don't object! I know my affliction and the children's canine carrying-on are not the same thing. I'm not sure I believe in curses, mind you . . . but it seems there's a curse out there that believes in Ashtons."

If only she could tell Lord Fredrick about Pudge's diary, and Madame Ionesco's warning, and all of it! But he was Edward Ashton's son, after all, and Edward Ashton was no friend to her or the Incorrigible children. To end the curse on his family had become his obsession, so much so that he had faked his own death and lived in disguise under the name of Judge Quinzy, to better conceal his actions. Whatever danger the children were in, Edward Ashton was the source of it. Of that she was certain.

"So it would appear, my lord," she ventured. "Perhaps if we knew more about this curse—the exact wording of it, for example?"

"The who and the why of it don't matter. Putting an end to it does. I've got to do everything I can for Constance, and for the child." He paused to gaze out the window, then let the curtains fall. "The girl may have married me for my money, and perhaps she does like me a bit, too, heaven knows why. I think I'm a bit of a bore, personally. But I'll tell you one thing: When she wed me, she didn't sign up to raise a barking baby Ashton. And if you don't come up with a cure before the first of May, a barking baby Ashton is just what she's going to have."

"The first of May!" she exclaimed. Now she realized what Madame Ionesco must have meant when she had said "time is running out." Edward Ashton had once told her that the curse could not be ended in his generation, but in his son's—meaning Fredrick's. Once the baby was born, would it be too late?

Worn out at last, Lord Fredrick crumpled into his chair. "Yes, the first of May, more or less. What a legacy to pass on to my son."

"But what if it is a girl?" Penelope blurted.

"It won't be. There have been no girls born in the family since . . . well, I don't know when." Lord Fredrick put down the cigar, and his hands grew still. "My only concern right now is for my wife, and my son. Poor lad! Come his first full moon, he'll howl those little mewling howls, like a newborn pup, and then what am I supposed to tell his mother? I know she's suspicious. 'Where are you off to this time, Freddy? Why must you go to your gentlemen's club again? Why are you so itchy? Why do you make those dreadful noises?' My pretending to get rashes and whooping cough is not fooling her anymore. Enough, I say. It's time to get to the bottom of it. The truth is, Miss Lumley, I've no one else to turn to."

He looked so forlorn sitting there that Penelope could almost—but not quite—forgive him for all the taxidermy. "I shall do my best, my lord. But I too have a request." She took a deep breath. "A trip to Brighton offers a cornucopia of educational opportunities—"

Lord Fredrick jumped up from his seat. "Right! That's the other thing. You're coming to Brighton. The Incorrigibles, too. No protests, please! I'm sick of hearing people complain about the weather. Put on a hat, for heaven's sake. You'd think we were going to the South Pole, the way the servants carry on."

All that Penelope was prepared to say regarding tides, seashells, and the life cycle of the hermit crab melted like candy floss in her mouth. "We shall be delighted to join you and Lady Ashton on holiday, sir," she answered meekly.

He squinted in her direction, as if trying to get a better view of her. "Well, good. Good! You're not a whiner, Miss Lumley. I like that about you. My wife and I leave later today, at one o'clock. Old Timothy will drive us in the carriage; I'll trust no one else to do it. The servants will go tomorrow by train, with the luggage. You can travel with them." He paused. "According to the almanac, the full moon's next Tuesday. Perhaps the wolf children can keep me company. Don't worry, I'll be no danger to them. But a bit of companionship would be a nice change."

"Very well, my lord," she said, keeping her voice steady.

His blurred gaze softened. "It's an extraordinary thing not to be judged, Miss Lumley. At least the Incorrigibles have one another. I've suffered alone, all these years." Abruptly he turned and pounded his fist on the desk, so hard the ashtrays rattled. "No child of mine will go through it! I swear it!" Wincing, he flexed his fingers, gave the hand a shake, and shoved it into his pocket. "That's all," he said gruffly. "You may go."

Penelope rose to obey, but she had scarcely made it to the door before Lord Fredrick called, "Miss Lumley, wait. Why did you come to see me? You wanted something, I expect. A salary increase? A day off? Whatever it is, the answer's yes. As if I care what people get paid. You can't imagine how much money I have. An army of Ashtons couldn't spend it all."

"I . . . that is . . . I had simply intended to say bon voyage," she stammered.

"Ha!" Lord Fredrick's laugh was short and sharp as a bark. "Bon voyage. That's French, what? *Arrivederci's* Italian. I wonder how wolves say good-bye." He threw back his head and playfully howled. "So long-*ahwoo*! I'm joking! It's not a full moon yet." He patted his jacket pocket, and his face fell. "Blast! It was right there a minute ago. Why is that curséd almanac always disappearing?"

THE THIRD CHAPTER

The children discover what the moon can do.

THE CONVERSATION WITH LORD FREDRICK left Penelope's head spinning. (Not literally, of course. To say a person's head is spinning is merely a figure of speech. Even an owl's head cannot spin, although, remarkably, it can swivel nearly all the way 'round. Human heads can safely be turned, but actual spinning should only be attempted by tops, globes, Russian ballerinas, and other items more suited to the task.)

She stopped on the stair landing to collect her thoughts. "How strange and unpredictable the Ashtons are," she said to the potted fern, the only other living creature present. "That Lord Fredrick will soon be a father has made him a new man in some respects. It is remarkable what happens when one begins to think of others, and not only of oneself. Still, he is an Ashton, and I must be careful for the children's sake. One never knows where danger may lurk."

She thought of Madame Ionesco's warning and frowned. How *were* the Incorrigibles mixed up in all this? True, they could be a bit barky and prone to howling when excited, but otherwise they seem untouched by anything resembling a curse. They were three happy, bright, and eager children, and the full moon had little effect on them, other than to inspire the writing of poetry in praise of its milky, faraway beauty.

"Then again, Madame Ionesco is a fortune-teller, and prone to spooky pronouncements." She turned her head to check the state of her bun in the landing mirror. The rich auburn color of her hair caught the light. For all the years that Penelope had been a student at Swanburne, Miss Mortimer had ordered regular applications of a hair poultice that kept all the girls' hair tinted the same dark, drab shade. It was only after leaving school that Penelope discovered the unusual hue of her own hair, which—oddly—resembled the color of the Incorrigibles' hair as closely as one pea matches another. (The children were not fans of peas in a culinary sense, but surely there is nothing distasteful about using peas as a figure of speech.)

"Dear Miss Mortimer," she thought. "Her reasons for ordering the use of the hair poultice remain mysterious, yet she is a private person in any case. Imagine her not telling anyone that Agatha Swanburne was her grandmother! I am quite sure I should never be able to keep such a secret."

Penelope adjusted a few stray hairpins and continued upstairs. At the nursery door she paused and sniffed, and took comfort in the smell of paint and turpentine and horsehair brushes, for it meant the children were happily and safely occupied.

Was it wise to take them away from the security of Ashton Place, to solve a strange curse cast long ago? Firmly she pushed away the fear. "Great-Uncle Pudge is the key," she thought. "Once we are in Brighton, somehow I must persuade him to reveal what happened on Ahwoo-Ahwoo, including the exact wording of the curse upon the Ashtons."

That Pudge had sworn to speak to no one about that ill-fated trip except the long-dead admiral posed a serious obstacle, but Penelope was not a Swanburne girl for nothing. "As Agatha Swanburne once said, 'The pony that shies at the fence today may take the jump tomorrow. If not, one can always take down the fence.' In any case, we shall cross that boardwalk when we come to it," she resolved as she opened the nursery door. "First . . . to Brighton!"

As planned, Lord Fredrick and his wife left that afternoon. A light snow fell as the carriage came 'round the long, curved driveway to the main entrance of Ashton Place. It was the clarence, the largest and most luxurious carriage owned by the estate, and it was pulled by the finest pair of grays in the stables. The seats were piled with lap robes, and a lidded metal bucket of hot coals nestled in sand had been placed inside to warm the carriage's interior.

Two lines of numb-fingered servants stood by the door holding umbrellas, so that not a single frozen flake would fall upon Lady Constance as she made her way from the house. She was wrapped in a fur-trimmed cloak fit for an Arctic explorer and leaned heavily on two young coachmen, one at each elbow. They would have the responsibility of lifting her up and inside the carriage.

Old Timothy struggled to keep the horses calm; he stood at their proud heads and murmured soothing words, but the sharp tingle of snowfall on their broad backs made them restless and easily spooked. At the slightest movement of the black umbrellas, their ears swiveled back in fear. Perhaps they believed a flock of giant ravens had landed nearby. They snorted steam from flared nostrils and stamped their hooves on the frozen ground.

Still, Lady Constance could not be rushed. Even as her gallant helpers lifted her, she paused in midair to give whispered instructions to a shivering Mrs. Clarke. "Make sure to have my summer gowns sent to *bella Italia*—to Genoa, or Rapallo, or whatever sunny, elegant resort Fredrick has chosen! Remind Madame Le Point to alter the gowns first, of course, for my tummy grows rounder by the day."

"Very good, my lady," Mrs. Clarke said through chattering teeth. "Of course, the weather may not be quite as warm as all that—"

"And send my fair-weather bonnets, the lace-trimmed ones, and a parasol to shield me against that strong Mediterranean sun. Oh, I cannot wait to see what fashions are on parade at the seaside resorts of Italy!"

Mrs. Clarke mumbled something about galoshes

and a woolen muffler, just in case, but Lady Constance only laughed and said *"Arrivederci,* Signora Clarke! See you at the beach!" She extended one airborne foot toward the snow-dusted carriage, and the uncomplaining coachmen finally were able to deposit her inside.

Once the carriage door was shut and latched, Old Timothy leaped into the driver's seat. "Hey, yah!" he called, flicking the reins.

He would have his work cut out for him keeping such high-spirited animals to a snail's pace, but Lord Fredrick's orders were clear. "No bumpety-bumps, now!" Lord Fredrick gave the old coachman a firm clap on the back before taking his seat inside the carriage, next to his wife. "Take it at a crawl, if you please. Think of her delicate condition, what? We'll go halfway today and stay over at a roadside inn. You manage the horses, and I'll manage Constance. Blast! I think you might have the easier job of it, Old Tim!"

"A TRIP! A TRIP! A trip*ahwooo*!" Penelope saved her announcement for the next morning, as she knew the prospect of a trip would have kept the children awake far past their usual bedtime. As she expected, they became wildly excited at the news. They pushed away their half-eaten breakfasts and ran to get their suitcases.

"Are we taking Bertha to Africa?" Cassiopeia asked. As much as the children liked having Bertha at Ashton Place, they knew an ostrich did not belong in England. The giant bird was to be returned home as soon as someone suitable could be found to take her.

"Not this time." Penelope lined up all their snow boots in a row for cleaning. "We are going on holiday with Lord and Lady Ashton, to a town called Brighton."

"Where is Brighton? North by northeast? South by southwest? Approximate altitude? Sorry, Beowoo, did not mean to kick your head." Alexander had climbed halfway up the drapes to get his compass, spyglass, and sextant down from a high shelf. He was fond of map-making and liked to keep track of where things were; besides, one never knew when one might be called upon to navigate. Simon Harley-Dickinson had taught him that.

"Brighton is by the sea—careful, Alexander! Next time you might simply pull a chair by the shelf to stand upon." Penelope dashed to the window and lifted him down to safety. How much he had grown this past year! He was almost too heavy for her to lift. "The easels will not fit in suitcases, Beowulf. We shall have to make do with sketch-books and pencils for the duration of the trip."

No easels! The children's disappointment was keen,

and a fresh bout of *weltschmerz* threatened to take hold. Then Penelope casually mentioned that if they caught any hermit crabs at the beach, she *might* consider letting them bring the curious creatures home as pets. That turned the tide in an instant. "Crabawoo, crabawoo!" they chanted happily as they tossed sock balls into their suitcases.

Penelope stood before the bookshelves with folded arms and considered what sort of lessons might be suitable for a trip to the seashore. "As Agatha Swanburne once said, 'The right question is the one that answers itself,'" she thought. Quickly she gathered some books about shipbuilding, the search for the Northwest Passage, and a nature guidebook titled *Favorite Shorebirds of England: A Seaworthy Guide to Plovers, Sandpipers, Gulls, and Terns (Footprint Identification Charts Included at No Extra Charge)*.

She even found a poem with a maritime theme. (No, not *The Wreck of the Hesperus*, but another, spookier poem that took place aboard a haunted ship.) It was a strange poem, frankly, and she did not understand it fully herself, but on the bright side it did contain a gloomy supernatural bird. (No, not *The Raven*, but a different gloomy supernatural bird. Why unhappy birds feature so prominently in poetry and

68

whether these two birds in particular perhaps knew each other are both intriguing questions. Alas, there is no time to discuss them now, for Penelope and the children are not done packing, and they do have a train to catch.)

The suitcases filled quickly, and Penelope had to be firm when the children begged to pack their bathing costumes and sun hats, just in case. "A beach holiday in January is not a beach holiday in August," she reminded them. Yet even as she tucked extra mittens in the suitcase corners, she too felt a pang of disappointment. "If only it were summer, so we could go sea bathing and walk barefoot on the sand, and watch our footprints be washed away by the surf!"

(Little did Penelope know how well she would soon get to know the sea and its currents and tides, its sickening swells and storm-tossed waves, its incomprehensible vastness and mystery! Alas, there will be much more on that topic later. For now, in the words of the plucky young governess herself: "First, to Brighton . . .")

Clang clang! Clang clang!

"All aboard the noon train to Brighton! Don't dawdle, now. We've a schedule to keep and there's snow on the tracks!" The conductor's bell rang up and down the station platform, but his efforts to rush the passengers along were in vain. Mrs. Nellie Clarke was in charge of the staff of Ashton Place, and they took orders from her, not the London, Brighton, and South Coast Railway. Truly, in a battle of wills between Mrs. Clarke and a shiny red Bloomer steam engine, the smart money would be on the housekeeper.

Under her leadership were the dozen or so servants she had personally selected for the trip. Some had hardly traveled at all before, and stood silent and wide-eyed as they anxiously waited their turn to board. Others chattered and joked. Margaret squealed like an unoiled hinge every time the idling locomotive belched a billow of steam from its stack.

The Incorrigibles were in high spirits and not at all nervous, for they considered themselves to be seasoned travelers. Once onboard, they settled into their seats. They smiled sweetly at the conductor and wriggled with joy as the train lurched into motion, with a marvelous accelerating *chug-chug, chug-chug* of the wheels. They pressed their noses to the window, but the scenery was dreary. The rolling fields were piebald as a Holstein cow, white in the hills and hollows where the snow had gathered, and dark where the bare earth peeked through.

After ten minutes passed, they began to pester their governess.

"Are we almost there?"

"How much farther, Lumawoo?"

"Can we play sled dogs on the train?"

"Can we have snacks?"

"Can we have treats?"

"Can we hear a poem, please?"

This last request she was willing to consider. However, the poem she had selected for their holiday studies was so perfectly maritime themed that she thought it really ought to be saved for Brighton, when she could intone its spooky refrains in the fresh salt air with the roar of the surf as accompaniment.

"Now is not the time for poetry. All this *chug-chug, chug-chug* of the wheels would interfere with our appreciation of the poetic meter." Even as she said this, the rhythmic sway of the train gave her an idea. "I know! Let us study the tides. That is a seaworthy topic, to be sure. Alexander, you might want to pay particular attention, for tides are important to navigation."

"Aye aye, Cap'n!" he said, and sat up straight. His siblings did as well.

"Tides are what make the water near the shore change its depth," she began. "The water goes up at high tide, and down again at low tide."

The children tilted their heads from side to side, trying to make sense of this. "Eureka!" Beowulf cried. "Like a bathtub! Someone goes swimming and the water goes up." It was a good guess, for Beowulf had personal experience with the way the water in a bathtub rises when, for example, three grubby children climb in to bathe.

Penelope smiled and shook her head. "If swimmers caused the tides, they would be higher in summertime, when many people go sea bathing, than in the winter, when hardly anyone does."

The children thought some more. "I know! Someone must be pouring water in the sea, and taking it out again." Cassiopeia spread her arms wide. "Someone very big."

Again, Penelope shook her head. "According to the tide maps, the water sweeps in toward the coast at high tide, and then sweeps out again, back to some faraway, opposite shore. It is as if a bowl were being tilted, first to one side, then the other."

Alexander frowned. "Who tilts the bowl?"

Penelope paused, for she was fast approaching the horizon of her own learning. "That is a very good question," she said. "Scientists believe that it has something to do with the moon."

The children laughed and clapped as if she had told a hilarious joke. "The moon moves the sea? Funny, Lumawoo!"

"Maybe it uses a big spoon." Cassiopeia giggled. "Moon, spoon! That is my tide poem."

Beowulf scoffed. "The sea is too big for spoons. A bucket at least."

"Two buckets," his sister agreed.

Alexander scowled; to him, the question of tides was serious business. "Shh! Let Lumawoo tell: How does the moon move the sea?"

Three curious faces turned to her, like sunflowers to the sun. She sat up straight and smoothed her hair. "I do not know exactly, but the moon can do many things, after all. It grows and shrinks. It is a different shape every day."

The children considered this.

"It moves around the sky," Alexander agreed after a moment.

"It rises and sets," Beowulf conceded.

"It makes Lord Fredrick howl," Cassiopeia offered.

All conversation in the train car stopped. The steady chug of the train wheels was the only sound left; that, and a rhythmic snore that came from Mrs. Clarke, who was now napping in her seat at the far end of the compartment.

Chug-chugga–snore!

Chug-chugga–snore!

"Did you hear what the child said about His Lordship?" one of the servants said at last. "The moon makes him howl! Did you ever?"

"The moon? Fancy that!"

"I thought I heard an odd noise once, during a full moon. Very howling-like, if you ask me. It was coming from the attic. . . ."

Penelope leaned close to her youngest pupil. "Cassiopeia, we do not discuss other people's private business in a crowded train compartment."

The little girl looked confused. "But I thought we were talking about the moon?"

All around them the gossip buzzed.

"Lord Fredrick–moon–howling–*snore!*"

"Attic–wolves–His Lordship–*snore!*"

Penelope stood and spoke at top volume, as if she could erase the whispers by shouting over them. "Yes, children, we *were* talking about the moon, and spoons, and macaroons! And next we shall talk of hermit crabs, for they are fascinating creatures! Did you know they change houses as they outgrow them?"

But it was too late. The tide of rumor was rising, and there was as little chance of stopping it as there was of stilling the sea. Oh, the perils of eavesdropping! Penelope felt woozy. She sank back into her seat and imagined herself being run through with a sword while hiding behind a curtain.

The children looked concerned. "Do you have chicken pox, Lumawoo?" asked Alexander gently. "You are white as an egg."

She counted backward from twenty to calm herself, which was an antipanicking skill she had been taught at Swanburne. "This talk of tides is making me seasick," she answered when she could speak. "Let us choose another activity." She reached into her travel bag and removed a knotted mess of yellow wool. It was the skein of yarn that had served as her Lady Constance hair; she had brought it along as a simple project to while away the time while traveling. "I shall need your help to rewind this yarn into a neat, tidy ball. Put out your hands, please."

The children looked skeptical, for the idea of having their hands tied up with yarn felt rather like being put on a leash. Penelope urged, "I have no intention of wasting a perfectly good skein of wool. Pretend it is a sled-dog harness that lashes you all together as a team. A *quiet* sled-dog team," she added.

This idea pleased them much better. "Mush, mush!"

they whispered to one another. But they could not race up and down the train aisles with yarn wrapped around their hands, and so the game had to be changed.

"Help!" moaned Beowulf, dramatically but at low volume. "We are caught in a butterfly net!"

Cassiopeia grinned devilishly and whispered, "No, spiderweb!"

"Butterfly net!"

"Spiderweb!"

"Butterfly net!"

"Spiderweb!"

Not to be outdone, Alexander began to thrash about and quietly call for help. "Ahoy, Captain! Drop anchor, I'm stuck in the rigging!" (As the sailors among you know, the rigging of a sailing ship is the complicated web of ropes and timber and sails that allows the ship to be propelled by the wind.)

"The yarn is getting even more tangled than before," Penelope cautioned. "You must hold your hands steady."

Cassiopeia raised her yarn-wrapped hands to the top of her head and opened her eyes wide, until they were very round indeed. *"Arrivederci!"* she trilled in a high voice. "That is Italian. It means 'I want to go shopping!'"

"Now, now," Penelope said quickly. "It is not polite to pretend to be other people—"

Before she could say another word, the children plopped the whole mess of yarn on Penelope's head. "Look at Lady Constance!" they cried, forgetting to be quiet. "Her hair is pretty and yellow as a daffodil in spring!"

This time their fellow travelers stared openly. Some stood up to get a better look. Once more the whispers began.

"Making fun of Her Ladyship, *tsk, tsk*!"

"Not very respectful, if you ask me."

"Sets a poor example for the children . . ."

Snore—

Disaster! Penelope wished she might crawl under her seat and hide for the rest of the trip. "If this gossip finds its way back to Lord and Lady Ashton, it would be enough to lose my position over," she fretted. "What an unfortunate misunderstanding that would be . . . hmm . . . now *there* is an interesting effect. . . ."

Her worried thoughts trailed off, for she had caught sight of her reflection in the train window. The window was scratched and clouded, and with the landscape whooshing by on the other side, the glass offered an imperfect reflection at best—but one that, ironically, made her look much more like Lady Constance than a mirror ever could.

Curious, she widened her eyes and tried to look silly. With all the blur and motion, the illusion was striking. "It is not that I look exactly like Lady Constance," she thought. "But I give quite a convincing *impression* of Lady Constance, at a glance." (Coincidentally, and only a few decades into the future, a group of French painters called the Impressionists invented a style in which landscapes and people were shown precisely as if they were glimpsed through the scratched window of a moving train. At first, no one knew what to make of these blurry paintings, but they soon became popular and now they, too, hang in the galleries of the world's great museums to this very day.)

Fascinated, Penelope turned her head this way and that, and stole quick glimpses of herself. "A professional thespian would hardly be surprised, but truly, it is amazing how a modest use of stagecraft can make one person resemble another. . . ." She swiped the yarn off her head. "Eureka!" she exclaimed. Everyone in the train car but the sleeping Mrs. Clarke was staring at her now, but she no longer cared.

"What did you discover, Lumawoo?" the children begged to know.

Penelope tapped one temple with a fingertip. "The answer to a riddle. The solution to a puzzle. The key to a conundrum."

"You mean, you discovered . . . synonyms?" Alexander asked, puzzled.

"I shall explain everything to you, later. Right now I must write a letter." Filled with inspiration, Penelope extracted a sheet of stationery and a matching envelope from her bag. (Along with a supply of clean pocket handkerchiefs, a respectable person of any age should always carry some decent stationery, for one never knows when one will be called upon to write a thank-you note.)

Beowulf could not contain his curiosity. "A letter to whom?"

"To Simon," she answered, taking out her fountain pen. "To Simon Harley-Dickinson."

"Simawoo!" the children half howled. Penelope did not scold them, for she too would have howled with delight at the prospect of seeing Simon, had she been in the least bit prone to howling.

"Will we see him in Brighton? He likes the ocean," asked Cassiopeia.

"And navigation," said Alexander approvingly.

Beowulf made a swashbuckling gesture that caused both of his siblings to duck. "And pirates."

"*Sort of* likes pirates," Cassiopeia corrected. (It was true that Simon had both happy and unhappy memories of his days as a pirate. This is called "having mixed feelings," and it is a condition we all find ourselves in sooner or later. There is no known cure except to eat a small amount of bittersweet chocolate. The chocolate does nothing to unmix one's feelings, but it does serve as a tasty reminder that bittersweet is a perfectly good flavor and can be enjoyed on its own merits.)

"We will see him soon enough, never fear." Penelope checked the nib of her pen and paused, for she did not know where in London Simon was staying. However, she knew a great deal about Simon himself, and that, she decided, would have to do.

In a bold hand, she wrote on the envelope: *Mr. Simon Harley-Dickinson, member in good standing of the Bards and Poets Society, the Professional Organization for Scribes, Playwrights, Scribblers, and Devotees of Thespis, care of the Theatrical Firmament, London, England.*

Proudly, she showed it to the children. "For an organization as well run and efficient as the London Postal Service, that is more than enough to go on," she told them, and then turned her attention to the letter.

Dear Simon,

For reasons best explained later, the children and I are on our way to Brighton. (Forgive the shaky penmanship! If you have deduced that this letter must have been written on a moving train, you would not be wrong.)

I believe I have discovered the means to convince G.-U. Pudge to reveal the tale of his secret boyhood adventure (you know the one). I trust you are still on friendly terms with the stage manager of Pirates on Holiday. *Borrow a costume from that dreadful show and bring it with you to Brighton as soon as you can. A garment in your size and suitable for the rank of admiral would be ideal.*

Deepest thanks for your loyal assistance! Reply to P. Lumley, care of the Brighton General Post Office. I will look for your answer there.

She paused, and considered how to end. "Wishing you good luck on your theatrical adventures . . ." "With best wishes, from your friend . . ." "From your faithful partner in crime . . ."

But it all sounded so formal, so familiar, so glib, so forced! It put her in mind of Goldilocks's porridge. "Everything I write is either too warm or too cold," she thought. Her pen hovered in the air. She and Simon were friends; why was it so tricky to find the right way to end a letter to him? She never had such trouble signing a letter to Cecily, her old schoolmate.

She took a deep breath to clear her thoughts. "I will use the trick that all the girls are taught at Swanburne. When faced with a difficult problem, imagine you are a person who knows exactly what to do. Then, do exactly as that person would. In this case, how would I say good-bye if I were the sort of person who never gave a second thought about what to say?"

That solved her dilemma at once. With a flourish, she wrote:

Arrivederci!
P.L.

THE FOURTH CHAPTER

*A holiday in Brighton gets off
on the wrong foot.*

MRS. CLARKE SNOOZED THE WHOLE way to Brighton and had to be awakened upon their arrival. Margaret did the honors; she shook the good woman by the shoulders, first gently, then more forcefully, until the housekeeper began to mumble, "Mind your toes around the hermit crabs, dear Hubert! Wouldn't want you to get a nasty pinch." Once fully roused, she explained, "I was dreaming of a long-ago beach holiday with dear old Mr. Clarke, rest his soul. How he would have loved a trip to Brighton!"

Brighton! Pudge! Ahwoo-Ahwoo! The letter to Simon was tucked in Penelope's coat pocket. Every few minutes she reached in to make sure it was still there, much the way Lord Fredrick fretted over his almanac. Would the London Postal Service live up to its sterling reputation? Would the adventurous young playwright even be in London to receive her correspondence, or had some fresh adventure whisked him to parts unknown? Simon was as loyal as a friend could be, but he attracted plot twists the way spilled honey attracts ants.

"I will remain optimistic, and wait for his reply," she decided, and not without cause. Even while kidnapped by pirates, Simon had written to her faithfully. He did this by tossing notes overboard after first slipping them into empty rum bottles, of which his pirate captors had no shortage. The fact that these bottles could hardly have been expected to reach her at Ashton Place was beside the point. Even by modern standards the mail delivery in Miss Lumley's day was swift and reliable, but alas, there was no Pirate Postal Service equipped to deliver letters from the briny deep. Tossing bottle-borne letters into the sea had been the best Simon could do under the circumstances, and truly, our best is all any of us can expect of ourselves, and each other.

"Come, children! Mind your step getting off," she said, guiding them from the train. Child-sized suitcases in hand, the three Incorrigibles clambered down the metal stairs and stood on the platform. The wind was strong, as it often is near the shore. They looked around, and sniffed.

"I smell seashells," Alexander said, "by the seashore." (Interestingly, these very words would become the basis of one of the most famously difficult tongue-twisters ever devised: "She sells seashells by the seashore." Credit for inventing this hard-to-pronounce phrase is most often given to Anonymous. Rest assured, Alexander Incorrigible was the first person to say it. Moreover, he clearly said, "I smell seashells," not "She sells seashells," which only goes to prove how thankless the burden of authorship can be.)

"I smell salt. And sand. And something else . . ." Beowulf closed his eyes and sniffed again. "Are there bears in the sea?"

"There are seahorses, and sea urchins, but I have never heard of sea bears. Perhaps you are thinking of walruses?" Penelope shepherded the children to one side of the platform, for all around them the luggage was piling up. With a sharp whistle that she blew between two fingers, Mrs. Clarke directed the efforts

85

to carry the trunks curbside, where a line of hansom cabs waited to transport them to the hotel.

"I smell stinky pirates," Cassiopeia said, with a flash of her teeth. "Or maybe just old sailors. But where is the sea?"

"It cannot be far. Once we have settled in the hotel and put away our things, we will take a walk and get our bearings, and drop this letter in the post as well." Penelope patted her pocket once more. One would think the letter to Simon was an anchor, the way it weighed upon her! The sooner they found the post office, the better.

Luckily, Mrs. Clarke overheard her. A moment later she pressed a slip of paper into Penelope's hand. "Here's the address of the inn where we're staying. Give Jasper your luggage. You take the children to stretch their legs and get a look at the ocean while the sun's still out. Remember to take nice deep breaths, dearies! The sea air is good for your health. That's one thing Dr. Veltschmerz and I agree on, at least!"

PENELOPE INQUIRED AT THE STATION and discovered that the Brighton post office was directly on their way. She could scarcely hide her excitement as she paid for the postage, affixed the stamp (which bore a charming portrait of Queen Victoria in her youth), and handed her letter to the postal clerk.

"How long will it take to arrive?" she asked.

The clerk peered at the address through the lower lens of his bifocals. "London takes one day, no more and no less. But 'Devotees of Thespis, care of the Theatrical Firmament' . . . let me check." He consulted a chart on the desk, and looked at her apologetically. "I regret to inform you that firmaments require an extra half day. That means your correspondence will arrive in the Friday four o'clock post. Guaranteed!" He tossed the letter in a great bin full of outgoing letters, and went on to help the next customer.

How staunch and unflappable were the employees of the postal service! And how simple yet inspired was Penelope's scheme! Frankly, she was amazed she had not thought of it before. "By means of a bit of stage-craft and costuming, we shall convince Great-Uncle Pudge that Simon *is* the admiral! Simon is a man of the theater, after all; I expect he will relish the chance to give such a performance." Really, the only flaw in her plan was that she would not be attempting the impersonation herself, "although it would be amusing to try," she thought. She took a few steps in a swaggering pirate gait to get the feel of it. "But I do not know how keen Great-Uncle Pudge's eyesight might yet be. Best to be on the safe side. Simon in no way resembles the men of the Ashton line, but between the two of us, he comes far closer."

That her letter would be delivered in Friday afternoon's post also struck her as encouraging. "The sooner Great-Uncle Pudge reveals the words of the curse, the sooner we can put all this mystery and danger behind us. Once the curse is gone, Edward Ashton will no longer have to scheme and plot against us to be rid of it—although why he thinks the children and I are mixed up in his family curse is anyone's guess."

Optimistic—or was it optoomuchstic?—as ever, Penelope's step grew so light it nearly turned into a skip. She doubted she and Edward Ashton would ever be friends, of course, but if her plan worked—and why wouldn't it?—at least she would rid herself and the Incorrigible children of an enemy. "And who knows?" she thought. "With the exact words of the curse in hand, Madame Ionesco could make short work of the whole business. With any luck at all, Tuesday's full moon could be the farewell performance of the curse upon the Ashtons!"

Once outside the post office, Alexander consulted his compass, adjusted his sextant, and made careful note of the speed and direction of the wind. Thus prepared, they were off. The air was cold with an unsteady breeze. Moments of calm were broken by gusts of wind so strong the four travelers could lean into them, arms spread wide like the crossbars of kites, and imagine they were airborne.

The children found the brisk weather energizing (as you might expect, three children who had been raised by wolves were not easily put off by the elements). Penelope wrapped her coat tightly around her, but she did not complain. It was not the Swanburne way to grumble about things that couldn't be helped, and the weather certainly fit into that category—a fact that remains true to this very day.

The houses they passed were modest and tidy. Many had whimsical names displayed on painted signs in their front gardens: THE HAPPY CLAM and THE SALTY SHORES and so on. There was even a house named GIDDY-YAP, SEAHORSE, which made Penelope clap her half-frozen hands in delight. At once the children insisted on having a seahorse race. They did this by galloping to the corner while holding their noses as if underwater. They were gasping for air by the time it was over, and Penelope quickly declared all three of them winners, for at least they had managed not to pass out.

In this pleasant way, Penelope and the children found so much entertainment on their walk that it came as a shock when they turned yet another corner to find, not more charming houses and shuttered storefronts, but a wide, wooden-planked promenade, beyond which lay—the sea!

Cassiopeia pointed and yelled. "Look, Lumawoo! The sea is alive!" One can hardly blame her for thinking so, for the sea never stopped moving. The waves rolled with a slow and ceaseless undulation, like an enormous carpet being shaken out by tireless giants. Beyond the breakers, the cresting swells rose and disappeared. The wind scurried gray clouds across a pale blue sky, and the cloud-cast shadows moved across the water. Where the sun broke through, the rolling swells glittered in the light, as if someone had scattered fistfuls of tiny diamonds across the water's surface.

Alexander's mouth fell open. "Behold the vasty deep," he intoned. "Is there anything more—more . . . *sealike* than the sea?"

"Perhaps the greatest of the earth's mountains would come close," Penelope said with reverence, for she, too, was awestruck. "Perhaps the Swiss Alps would feel nearly as vast, if one stood at the bottom looking up."

"It is so beautiful. So mysterious." Whatever vague

ambitions Alexander might have had to be a navigator were given form and purpose that moment. His destiny was written in the waves, as if the sea's froth were the tea leaves in the bottom of a soothsayer's teacup.

"The sea is nice," Cassiopeia said, not nearly as impressed. "But the moon is more beautiful and mysterious."

"I think paintings are the most beautiful and mysterious," Beowulf said firmly. "Paintings and poems."

"It is a remarkable world, that has the sea and the moon and art, and spring flowers, new babies, and tasty biscuits, too," Penelope interjected, to keep peace among them. "We are lucky to live in it! But remember what Mrs. Clarke said: We must take deep breaths. Breathe in as much as you can, children." She demonstrated, inhaling so deeply that it felt like the salt air filled her to the bottoms of her feet.

(Nowadays, medical science has all kinds of ways to make sick people well, and to prevent well people from getting sick in the first place. But in Miss Penelope Lumley's day, it was widely believed that fresh air itself had medicinal properties. The sick were routinely sent to take deep breaths at seaside resorts, where they might also enjoy mud baths, saunas, natural hot springs, medicinal tar pits, and the like, all of which, it

91

was hoped, would restore them to good health.)

The children did as they were told, drawing the cold salt air all the way in and then blowing it out again. "How invigorating!" she declared. "Now let us go near the water and gather some shells." Penelope headed for the stair that led down from the promenade to the pebbly beach below. The children hesitated.

"I still smell bears," Beowulf insisted. The other two were not as certain, but agreed there was a whiff of something peculiar in the air.

Penelope knew from experience that the children's sense of smell was far keener than her own. There was nothing magical about it; they had simply been trained from an early age to use their noses the way a wolf might. Years of practice had made them good at it, just as years of practicing the violin would give someone the ability to play beautiful music, whereas someone new to the instrument might manage only a tuneless shriek. But sea bears? That was clearly impossible. In any case, Penelope was so eager to gather her first seashell that she could not wait another minute.

"Never fear, my dear Incorrigibles. I shall go in front." Confidently she marched down the stairs and took her first thrilling steps onto the sand. "Even in January, it is too warm for walruses in Brighton. They prefer Arctic regions, not English seaside resorts, and I believe they are peaceful creatures in any case. This way, please!"

Warily at first, the children followed. The beach was empty, save for the shrill-voiced gulls wheeling overhead and whatever snails and hermit crabs might have lurked among the rocks. Soon the children forgot their caution. They stood with mittened hands on their hips, gulping in the salt air. They ran in circles, making boot prints in the sand and boasting about how healthy they felt. Cassiopeia insisted she was growing taller with each breath, and her brothers indulged her by lifting her up onto Alexander's shoulders.

"Look," she said, pointing out to sea. "Someone is swimming."

Penelope shivered at the mere thought of it. "It must be a trick of the light. It is much too cold for swimming."

"Not for the fish." Beowulf lifted a hand to shield his eyes from the glare of the sun across the water. "But Cassawoof is right. That is no fish."

Penelope squinted toward the horizon. For a moment she thought she glimpsed a massive whiskered head breaching the surface. "It may be a walrus after all," she exclaimed. "How remarkable to spot one so far south!"

By now Alexander had his spyglass up. "Man overboard! All hands on deck!" He threw down the spyglass, crouched low to let his sister slip to the ground, and ran headlong toward the water.

Beowulf and Cassiopeia raced after him. "Wait!" Penelope yelled. She retrieved the spyglass from the sand and scanned the waves until she could see the swimmer, too. He was far out, well past the breaking surf, but he swam with strong, rhythmic strokes and seemed in no distress.

The children were at the water's edge. As far as Penelope knew the Incorrigibles had never once been swimming in their lives. Now all three looked ready to plunge into the icy sea to rescue this strange man. "Children, stop! He is not drowning," she called as she ran to them. "It appears he is swimming back to the beach." Fascinated, they stood and watched as the mysterious swimmer churned his way through the water. When the waves rose up, they lost sight of him, but each time he reappeared, lifted by the crest of a swell, he was that much closer to the shore.

Before long, it was apparent that he wore no bathing costume whatsoever.

"My goodness! Let us avert our gazes," Penelope instructed, for now it was too late to leave, and the man might yet need help, or a hot cup of tea at the very least. "I expect our swimming friend will be just as surprised to see us as we are to see him." The four of them turned their backs to the sea and covered their eyes. Soon there was a splashing sound, and a series of low-pitched grunts.

Penelope called over her shoulder. "Good afternoon! Please forgive our intrusion. We did not expect to encounter any swimmers here today. Do you require assistance?"

"Ah. Ha. Hah." His slow, deep laugh was like three strikes on a bass drum. "Wait. My clothes are by rocks. Don't peek."

His footsteps were silent on the sand, but in a voice low as thunder he narrated his progress. "First, pants. Then, boots. Then, shirt. Last, cape. Now you look."

Peeping shyly above their hands, Penelope and the children turned around. The man was tall, with thick black hair that ran rivers of seawater down his broad face. His shoulders were wide enough to have sat two Incorrigibles on each side. His mustache and sideburns bristled like the body brush Old Timothy used to groom the horses. His long bearskin cape hung to

*His shoulders were wide enough to have sat
two Incorrigibles on each side.*

the top of his boots, which had a military look to them, with the trousers tucked neatly inside.

Beowulf sniffed and pointed at the cape. "*That* is the bear I smelled."

"Smart boy. Russian bear very strong. Fur, very soft." The man shook his head like a great dog to get the water out of his hair, and spat seawater from his mouth. Then he bowed. "Captain Ivan Victorovich Babushkinov. At your service!" He straightened and clicked his boots together sharply enough to make a loud *clack!*

"It is a pleasure to meet you, Captain. I am Miss Penelope Lumley." Penelope did her best to curtsy on the uneven slant of the beach. "These children are my pupils. May I present Cassiopeia, Beowulf, and Alexander Incorrigible."

All three children eagerly offered socially useful phrases, as they had been taught to do when being introduced to a grown-up.

"How do you do, Captain Walrus Mustache?" Cassiopeia said grandly.

"Eternally obliged for you putting on your clothes, sir!" Beowulf said.

"All hail the captain!" Alexander offered a crisp salute. They all tried to click their heels as Captain

Babushkinov had. It was no easy thing to do in the sand, and they nearly knocked themselves over in the attempt.

"Alexander. Like the tsar. I approve of this name. But you two"—he gestured at Beowulf and Cassiopeia—"your names are too hard to say. I call you Boy and Girl instead." The captain lifted one black eyebrow at Penelope. "So. You are teacher?"

"Yes, I am the children's governess."

He lifted the other eyebrow. "You are here to teach them to swim?"

"Heavens, no! It is much too cold. . . ." She stopped, embarrassed. "That is to say . . ."

But he was already laughing that booming bass-drum laugh. "Ah. Ha. Hah. Too cold for you, maybe! I go back to hotel now. Cold swim makes hungry captain." He bowed at the waist. *"Do svidaniya."*

The children tried to say it, which made him laugh again.

"Is Russian. Means, 'See you later.'" Still laughing, he strode up the beach. *"Do svidaniya.* See you later!"

"I assure you, there are no Ashtons here, miss. We've no guests at all, not one. It's not what you'd call a profitable state of affairs, but that's the management's business, not mine." The hotel clerk leaned forward on the reception desk and peered unhappily at the Incorrigible children. "Personally, I appreciate the quiet. Gives a man time to think."

"Or take a nap," Penelope thought but did not say. It had taken nearly ten minutes for the clerk to respond to the brass bell that sat on the countertop, next to a sign that read WELCOME TO THE LEFT FOOT INN! WE APPRECIATE YOUR BUSINESS. PLEASE RING FOR PROMPT AND CHEERFUL SERVICE. On the bright side, the lack of a quick response had given the children many turns each to ring the bell, which they greatly enjoyed (although, upon reflection, the incessant *clang clang! Clang clang!* may have partly accounted for the clerk's ill temper).

"I have no wish to disturb your contemplations, sir, but my instructions are clear." Penelope glanced at the slip of paper Mrs. Clarke had given her. "We were told to meet our party at the inn on Front Street. The directions say, 'Look for the sign of the'—after which there is a drawing of a human foot." The inn fit the description perfectly, for the sign that hung above the door depicted a large bare foot sandwiched between the words THE and INN.

"Terribly sorry to disappoint you," the clerk said, sounding neither sorry nor disappointed. "As I said, the Left Foot Inn is vacant. Whoever you're looking for is not here. If you insist on staying, I suppose we could accommodate you. Unless you intend to be demanding! That would never do, as there's only me here this time of year, and a part-time housekeeper, and a cook on alternate Sundays. Frankly, we prefer to be left alone during the off-season."

Penelope turned and surveyed the hotel lobby. Other than the Incorrigibles and the clerk himself, there was not another soul in sight. "They should have checked in this afternoon," she insisted. "A dozen household staff, in the service of Lord Fredrick Ashton."

"Maybe they got lost on the way from the station." Alexander shook his head ruefully. "I should have navigated!"

"Maybe something ominous happened," Beowulf suggested. "Ominous weather?"

"Ominous pirates," Cassiopeia said knowingly.

The man looked at her askance. "Even pirates have the sense not to holiday at the beach in the off-season. If you'd come in July, we'd be full up. I'd have to turn you away, and wouldn't that be a pleasure! But Brighton, in January? Empty as a pauper's bank account."

In answer, the children clicked their heels together and imitated the captain's bass laugh. "Ah. Ha. Hah," they intoned, in their deepest voices.

"Not quite right, are they?" the clerk said sympathetically, to Penelope.

Penelope's spine went straight as the handle of a whip. "The children are merely observing that Brighton in the off-season is not as empty as you claim," she retorted. "We have scarcely been in town an hour, and already we have met a visitor from Russia. He is a military captain, of tremendous dignity and command."

"He had no clothes on," Cassiopeia explained.

"He had hair like a walrus." Beowulf stroked the sides of his face to indicate a fearsome growth of whiskers.

"He said I was like the tsar." Alexander snapped his heels together. This time it made such a loud and satisfying *clack* that he immediately checked his shoes to make sure they were still intact.

The hotel clerk gasped. "You don't mean the Babushkinovs? That horrible family! They were guests here last week, it's true, but there was . . . an incident. The management had no choice but to ask them to leave. If the Babushkinovs are still in Brighton—well, there's only one other hotel that's open. They must be staying there. Perhaps that's where your missing Ashtons are as well." He shuddered. "Sharing a hotel with those dreadful Babushkinovs!"

He looked around in terror and lowered his voice, although there was no one near to eavesdrop. "My advice is to avoid them at all costs. And whatever you do, don't mention Napoleon! It seems to set them off." (As the historians among you know, Napoleon Bonaparte had once been the Emperor of France. After conquering most of Europe, he decided to invade Russia, and a terrible war ensued. Russia prevailed over the French in the end, but it was a brutal conflict lasting many months, and hard feelings remained on both sides, even years later.)

"We shall do our best to avoid the topic," Penelope said impatiently. "Now, if you might direct us to the other hotel—"

But the clerk was not listening. "Horrible Babushkinovs!" he said, in a tremulous voice. "You'll know who they are, trust me. They're hard to miss, with all those badly behaved children."

At the mention of children, the Incorrigibles began to elbow one another and whisper in excitement. Penelope quieted them with a look. "If you please, sir," she said pointedly, "what is the name of the other hotel?"

"I'll write it down." From behind one ear he produced a pencil. "Can't miss it. It's just a few blocks down on Front Street." He took the note with the directions from Penelope and began to write on it, then stopped. "Well, that's your problem right there, miss. Look at that foot." He handed the paper back to her. "You've come to the wrong hotel. This is the Left Foot Inn. See?"

Penelope could not see, not until she thanked the man and led the children outside again. Then she looked at the paper, and up at the sign above the entrance to the inn. Both displayed feet, but they were not the same feet.

"On closer examination, it seems our stay in Brighton has gotten off on the wrong foot," she explained to the children. "Honestly, the clerk might have simply said so. Off we go, to the Right Foot Inn this time. Step lively, now!"

THE CHILDREN AMUSED THEMSELVES BY trying to walk forward with their right feet only. Unsteady hopping ensued. It slowed their progress, but as they did not have far to go, Penelope saw no harm in it.

Privately she could not stop wondering about the clerk's stern warnings against the Babushkinovs. The children must have been having similar thoughts, for soon Cassiopeia hopped over and tugged at Penelope's sleeve. "Are Horrible Babushkawoos pirates?" she asked, pirates being the most horrible sort of people she could think of.

Beowulf, too, hazarded a guess. "Badly behaved bank robbers?"

"I say horse thieves." Alexander balanced on his left leg long enough to add, "And failure to write thank-you notes."

"Or perhaps there was an unfortunate misunderstanding," Penelope cautioned. "We ought not to jump to conclusions based on gossip. Let us meet the Babushkawoos—I mean, Babushkinovs—with open minds, and see for ourselves what sort of people they are. As Agatha Swanburne said, 'There is no harm in carrying a borrowed umbrella, but toothbrushes and opinions should always be one's own.'"

The children liked this reply; in fact, the mere possibility of befriending a family of pirates, bank robbers, or horse thieves struck them as both thrilling and highly educational.

As for being "badly behaved," the Incorrigibles were in swift agreement: If the Babushkinov children were not already in the habit of writing prompt thank-you notes, it would be simple enough to teach them. After all, it was not so very long ago that the Incorrigibles themselves learned the difference between a salad fork and a fountain pen, or how to curtsy and bow and say a friendly hello when being introduced, rather than growl and hide in a corner. Such minor lapses in a person's education were easily corrected, given a bit of time and patient instruction.

Satisfied, the children continued hopping down Front Street until the Right Foot Inn came into view. At the sight of it Penelope froze. "I wonder if the Babushkinovs employ a governess?" she blurted. The children performed quick calculations—three Incorrigibles plus two Lumawoos and an unknown number of Babushkinovs sounded like marvelous fun to them—but Penelope was overcome with a sudden shyness, for the truth was she had never met another governess before.

On one foot—that is to say, hand—it would be pleasant to have a more grown-up companion with whom to pass the time, and perhaps swap teaching tips for the trickier bits of the multiplication tables. But on the other foot—hand!—what might a proper, professional, thoroughly Russian governess think of Penelope? A mere sixteen-year-old girl at her first position, who used biscuits to train her pupils, and recited poetry aloud in a dramatic voice even when no one was listening? Who could still—on occasion—be moved to tears when reading a children's storybook about ponies?

"As Agatha Swanburne said, 'Never assume, but if one must, never assume the worst,'" Penelope sternly reminded herself. "It is just as easy to imagine nice things as the opposite, so that is what I shall do."

To the children's delight, she joined them in hopping the last little way to the Right Foot Inn. "If there is a governess, I expect that she and I will get along famously," she announced, hopping double time to catch up. "When we all return to our homes, perhaps she will even wish to be pen pals." *Hop!* "I hope so! It would be fascinating to"—*hop!*—"learn a bit of Russian."

"Do svidaniya," the children boomed. "See you later!"

"Yes, *do svidaniya,*" Penelope repeated. "And how splendid it would be to hear all about the Imperial Russian Ballet, in Moscow. I wonder if"—*hop!*—"our new friends have ever seen them"—*hop!*—"perform?"

The Fifth Chapter

The horrible Babushkinovs
appear at last.

THE SIGN ABOVE THE ENTRANCE to the Right Foot Inn was nearly identical to that of the Left Foot Inn, with the sole exception that it showed a right foot, rather than a left. (To call it the "sole exception" is an example of a pun. As Lady Constance suspected, a pun is a word used to suggest more than one meaning at the same time. In this case, "sole" means "the only one," but it also means "the bottom of the foot." Curiously, a sole is also a type of fish. How one word came to mean three such unrelated things is a question too profound to grapple with at present. Alas, such mix-ups are common in every language and remain the cause of unfortunate misunderstandings to this very day.)

In any case, Alexander did not have to consult his compass, spyglass, or sextant to know that the Right Foot Inn was the right inn, for there in the lobby was Jasper, supervising the distribution of the luggage. He grinned to see them arrive.

"So you've turned up at last, you brave explorers! Mrs. Clarke told me to keep an eye out for you. Did you find the beach?"

The children nodded. They were no longer hopping, but they each stood on one leg, like a trio of flamingoes.

"What's happened to your other feet?" Jasper heaved the last of the trunks onto a luggage trolley. "I hope the hermit crabs didn't get hold of your toes."

"Ah. Ha. Hah," the children boomed. They each tried to click their heels while standing on one leg, but the sound of one foot clicking proved elusive, as they swiveled in vain on their sole remaining soles. Naturally Jasper thought they were demonstrating how to dislodge a hermit crab from one's toe.

He ruffled their three heads. "That'll show them crabs, eh? Go bite someone else's toe, you big-clawed bully! Hop on, I'll give you a ride."

The Incorrigibles gladly climbed aboard the luggage trolley and pretended to row with coat-hanger oars as Jasper pushed them along. "You're in room fourteen, in the east wing of the hotel," he said to Penelope, who had declined to ride, although it was tempting. "Lord and Lady Ashton are in the west wing. Mrs. Clarke thought it best to put a bit of distance around Lady Constance. Heaven knows what she'll do when she figures out that Brighton isn't going to turn into the Italian Riviera anytime soon!"

His remark puzzled Penelope, who knew nothing about Lady Constance's unfortunate misunderstanding. Jasper quickly filled her in.

"Let me see if I understand you properly, Jasper: Lady Constance pretends to believe we are taking our holiday in Brighton, which is true, although she thinks it is false. Meanwhile, she is convinced that the entire staff is playacting in order to conceal from her a trip to Italy that does not, in fact, exist." Penelope shook her head. If only solving the mystery of the Ashton curse was this straightforward!

"That's about the size of it," Jasper agreed. He leaned back to stop the trolley from rolling any farther, for they had arrived at the end of the hall. "All ashore!" he called to the children, who jumped off and began hauling the suitcases to the door. To Penelope he quietly added, "I wouldn't waste your time unpacking, Miss Lumley. My guess is we'll be on the next train back to Ashton Place once Lady Constance figures out the truth."

Penelope lost her balance as surely as if she had been standing on the deck of a ship in a squall. *Would* Lady Constance demand they all go home, despite the doctor's orders? With Simon still on his way to Brighton and a pesky curse yet to undo? Not if she could help it.

She turned to Jasper. "Thank you for your assistance with the luggage. As for Lady Constance, we must all do our best not to upset her. In fact," she added, thinking quickly, "I recommend that all of us 'play along' with her unfortunate misunderstanding."

"But surely that's just setting her up for disappointment." Jasper looked dubious, but Penelope was, after all, a governess. The opinion of such a highly educated person carried a great deal of weight among the staff. "Plus it's a bit complicated to pull off, don't you think?"

"Nonsense, it could not be more simple." Penelope stood straight and tall, and imagined herself a great orator from the days of antiquity, inspiring reluctant troops to undertake an impossible mission. "All you need do is pretend that you are pretending we are staying in Brighton, while at the same time revealing that you are concealing a trip to the Italian Riviera. Think of her health, Jasper!" she pressed. "Given her delicate condition, we must not deliver bad news unnecessarily. And surely there is no harm in expecting nice things to happen."

"No, of course not. Until they don't," he answered with a frown. "That's when the trouble starts. But if you think it's the right thing to do . . ."

"Right foot in!" the children cried, and jumped onto their right feet, for Jasper had said the word "right," and this was their new game.

"I know it is, Jasper," Penelope said. She smiled reassuringly. "I will leave it in your capable hands to persuade all the staff to do the same."

"I'll do my best," he said. "But I'm starting to wish we'd never left home."

"Left foot in!" the children shouted, and switched feet.

JASPER PRODUCED THE KEY AND dragged their suitcases inside. It was a cozy room, clean and tidy—shipshape, one might say—with a pleasingly nautical theme.

Paintings of sailing ships hung on the walls, and the bedroom window was in the shape of a porthole. There were two double beds, so that Penelope could share one with Cassiopeia, and the boys could share the other. The beds were comfortable, neither too soft nor too hard, and the bedcovers had a crisp navy-blue stripe running around each edge. The detail reminded Penelope of the Swanburne school uniforms, which she took as a lucky omen.

Confident that her instructions to Jasper had settled this business about making a quick exit from Brighton, Penelope had the children unpack and put away all their things, just as if they were at home. She arranged for dinner to be delivered to their room. (As it happened, the evening's dinner special was a tender fillet of sole, swimming, as it were, in a sea of buttery sauce.)

All the while they were unpacking, and eating, and even as they readied themselves for bed, the Incorrigible children could not stop talking about the Babushkinovs. They wondered how many children there were, how many boys and how many girls, what they looked like and how they dressed. They wondered what their favorite books and poems were, what games they knew, and how they felt about navigation, paintings, and pirates (you may easily guess which of the Incorrigible children wondered which of these things).

Most of all, the Incorrigibles wondered how soon they might meet this fascinating family, and how long it would take for them all to become the very best of friends.

"Questions may be asked at will, but answers will come when they wish," Penelope said as she tucked each curious, drowsy Incorrigible into bed.

"Did wise flounder Agatha say that?" asked Cassiopeia, who still sometimes mixed up the words "founder" and "flounder." (To clarify: Founder means the person who first built or created something, and flounder is a type of fish that is often mistaken for sole. The word "flounder" has other meanings as well, but there is no time to delve into that now, as the Incorrigible children are sleepy and must be put to bed.)

"Agatha Swanburne said many things, and that may have been among them," Penelope replied, for she herself could not remember if she had heard that saying before, or had simply made it up on the spot. "Good night, one and all."

She blew out the last of the candles and settled in a chair near the porthole-shaped window. Her mind, too, was filled with questions, although not about the Babushkinovs. Was the Home for Ancient Mariners close enough to walk, or would she have to persuade Old Timothy to drive them in the carriage? Was the Brighton postal clerk being optoomuchstic to promise that her letter to Simon would be delivered on Friday, despite its poetic form of address? And would a borrowed pirate costume from a flop West End operetta be enough to fool Great-Uncle Pudge into revealing the secrets of Ahwoo-Ahwoo?

It was then that the moon finally peeked out from behind the clouds. "Waxing gibbous, a few days short of full," she thought, gazing out the window. "If my plan succeeds, the bouncing Baby Ashton will never feel a twinge of the Ashton curse. Although I suppose a knack for baying at the moon is hardly the worst thing that can happen to a child! Just look at the Incorrigibles. They can bark and howl with the best of them, and never give it a second thought."

Penelope stifled a yawn and glanced at the sleeping children. The boys lay curled on their right sides, neat as two spoons in a drawer, but Cassiopeia had sprawled like a starfish and took up the whole bed. Luckily, the girl was a sound sleeper and did not awaken as Penelope gently rearranged her limbs, by first tucking the left foot in, and then the right. Then Penelope slipped her whole self in, under the covers. Soon she was as deeply asleep as the rest.

By the following afternoon the children had explored the entire hotel, with the sole exception of the west wing, where they had been told not to set foot (neither right foot nor left, it was made clear by Mrs. Clarke).

With their cheerful spirits, good manners, and socially useful phrases, the Incorrigibles charmed everyone they met. The front-desk clerk let them ring the bell as much as they liked. The bellhops gave them rides on the luggage trolleys, and they even convinced the cook to let them help peel potatoes in the kitchen. "Such lovely, well-behaved children," members of the hotel staff whispered to one another. "Not like those terrible Babushkinovs!"

Naturally, hearing this made the Incorrigibles even more eager to meet their future friends, but the morning came and went, and they caught no sight of them. Nor, despite some vigorous sniffing, did they detect any smell of bears.

Still, Penelope kept them occupied. After lunch they put on their coats and walked back to the post office.

There Penelope left instructions that all incoming mail for P. Lumley ought to be delivered to the Right Foot Inn. She took extra care in describing how only the Right Foot Inn was the right inn, so that no letter might be wrongly left at the Left Foot Inn, which was the wrong inn. Naturally, the postal clerk understood it all perfectly.

By the time they were done at the post office, the sun had broken through the clouds, and they decided to walk to the end of the chain pier, which jutted out over a thousand feet into the Channel. It was called a chain pier because it was structured much the way a suspension bridge is, with towers placed at either end and spaced along the length of it. The towers sat upon strong oak piles sunk deep into bedrock, and heavy chains draped between the towers supported the weight of the pier.

After making it to the end of the pier and admiring the view of Brighton from the sea, the Incorrigibles pleaded to go back to the beach for more deep breaths, and to search for hermit crabs among the rocks. Alas, they found none, and wondered if it was simply too cold for the little creatures.

"Perhaps they are shy. Hermits are known for being solitary," Penelope explained. (If her teeth had not been chattering with cold, she might have further explained that the word "hermit" comes from the Greek word *eremos*, which means desert. "But hermit crabs do not live in the desert," you say. You are correct; they do not. However, in ancient times there were people who spent their days in solitude, thinking and having epiphanies. They often chose to live in the desert, away from the distractions of the world, and so the word "hermit" came to describe a person who prefers to be alone. That crustaceans in the sea are named after people in the desert is yet another example of how slippery words can be. Fortunately, when one tires of words, one can always look at paintings, which manage to have their say without using any words at all.)

Everywhere they went, the children practiced clicking their heels and imitating the captain's unmistakable basso laugh. Only when they were shivering too much to even say "Ah. Ha. Hah!" was Penelope able to persuade them to go back to the hotel. They stood in the lobby with coats on, thawing themselves gratefully by the hearth.

"Surely there is nothing so pleasant as coming close to the fire when one is chilled to the bone!" Penelope finally dared to peel off her gloves. "I think we have each earned a cup of hot tea, and some biscuits, and perhaps a nap."

"Ah. Ha. HAM!" Cassiopeia said to Beowulf, for while they were out, Penelope had casually mentioned that they might soon be paying a call to the Home for Ancient Mariners, or the HAM, for short.

"Ah. Ha. HAM!" he boomed back. They clicked their heels and fell to the ground. *"Do svidaniya!* See you later!" they said, giggling, and got up to do it again.

They were so busy laughing and clicking and falling that they did not notice that the doors to the hotel lobby had opened to let in a remarkable parade. First in was a silver-haired woman in a wheelchair, seemingly asleep. A heavy lap robe was tucked around her legs, but still one could see she was grandly dressed, with both hands plunged into a fur-trimmed muff and a lacquered brooch pinned high on the lapel of her coat.

The wheeled chair was pushed by a man, somewhat younger than the captain. His round-rimmed glasses gave him an intent, owlish expression, as if he were thinking profound thoughts. His dark hair was wild from the wind, and long enough to curl around his collar.

Behind them came a large baby carriage, pushed

There may have been a baby in the carriage, or maybe not.

with effort by a young woman in a long, slim-fitting coat. She was slight, pale in complexion but pink-cheeked from the cold, with nervous, darting eyes and mouse-brown hair that hung down her back in a single loose braid. There may have been a baby in the carriage, or maybe not; it was piled so high with blankets that it was impossible to tell.

The swirl of cold air that accompanied this group caused the hearth fire to flare up, and that is what finally caught the attention of Penelope and the Incorrigibles. They turned in time to see a girl race in and dart in front of the baby carriage, as if she were being chased. She looked to be around Alexander's age. She wore a scarlet wool coat with a fur-trimmed collar and brass buttons that ran all the way down the front, and a matching hat with flaps that covered both of her ears. Even her gloves were scarlet. Her hair was pale as wheat, and hung in ringlets on either side of her face. It was plain she had been crying.

Two younger boys ran in after her. They were identical twins and dressed alike, too, but they were not difficult to tell apart, as one of them had a ferocious black eye.

"You rotten boys," the girl shrieked. "Words cannot describe my hatred of you. Noisy and Vulgar! That is what you should have been named."

"Be quiet, Veronika," one of the boys spat back. "Or we shall dip your hair in ink while you sleep."

"And put bugs in your shoes," said the other.

"And spit in your soup."

"And steal your diary and read it aloud! Oh, I wonder! Who is Veronika in love with today?"

Gleefully they stuck out their matching tongues. Poor Veronika sank to her knees, weeping. "Grandmamma!" she wailed, and collapsed fully to the ground. "Make them stop!"

The old woman in the wheelchair stirred. Slowly she withdrew her hands from the muff. Each bony finger bore a precious stone the size of a duck's egg. She unfurled a bejeweled claw and crooked it at the twins, who gulped and fell silent.

"*Nyet!*" she growled.

The boys sniveled, and Veronika beat her fists against the carpet and wept passionately from the floor. A piercing infant wail added itself to the mix, prompting the anxious young woman with the braid to rush to the front of the carriage, cooing and scolding. "Look what you've done, you awful children! You have woken Maximilian! Come to Julia, darling Max! My sweet, tiny Max, my delicate infant, my prize . . ."

She dug through the blankets until the child was revealed. He was neither tiny nor an infant; in fact, he was old enough to sit up and yell, and that is what he now did. His face was round as a full moon, and his mouth opened like a perfect O. The sound that came out would have been impressive for a trumpet; for a baby, it was nothing short of remarkable. As he yowled, his chubby fists flailed by his sides, but he was bundled in a coat so thick that his arms hardly moved. More than anything, he looked like a baby dodo flapping its useless wings.

The man who pushed the wheelchair did not turn his head or raise his voice when he spoke, but his voice was so sharp with annoyance it easily cut through the din. "Constantin Ivanovich! Boris Ivanovich! If you continue to behave like wild animals, I will make arrangements to donate you to an English zoo. Would you like that, I wonder? Your parents would thank me, I'm sure."

"Papa will not let you!" the boys screeched as one, but clearly they were afraid, and their sniveling turned to full-throated bawls.

The baby cried harder and beat his arms, until his moon face went scarlet as Veronika's coat. Julia lifted his overheated bulk from the carriage and bounced him on her hip. "Maxie, precious! Ignore your brothers, they are monsters. Someday you will be bigger than them. Then you will teach them a lesson!"

At the sight of the unhappy baby, the Incorrigibles rushed over to help. Cassiopeia patted one flushed and sweaty hand, and Beowulf jumped back and forth in front of him, playing peekaboo.

"Ah. Ha. Hah!" Alexander said, to make the baby laugh. The child stopped crying and gave him a puzzled stare.

The twin with the black eye (it was Constantin) also stopped bawling and scowled. "What are you saying?"

"He is mocking Papa!" the other one, Boris, cried.

"Mocking!" Constantin agreed. "Mocking Papa!"

As one, the furious twins ran up to Alexander as if to strike him. Instead, they ripped off their mittens and hurled them to the ground at his feet.

"A duel! We challenge you to a duel!" they cried. "This insult cannot go unanswered!"

"You dropped your gloves," Alexander said helpfully, and stooped to pick them up. When he bent over, the twins pushed him to the ground. Beowulf and Cassiopeia began to growl, but Alexander looked more startled than hurt.

"You terrible boys!" Julia had to shout over Baby

Max's earsplitting wails. "That is no way to introduce yourselves."

"Beowulf! Cassiopeia!" Penelope rushed forward and helped Alexander to his feet. "No growling, if you please! These children are visitors from a far-off land, and their customs may be different from ours. Let us make our friendly intentions known." Hastily she curtsied to the grandmother. "I beg your pardon, madame! It seems there has been an unfortunate misunderstanding. . . ."

With sudden strength, the grandmother wheeled herself close enough to the twins to give each of them a pinch. "No duels, do you hear me?" she said. "Do you want to get us thrown out of another hotel? I will tell your mother and father that you are acting like savages! Then what, eh? You know the captain's temper."

Constantin and Boris went limp as rag dolls and hung their heads. "Sorry, Grandmamma," they mumbled, and began to weep afresh, but silently this time. In friendlier circumstances, the Incorrigibles would have offered their pocket handkerchiefs, but in a situation so fraught with confusion it seemed better to wait.

Penelope turned to the grandmother. "Madame, I apologize for this poor first impression. We mean no offense. I am the children's governess, Miss Penelope Lumley—"

The old woman held up her hand. *"Nyet!* I am too old to meet people. Veronika! Get off the floor and speak to this English girl. Why your father insisted on coming to this place I don't know. The Black Sea! Now, that's a good beach."

Veronika, who had been thrashing in misery this whole time, leaped gracefully to her feet. She seemed perfectly cheerful now that her three brothers were all crying. "Good afternoon! My name is Veronika Ivanovna Babushkinova. I am twelve years old. I am so very pleased to make your acquaintance." Then, rising to her toes as much as a person can do in winter boots, she spun around twice, in a perfect double pirouette.

Penelope clapped her hands. "How marvelous! Did you see that, children? We have a ballerina in our midst."

Beowulf looked unimpressed. Cassiopeia still glared at the twins.

"My ballet shoes are in my room," Veronika trilled. "Shall I run get them now? In them I would dance *en pointe.*"

"On pwah," her brothers repeated sarcastically through their tears. "Ugly Veronika and her smelly toe shoes!"

"These are my awful brothers," Veronika said brightly.

125

"How I wish they had never been born! May I present Boris Ivanovich Babushkinov and Constantin Ivanovich Babushkinov. They are twins. Eight years old. Savages!" At the sounds of their names, the twins clicked their heels and bowed. Then they went back to sniveling.

Veronika gestured toward the baby. "This is my youngest brother. Maximilian Ivanovich Babushkinov. We call him Baby Max. Julia is his nurse." Julia smiled nervously as she switched the massive, squalling baby to her other hip. "And this is our grandmamma, the Princess Popkinova. I think she has fallen back asleep." The old lady's eyes were closed once more. Her chin had dropped on her chest, which rose and fell in time to a gentle snore.

"Don't forget your tutor." Julia threw a sideways glance at the dark-haired man behind the wheelchair.

"I apologize, of course! How could I forget?" Veronika's cheeks flushed. "This is our tutor, Master Gogolev."

"Good afternoon," the man said. His tone was quiet, almost indifferent, but his owlish eyes seemed to miss nothing. "I am Karl Romanovich Gogolev. At your service, Miss Lumley."

"I am pleased to make your acquaintance, Master

Gogolev," Penelope answered. So the Babushkinov children had a tutor, not a governess! Already she found herself wishing he had spent more time teaching good manners to his pupils.

The twins were now whispering "Smelly toe shoes, smelly toe shoes," over and over.

"My brothers are barbarians," Veronika explained. "They are not gentlemen, like *you*." This last remark was directed at Alexander. She curtsied as a ballerina would at the end of a performance, one knee touching the ground, head bent low, and her arms swooping wide like wings. Then she popped up again and giggled. "Tonight we are to go ice skating. You will come. Yes? Yes!"

Alexander gazed up at Veronika, for she was a head taller than he was. There was an odd, stricken look on his face, and Penelope worried that he might have hurt himself when he was pushed by the twins. "Are you all right?" she asked, but he seemed not to hear her.

"Alexander Incorrigible Incorrigible," he managed to say, and clicked his heels. "At your service, Miss Veronika Ballerina Babushkawoo!"

THE SIXTH CHAPTER

A friendship is formed on thin ice.

SO THESE WERE THE HORRIBLE Babushkawoos! They were a lively bunch, to be sure. "Veronika is a talented dancer, and the twins are full of pep," Penelope conceded, when the Incorrigibles asked her what she thought of their new acquaintances. "And Baby Max's lung capacity is nothing short of remarkable. He could easily grow up to be an opera singer, with proper training and years of practice, of course."

Penelope and the children had retired to their room for a well-earned rest; as you can see, she was still trying hard to keep an open mind about the Babushkinovs.

But, honestly! The baby was louder than a Bloomer steam engine pulling into the station. Veronika was an attention seeker of the first order, and those cruel, whining twins would be enough to drive anyone mad. What a job it would be to have to teach them! Their tutor, Master Gogolev, was an odd duck too, dour and sharp-tongued, but Penelope could hardly blame the man for having a touch of *weltschmerz* about him. One could only imagine the difficulties he had to contend with every day.

Penelope's own pupils made no such effort to keep their minds open; in fact, the Incorrigibles had already formed an unshakable opinion of their fellow guests at the Right Foot Inn. "They are dreadful! Savages! Barbarians! We *love* the Babushkawoos," they declared, clearly in awe of this strange, violent family.

That three well-behaved children who had been raised by wolves would be so charmed by the utterly untamed Babushkinovs struck Penelope as ironic, but she thought it best not to say so, other than to offer a gentle warning. "Do not forget yourselves, my dear Incorrigibles. You must act with courtesy, no matter how—well, *expressive* your new friends may be. That is their way, and we have our way. Do you understand?"

The Incorrigibles assured her that they did understand, and that they would use the evening's ice-skating trip as a chance to show off their finest behavior: good manners on ice, one might call it.

Satisfied with this reply, Penelope slumped in the chair by the porthole window. Ice-skating! As if hunting hermit crabs in January had not been bone-chilling enough! She desperately wished there were a way to get out of it, but of course the Incorrigibles were dead set on going, each for his or her own reason.

Daredevil Cassiopeia longed to rocket across the ice with razor-sharp blades strapped to her feet. To her, it seemed the ideal mode of travel. Aloud she wondered if they might someday move to wildest Canada and live as the Eskimaux do, with their igloos and sled dogs.

It was the frozen pond itself that fascinated Beowulf. He was deeply curious about how such a large, flat sheet of ice might catch and reflect the moonlight, and pondered how an artist like himself might represent such ethereal loveliness in paint.

Alexander mumbled something about "cardiovascular exercise" and "preparedness for Arctic exploration," but neither of these explained the care with which he chose his outfit for the evening (that his clothes would be hidden beneath his coat seemed not to factor into his thinking). Nor did they account for his many fruitless attempts to smooth his hair, which had been made hopelessly unruly by a long day in a close-fitting hat.

Evidently, Veronika Ivanovna Babushkinova was the main attraction as far as Alexander was concerned. This fact was not lost on his siblings. Cassiopeia teasingly began calling him the Tsar of Love, but Beowulf was more sympathetic to his brother's plight. He offered to compose some love poetry on Alexander's behalf, and set about trying to find words to rhyme with "Veronika." After a quarter of an hour's hard labor, all he had come up with was the woefully unromantic "harmonica," which he declared too shrill and reedy for use in a love poem.

"Tell her to change her name," he suggested.

For some reason Alexander took great offense at this. His mittens had been hung by the fire to dry; instead he yanked his handkerchief out of his pocket and hurled it to the ground. "Veronika she is, and Veronika she must remain! This insult cannot go unanswered! I challenge you to a—"

One stern glance from his governess restored him to his senses. "A game of chess," he finished, his head hung low in shame. Beowulf accepted the challenge, and the two brothers sat down to play. With Penelope's watchful eye upon them, they conducted themselves with impeccable sportsmanship.

"Excellent move, little brother! I did not see that coming."

"You're playing well, too, big brother! Sorry to capture your knight. Couldn't be helped."

"Not at all. On the bright side, I still have both bishops. Whoops! I fear I've got you in check for the moment. Sorry about that!"

Penelope leaned back in the chair and closed her eyes, and reflected on the fact that bad behavior was nearly as contagious as puns. "And now we have a whole evening to spend with those horrible—I mean, those interesting Babushkinovs. But blast! Why must it be ice-skating?" She had only been ice-skating once, some years before, when a bitter cold snap caused the largest pond in Heathcote to freeze all the way across. It was a rare event, so rare that Miss Mortimer canceled all classes and declared a Totally Unplanned Skating Holiday. Little, shivering Penelope had spent the day of the TUSH falling on her bottom and desperately wishing for a cup of hot tea.

"Lumawoo?" Cassiopeia was practicing her skating technique by hopping from one leg to the other. "Why do Babushkawoos have three names?"

Reluctantly Penelope opened her eyes. "That is how Russian names work. The first name is your own, the second is based on your father's first name, and the third is your family name. The endings of the second and third names change a bit depending on whether you are a boy or a girl."

Cassiopeia gave another hop. "What would *our* Babushkawoo names be?"

"That would depend on the names of your parents," she replied uneasily.

Alexander and Beowulf looked up from their chessboard. Due to their extreme courtesy, the game had quickly ended in a draw, as neither player could bear to checkmate the other.

"But what *are* the names of our parents?" Alexander asked.

Three trusting faces gazed at her for an answer. "Well . . . that is to say . . . I do not know," Penelope admitted. "I am afraid the identity of your parents is somewhat of a mystery at present."

The children were silent for a moment, then talked quietly among themselves. In the end they decided to use Woof as their second name, in honor of Mama Woof, the very large and frankly very unusual wolf that had cared for them during their days in the forest. Incorrigible was the family name given to them by Lord Fredrick. He may not have meant it as a compliment at the time, but now they could not imagine being called anything else.

"Cassiopeia Woofovna Incorrigiblovna!" It was a great deal to pronounce, but Cassiopeia nearly managed it. She took a low, ballerina-style bow at the end.

"Beowulf Woofovich Incorrigiblov!" Beowulf bowed crisply at the waist.

"Alexander Woofovich Incorrigiblov, at your service!" his brother said, with a sharp *clack* of his heels. "Ah. Ha. Hah!"

Cassiopeia looked up from the floor, where her bow had landed her. "What would your Babushkawoo name be, Lumawoo?"

Penelope's brow creased in thought. "It would be Penelope . . . Penelope . . ." But the Long-Lost Lumleys had been lost for so long that minor details like their first names had all but faded into the mist. She stared up at the ceiling to help her concentrate. "My father's first name . . . I am nearly certain his first name was—"

"Was?" Beowulf interjected. "Is he extinct?"

"Hans" is what she was going to say, but Beowulf's question plunged her into icy seas.

Cassiopeia sprang up and tugged on her sleeve. "Don't look sad, Lumawoo. You can be a Woof Incorrigible, too."

Penelope tried to smile. "Penelope Swanburnovna Lumawoovna," she said, when she could speak. "That is what my Babushkawoo name would be."

At six o'clock, after an early supper, all of the eager ice-skaters, and those who were less than eager, gathered in the hotel lobby to walk to the pond as a group. The three elder Babushkinov children were there, and Max rode in the carriage with Julia pushing. Master Gogolev was present as well.

Once more Veronika was dressed in a fur-trimmed coat with matching hat and muff, but this time she was in pure white, from head to toe. "I shall be a dancing snowflake upon the ice," she sang out as she rose to the tips of her white leather boots. The remark made Alexander sigh and press his hands to his heart, while Beowulf and Cassiopeia were moved to improvise a short ballet they called *Dance of the Melting Snowflake*. It was lovely and brief, and ended tragically for the flake.

Master Gogolev ran his hands through his unkempt hair. "There is no need to wait. The captain is not coming, alas." His remark seemed directed at Julia.

"Nor is his wife. Alas for you!" she retorted, a hint of sharpness in her voice. "Nor the princess."

"Does Grandmamma skate?" Cassiopeia asked, who had just realized that riding a wheeled chair on ice would be doubly slippery, and therefore twice as exciting.

Julia rocked the carriage, for Max was already beginning to fuss. "The Princess Popkinova has retired for the evening," she said.

"Grandmamma is very old," Veronika explained. "Older than she looks."

"She must be two hundred, then!" Beowulf said, impressed.

"She could live in a HAP," Alexander quipped. "A Home for Ancient Princesses."

Veronika laughed and twirled. "I do not know what that means! English is so difficult. Yet Master Gogolev says my English is . . . I have forgotten the word— *incredible*, is that it?"

"Your English is not bad," Master Gogolev said drily. "It is your thinking I find incredible."

Veronika giggled at what she took to be a compliment. Against the backdrop of her white coat and hat, her blushing cheeks stood out like a pair of apples dropped in the snow.

"Let us go," said Julia anxiously. "Before the baby starts to cry." Poor Max was helpless as a trussed goose in his carriage, overdressed and sweating in his coat and hat, and smothered in blankets all around. Master Gogolev gave a nod, and the hotel doorman pulled open the door, letting in a blast of cold air that scattered all the papers on the front desk.

"Wait," roared a deep bass drum of a voice. "We come, too."

Captain Babushkinov's stride was deliberate but covered a great deal of ground; in three steps he had crossed the lobby and loomed before them. In his wake, moving at her own pace, was a woman who seemed to embody the various qualities of all the Babushkinovs rolled into one. She had excellent posture, like Veronika, and wore a great deal of jewelry, like Grandmamma. Like Max, she was dressed for the Arctic winter, and (as was about to become evident) like Boris and Constantin, she had no qualms at all about hurting people's feelings.

"Mama!" the twins cried, and rushed to hug her around the waist. "Will you skate with us? Will you?"

"Nyet." She peeled their arms loose. "Me, on the ice? I would rather die! But your father insists. Perhaps he

wishes to torment me."

"Natasha, never!" The captain reached for her hand, which she quickly drew away. "Your tongue is more sharp than my sword. Be sweet, my darling."

"If I am sharp, Ivan, *you* know why," his wife retorted, and turned her back on him. To Penelope, the swerve into argument seemed unprovoked, but she knew from her time with the Ashtons that other people's private lives were just that: private, and full of secrets.

MASTER GOGOLEV MADE BRIEF INTRODUCTIONS, and they were off. A porter from the hotel led the way with a torch, for it was already dark. Veronika seized her father's hand and walked next to him, swinging both their arms and chattering ceaselessly as a monkey. Now unescorted, Madame Babushkinov insisted on taking Master Gogolev's arm. Stiffly he obliged.

"Perhaps we ought to turn back," she said shortly. "I fear Master Gogolev has forgotten his hat." The tutor was bareheaded, as before, and his hair blew every which way in the wind. Despite the cold night air, his scarf hung loosely around his neck, and he made no move to tighten it.

"No offense, madame," he replied mildly. "But as you know, I do not wear hats. The pressure on my skull limits my thinking."

"You will catch cold, then. And what good is your thinking if you die of pneumonia?" She turned to Penelope. "Master Gogolev and I have this argument daily. I think he likes to provoke me. Hats were the source of our family's fortune—or what is left of it," she said with sudden bitterness. "Boris, Constantin, do you remember the family motto?"

" 'Let no head go uncovered!' " the twins bellowed as one.

"Yes! Let no head go uncovered!" She laughed, sharp and joyless. "Until not so long ago, hats made us rich. Every time the snow fell, it was like rubles falling into the pockets of the Babushkinovs. But then . . ."

"Madame," Master Gogolev said abruptly. "If it pleases you, I will return to the hotel and put on a hat."

She patted his arm. "No, my dear Gogolev. Your skull suits you the way it is. Free, and unencumbered. But I warn you, if you get sick we shall be in the market for a new tutor."

"You break my heart with such threats, madame," he answered, smooth as milk. "How could I manage without my dear pupils? I live for your children, as you know. They are sweetness incarnate."

Penelope walked just to the side of these two, with

the Incorrigibles directly ahead of her. She knew she ought not to be eavesdropping, but really, she could not recall ever being privy to such a fascinating conversation! How strange these Babushkinovs were, with their bitterness and misery! And yet everyone was pretending to be happy, at least some of the time, while saying the opposite of what they truly meant.

"Look!" Despite being told not to, Constantin and Boris had raced ahead to see how much farther it was to the frozen pond. Now they came roaring back. "The ice is on fire! Come look!"

The twins were guilty of hyperbole, but for good reason. A bonfire blazed at one end of the pond, and torches that stood nearly as tall as the captain had been planted in the ground all around the pond's edge. The reflection of their leaping flames turned the perimeter of the ice a brilliant rosy hue. Ice skates in various sizes had been laid out on blankets near the fire, and their metal blades also caught the light, until the skates themselves were edged in flame.

Beowulf was entranced by the play of firelight on the ice. Eagerly he strapped on a pair of skates. "I am fire skating!" he cried, wobbling his way onto the ice. Cassiopeia and Alexander quickly joined him. It took a few minutes of slipping and sliding and hanging on to one another, but the Incorrigibles were naturally quick and agile, and soon enough all three were gliding capably along.

The Babushkinov twins each grabbed one of the same pair of skates and nearly got into a brawl over it, but once that was settled they were twin blurs crisscrossing the ice, fast and aggressive. A pair of tiny double-bladed skates was found for Baby Max. Julia hovered near him, begging him to let her hold his hands, but it turned out he could skate better than he could walk, and his outfit was so padded that his frequent falls only made him laugh.

And then there was Veronika, who did not merely skate, but danced on the ice. She could sail across the full length of the pond with one leg extended high behind her. She arched her back and made graceful sweeping movements with her arms, then spun like a coin set on edge. When she stopped, she was hardly out of breath, and she wore a dazzling smile.

"Again, again!" the Incorrigibles cried. Alexander in particular could not stop clapping. "Encore!" he yelled. ("Encore" is simply the French word for "again." It is shouted with appreciation during the applause to urge a performer to offer one more song, soliloquy, pirouette, puppet show, magic trick, or what have you. A polite cry of "Encore!" can also be used to demand a second helping of dessert, particularly a French dessert, such as an éclair, a mousse—which is not to be confused with an elk—a tarte Philippe, or even some tasty petites madeleines.)

Veronika bowed so low that the fur trim of her hat brushed the ice. "I ought to say no, my ballet master says skating is bad for my feet—but all right!" She soared through another gorgeous turn around the pond. Her brothers paid no attention, but the Incorrigibles watched in awe, until an even more impressive sight caught their attention.

"Look! Lumawoo on skates!" Cassiopeia cried, pointing.

And it was true. After giving the matter some thought, Penelope had decided to give ice skating one more try. She was a Swanburne girl, after all, and as Agatha Swanburne once said, "Resist temptation, embrace adventure, and learn how to tell the difference!"

Awkward as a chick newly out of its egg, she stood wobbling on the ice and willed herself not to fall. She took tiny, halting steps across the slippery surface, or tried to. "Oh!" she cried, cartwheeling her arms for balance. "Whoops!"

As she toppled, a set of arms swooped in and caught her from behind. It was Master Gogolev. They skated on together, with one of his hands lightly supporting her elbow and the other firmly around her waist. At first Penelope was alarmed, as he took her around the pond much faster than she would have liked. But his grip was firm, and to have someone steady her while demonstrating the smooth, steady rhythm of correct skating technique made all the difference.

By the time they finished a third lap, she felt able to maneuver slowly but reliably across the ice. Master Gogolev seemed to intuit as much, and let her go without a word.

"Thank you," she called as he glided away. He did not answer; perhaps he was already lost in some deep internal philosophical debate. Penelope completed a few cautious loops on her own. She was no longer cold, quite the contrary; but her legs were tired and the skates were beginning to pinch. Satisfied that the challenge of ice skating had been met and mastered, she left the ice, removed her skates, and made her way back to the bonfire. Porters from the hotel had set out chairs nearby, and were now preparing some sort of warm drink in a large kettle hung over the fire.

Captain Babushkinov stood by his seated, bored-looking wife. He smiled at Penelope's approach. "Still too cold for you, teacher?"

She peeled off her gloves and held her hands to her face. Her cheeks were warm with exertion. "On the contrary, I am rather flushed."

"Is swimming weather, not skating weather. Ah. Ha. Hah!" The captain's laugh boomed like cannon fire. "English beach in January is like Russian spring!"

Penelope did not want to argue, although she certainly had no intention of going swimming anytime soon. "I am sure you are correct, Captain. When I was at school in Heathcote, the pond froze over so rarely that the one time it did, it was the occasion for a school holiday. . . ."

Her words trailed off as a terrible realization overtook her. Yes, the past few days had been brisk, but that memorable, long-ago day of the Totally Unplanned Skating Holiday in Heathcote had been far colder. In fact, the winter of the TUSH had been one of the coldest winters she could remember.

She turned and addressed the two hotel porters who tended the kettle. "Pardon me. Would I be correct to assume that you two gentlemen are responsible for the excellent preparations made here: the torches, the chairs, the bonfire? Not to mention this tasty-smelling beverage that is even now simmering away in the kettle?"

Proudly they stirred. "That we are, miss," one of them said with a confident smile.

She smiled back. "I thought so! One question. Upon your arrival at the pond, did either of you think to measure the thickness of the ice?"

They looked at one another, somewhat less confident. "We were told the pond was frozen," one of them answered.

"Well frozen," the other said. "Frozen solid, practically."

"You were told?" Penelope's face lost all trace of friendliness. "By whom?"

The first man shrugged. "It was a fellow from the BIP. Brighton Ice Patrol. He came by the hotel and told us it was safe for skating."

"Did you know this man?" she said sharply.

"Nope. Never heard of the BIP before, either. Must be something new. But his uniform was quite proper. Very impressive."

"Sharp uniform, yes," his companion agreed. "Official looking."

145

"But no one checked the ice. . . ." She turned and looked at the pond. The Incorrigibles were out there still, happily skating. Boris, Constantin, and Veronika were there. Master Gogolev wove endless figure eights with his hair flying, while Julia chased after chubby, clumsy Max, who did everything in his power to escape her.

Unconcerned, the porter stirred the kettle. "We trust the BIP. If you'd seen that uniform, you'd trust it, too. And we did a nice job with the bonfires and the torches, don't you think? And there'll be a nice warm beverage, soon enough. . . ."

"'The wolf babies are in danger. . . .'" Madame Ionesco's warning flashed through Penelope's mind like a lightning strike. A moment later she was at the pond's edge, waving her arms.

"Alexander! Beowulf! Cassiopeia!" she yelled. "Be careful!"

The two boys were practicing an elaborate skating routine they had just devised. Near them, Cassiopeia skated back and forth in a long, straight line, with her head down and hands folded behind her back, trying to see how fast she could go. The panic in their governess's voice made all three children look up.

"We are careful, Lumawoo," Alexander reassured her, as he and his brother stepped and glided together.

"See? We are doing the Skateesh!" Their routine was based on a dance step they had once learned called the schottische. It was a fine dance on dry land, but positively dazzling on ice.

"And I am faster than Bertha!" Cassiopeia yelled as she zoomed back and forth.

"Bertha on land, or Bertha on skates?" Beowulf inquired as he skipped and turned.

Whether an ostrich could be taught to ice-skate was an intriguing question, but one best saved for a less perilous situation. "We shall discuss it later, back at the hotel," Penelope said firmly. "That is enough ice-skating for now."

"But we are not done learning the Skateesh!" the boys protested.

"And I am not done racing, whee!" Cassiopeia called, whizzing by once more.

The worried governess used her sternest, most Swanburnian tone. "Ice-skating is over. Come off the ice at once, please. Please bring your friends as well."

The children hesitated. "But *why*?" they asked, as one.

"Because . . ." Penelope looked around, desperate for an answer that would not cause a stampede of panic. "Because . . ."

Luckily, at that very moment a delicious aroma wafted across the ice. All three children sniffed deeply, and their eyes grew wide.

"Because the chocolate is ready," Penelope answered gratefully. "Come, everyone! Time for chocolate!"

WHAT PENELOPE CALLED "CHOCOLATE" WOULD nowadays be called "hot chocolate" or even "hot cocoa," but rest assured, all three names describe the very same warm and creamy wintertime drink. The porters had scraped shavings of dark chocolate into boiling milk, with plenty of sugar mixed in. Once the chocolate had melted, the mixture was beaten with a whisk until the top frothed like the foam-tipped swells of the sea. The result was a kettle full of steaming, sweet, delicious chocolate for all.

Mesmerized, the Incorrigibles staggered toward the delectable aroma. "No broken ankles, if you please! Skates off first, then chocolate," Penelope admonished. "Undo the buckles properly and put the skates back where they belong."

By now Boris and Constantin smelled it, too. They carelessly kicked off their ice skates and left them lying on the ground where anyone might trip over them. They pushed their way to the front of the line and insisted on taking two mugs each, for a total of four. If they had been triplets instead of twins, no doubt they would have insisted on six.

Veronika lingered on the ice, performing one last, unseen pirouette. "Stop dancing and take off your skates, silly girl. No one is watching you. Don't you want a mug of chocolate?" Julia called to her, already in line by the kettle.

"Perhaps." Reluctantly Veronika came to the pond's edge. Watching her step back to the earth was like watching a swan dissolve into a dodo, for the same skates that allowed her to fly over the ice made her clumsy and slow on land. "I don't want to get chocolate on my white coat."

It was the wrong thing to say. "Oops, I hope I don't spill any chocolate on my sister," Constantin teased, holding a steaming mug of chocolate toward her like a weapon.

She took an awkward step backward, only to find Boris waiting behind her. "I hope I don't spill any chocolate on *my* sister," he singsonged.

"Stop it." Her eyes grew wide and instantly filled with tears. "Stop it, stop it!"

"If you cry, I'll throw my chocolate on you." Constantin raised his mug high.

Veronika bit her trembling lip.

"If you *don't* cry, I'll throw *my* chocolate on you," Boris crowed.

Thus trapped, Veronika opened her mouth and let out a wail of misery that could have started an avalanche. Luckily, there were no snow-capped mountains nearby. Nor was Alexander Woofovich Incorrigiblov close enough to witness this unpleasant scene. He knelt by the fire with his back to the pond, patiently helping Cassiopeia take all the knots out of her laces so she might put her skates away properly and enjoy a mug of chocolate.

But one did not need wolf-keen senses to hear Veronika's dramatic, ear-splitting howl. Alexander turned in alarm. There she was, a vision in white, teetering helplessly on her skates, while her two sneering brothers circled her like hyenas.

"Cry!"

"Don't cry!"

"Cry!"

"Don't cry!" they taunted.

Boris dipped one fingertip in his chocolate and prepared to flick a drop in Veronika's direction.

"GRRRRRRRRRAAAHHHWOOOOOO!" Without question it was the most terrifying sound Alexander

had ever produced. He sprinted, then leaped into a flying pounce that carried him through the air until he landed directly upon Boris. The younger boy slammed to the ground on his back. Alexander crouched above him on all fours, snarling viciously.

"Help! He's drooling on me!" Boris shrieked.

Constantin came running to knock Alexander off, but Alexander was quicker. In a single motion he was up and out of the way, and Constantin landed on his brother with his full weight. The two twins thrashed on the ground, a tangle of elbows and knees and chocolate-milk mustaches.

"Ow! My eye!" Boris yelled.

"Savages," Master Gogolev remarked under his breath, and took a sip of chocolate. Truly, it was a delicious beverage.

"Natasha, you must discipline those boys," Captain Babushkinov said to his wife.

She too was sipping the hot chocolate, though the expression on her face could have frozen over the sea itself. "They get their foul tempers from you, Ivan, not me—"

"Where is Maximilian?" Julia asked, suddenly anxious. In the confusion, the baby had wandered off. Everyone looked around, but outside the halos of light cast by the torches and bonfire, all was pitch-dark, for the moon had not yet risen.

"There he is!" Penelope cried. Still in his skates, Max had toddled back onto the pond. He was tracing long, spiraling loops around the scarred ice, each one bringing him nearer to the center.

"What a big, brave boy, skating by himself!" his mother said, not bothering to get up from her chair.

"He is a Babushkinov, through and through. Strong. Fearless! Like bear cub," the captain agreed, and turned back to the fire.

Then Maximilian fell, sprawled on his belly like a seal. He could not manage to right himself on the slick ice. He yowled in frustration, but there was no one to help him.

"Go fetch him, Julia." Madame Babushkinov took a sip of chocolate and waved her free hand. "He is going to ruin his new coat, carrying on like that."

Julia scowled and sighed, for she, too, was enjoying her chocolate and was loath to put it down. "Yes, madame. One moment, please; I must put my skates back on. . . ."

Meanwhile Max thrashed and tantrummed. He lay on his belly, red-faced, pounding and kicking. His fat baby fists did no damage, but the sharp blade tips of his skates were like two pickaxes driving into the ice as he kicked, and kicked, and kicked some more.

"Lumawoo?" Beowulf frowned. "I hear crunching. I smell—water."

"Water?" But a lump of fear had already formed in Penelope's throat. She looked around. Julia was still trying to find a pair of skates that matched, but the twins had made such a mess of things it was impossible. No one else was even paying attention—

Crack!

The sickening noise echoed through the dark. Then came a terrible ripping sound, like the roots of a falling tree tearing agonizingly from the earth as it heaves and topples to the ground. The pond's surface, perfectly smooth when they arrived, was now spider-webbed with cracks, like a dropped mirror.

"Waaaaaaaa!" Baby Max yelled. The ice beneath him rippled, and a hand's-width gap had opened near his feet. The sloshing water below was inky black.

"Man—I mean Max—overboard!" Alexander yelled. "Incorrigibles, ho!" In a flash he and his two siblings formed a human chain belly-down on the ice, hands gripping on to ankles. As the smallest and lightest, Cassiopeia served as the outermost link. Slowly, with great care, her brothers swung her out across the fragile ice

The pond's surface was now spiderwebbed with cracks.

into the center of the pond. Max was too frightened to do anything but scream, and she had to dodge his razor-sharp kicks, but at last she managed to get a grip on the child.

"Pull!" she yelled to her brothers. "Pull!" His face hit the water just as Cassiopeia grabbed the back of his coat. "Swim, Maxawoo!" she yelled encouragingly, but he could barely move his arms, and his wet clothes were like lead.

"Hang on, Cassawoof! Hoist anchor, men!" Alexander commanded. With the captain and Master Gogolev aiding their efforts by grabbing Alexander's legs, the Incorrigible rescue chain managed to haul the soaked, frightened Baby Max out of the water and across the rapidly disintegrating ice. His lips were faintly blue, his eyes wide, and he was terrifyingly quiet.

"Call for a doctor!" his mother cried, finally on her feet. "Is there a doctor, please?"

"No, but there is a Swanburne girl." Penelope had not taken Swanburne's required class in the rudiments of first aid for nothing. She rolled the soggy toddler onto his side and pried open his lips. Icy pond water trickled out of his mouth, and he began to cough.

"Excuse me, Max," she said, to be polite. Then she crouched over him and blew a little puff of air into his mouth. He coughed again, and Penelope repeated the maneuver a few more times. Soon he was screaming robustly on his own.

"He is cold and frightened, not drowned. Take off his wet clothes and wrap him in a dry blanket." Relieved, Penelope sat back on her heels. She was quite wet herself by now. "Keep him by the fire until he warms up. Someone—you," she said, pointing at one of the gaping porters from the hotel. "Run back to the hotel at once and have a doctor sent for, so he can meet us there upon our return. Now, go!"

Everyone jumped to do as she said. Max protested loudly as his mother and Julia stripped off his wet clothes. Julia also wept, for was she not his nurse? How had her precious charge ended up alone on the ice? Was not the whole near catastrophe entirely her fault, and all because she was distracted by chocolate? Her hysteria only upset Max further.

"I will do it myself, Julia," Madame Babush-kinov snapped. "Let me care for my son! Surely you have shown enough negligence already." The rebuke prompted a fresh bout of misery from Julia, who slunk off, sobbing, into the darkness. Master

Gogolev followed, perhaps to comfort her, but when he returned moments later, he looked in need of consolation himself.

All this anger and misery was in no way lessened by the fact that everyone except Max and Penelope now sported a chocolate milk mustache. The adults were so upset that even the twins forgot to keep fighting. Veronika performed a sad little dance alone near the fire, but no one cared, or saw. The Incorrigibles helped themselves to extra mugs of chocolate, and took one for their governess, too, to warm her. It was more than thanks enough for them, for they had only done what they thought right.

Now that his son was safe, the captain's mood turned violent. "In Russia, ice means ice!" he raged. "Frozen means frozen! What kind of place is this, where my children are sent to skate on water? Someone is going to pay!"

His wife came and handed him the baby, and spoke quietly and rapidly in their native tongue. If only Penelope had studied Russian at school, instead of French and Latin and a smidgen of Greek! It was a pity, as this was one of those rare cases where a bit of eavesdropping might have saved a great deal of trouble later on.

"The English governess is very capable, and her charges are clearly well trained. Did you see how our Julia wept with fear? While that pale, serious child— she is hardly more than a child herself—showed such pluck! If not for her, and her brave pupils, our sweet Maximilian would be . . . would be . . ." But Madame Babushkinov could not say it; it was too awful.

"You are right, beloved." The captain hoisted the sleepy child from one arm to the other as if he weighed no more than a kitten. "It seems my friend the judge was right to praise English governesses. My mind is made up. The judge will know the legalities of it."

"It was Providence that brought you and that judge together!" his wife said with feeling. "Truly, what are the odds that a man of such learning and wisdom would be in Brighton during the off-season?"

Together they looked up and took stock of the clever English governess. Penelope noticed she was being scrutinized and mistook the reason why, for of course she had not understood a word of the conversation between the captain and his wife. Embarrassed, she quickly dabbed her own choco-late milk mustache with a pocket handkerchief and smiled apologetically.

The remaining porter extinguished the bonfire and

torches, and the whole party began a somber march back to the hotel. Master Gogolev pushed the empty carriage, and the captain himself carried Max, who was alert and swaddled in as many dry blankets as could be found. For once the baby seemed content.

The Seventh Chapter

*Curiosities, antiquities,
rarities—and more.*

The Right Foot Inn got one thing right, at least: By
the time the parade of bone-weary guests had reached
the hotel, the abruptly summoned doctor was already
on the premises. His silver hair was askew and he was
dressed in his nightshirt and nightcap over tall winter boots. His medical bag overflowed with tinctures,
ointments, bandages, tourniquets, and even surgi-
cal instruments, for he had not been told what sort
of medical emergency he was about to confront, and
came prepared for every eventuality.

Everyone spoke at once to tell him about Baby Max's mishap on the ice; once he sorted out the tale, he sprang into action. He gave the baby a thorough examination and declared him "a robust specimen, in perfect health. All the child needs is some warm milk and careful supervision. Someone ought to stand guard over this little adventurer!" The captain and his wife exchanged a knowing look at that.

Dr. Martell (for that was his name) insisted on examining Boris as well; by now one of the boy's eyes had swollen half shut. "Ice will take down the swelling, but he'll have a whopper of a black eye by morning. You'll be a matching set," he said, ruffling Constantin's hair, for of course Constantin still sported a magnificent black eye of his own.

Curious, the doctor looked over the whole array of young people, Penelope and the Incorrigibles and the Babushkawoos, too. "Eight children," he marveled. "A nice big family. You've got your hands full, madame!"

"Only these are mine, and the baby." Madame Babushkinov drew in the air with one bejeweled finger; at once, Veronika and the twins dashed over and clung to her legs. Max had fallen asleep in his carriage.

"Ah, yes. Now I see the resemblance," Dr. Martell remarked, but he was looking at Penelope and the

161

Incorrigibles when he said it. "It's unusual for the inn to have so many visitors in January. There's not much to do in Brighton this time of year. Perhaps you'd all like to visit my museum tomorrow?"

"A mew-eezum, hooray!" Cassiopeia cried, using her baby word for it.

"Does it have Ominous Landscapes? Mythic Figures? Overuse of Symbolism in Minor Historical Portraits?" Beowulf asked eagerly, naming some styles of painting he had seen and enjoyed in the past.

Dr. Martell already had his coat on. Now he tucked his nightcap beneath a warm winter hat. "There might be a picture or two lying about, but it's more of a scientific collection. It's an oddities museum. You'll find some, well . . . *unusual* items there. It's closed during the off-season, but I'd be delighted to open the doors for you, since you're here. A museum is meant to have visitors."

The Babushkinovs were indifferent, but the Incorrigibles expressed so much enthusiasm that the doctor's invitation was quickly accepted. "Splendid," he said, stifling a yawn. "Don't arrive before eleven o'clock, if you please. It's been a late evening for me, and I do prefer early bedtimes, as you can see from my attire." After waving away the profuse and weepy thanks of

Madame Babushkinov, and bravely enduring the bone-crushing handshakes and backslaps of the captain, the sleepy doctor took his leave.

By now the Incorrigibles were yawning, too, but the twins refused to say good night until they had done one vitally important thing. "You saved our brother's life!" Boris and Constantin declared. "We pledge to you our eternal friendship! Our lives and fortunes are yours!" They fell to their knees and bowed their identical heads, and Veronika wept and clutched theatrically at her heart.

It was one extreme or the other with these Babush-kawoos, but eternal friendship was a far more pleasing notion than duels to the death. Gladly the Incorrigibles accepted these vows of loyalty and friendship, and offered appropriate promises in return.

"We shall paint your portraits and hang them on the wall!" Beowulf said with feeling.

"Our biscuits shall be your biscuits!" Cassiopeia swore.

Alexander closed his eyes in concentration, as if he wanted to offer something particularly memorable. "Our bond shall be unchanging as the moon!" he cried at last. However, despite being a spot-on example of iambic pentameter, this was a poor promise, for of course the moon changes every day, as his siblings quickly pointed out.

Quickly he revised his vow to "Our bond shall be eternal as the moon!" And although the moon is not, technically speaking, eternal (as you know, only eternity can fairly lay claim to that), it certainly has lasted a long time and shows every sign of continuing to do so. This was deemed close enough. All were pleased with the sentiments expressed, and parted with warm cries of "See you tomorrow!" and *"Do svidaniya!"* and "To the mew-eezum we go!" and other, similar phrases of friendly farewell.

DR. MARTELL WAS RIGHT. By morning, the skin around Boris's eye had turned purple as a grape. Constantin's bruised eye was on the left, and Boris's was on the right, but in practical terms it was now impossible to tell them apart, and no one made the attempt, not even their parents.

Unlike the Ashtons, the Babushkinovs took their meals together: parents, grandmamma, children, nurse, and tutor. This morning they asked Penelope and the Incorrigibles to join them, and now they all sat at the same long table in the dining room of the hotel. Julia's seat was empty and her food untouched; she was in hot pursuit of Max, who would not sit still and toddled precariously around the room.

The captain was in good humor, his hair still damp from an early morning swim. "Savages!" he bellowed, addressing the twins. "One of you, pass the salt." Both boys reached for the salt shaker at the same time.

"Excuse me, savage!" said one.

"Be my guest, savage!" said the other.

"Thank you, savage!"

"My pleasure, savage!" Clearly the nickname pleased them.

"My husband is a madman! He loves to swim in the cold sea," Madame Babushkinov said, fondly patting his hand. Despite the near-tragedy of the previous evening, both Madame and the captain were in excellent spirits, and their attention seemed fixed on Penelope. Every time she glanced up from her food, one or the other of them would be looking at her, smiling and nodding.

She smiled and nodded in return, as was only polite, but she hoped the Babushkinovs would soon get over this excessive gratitude about the way she had used her rescue skills on Max. "Truly, I did no more than I was taught to do in the class I took at school, called A Swanburne Girl Is Good in a Crisis," she thought as she helped herself to a second piece of toast. "Any of my schoolmates would have done the same."

It was Princess Popkinova who would not let the incident go. She watched, aghast, as the children dramatically reenacted the ice-skating catastrophe for her.

"Someone knew that the pond was not fully frozen." The old woman poked a gnarled finger in the air for emphasis. "Someone *knew*. There is an enemy afoot. Be on your guard!"

"My mother-in-law likes to predict disaster," Madame Babushkinov said lightly. But the princess's words reminded Penelope of the suspicious tale the porters had told about the man from the BIP, and of Madame Ionesco's warning, too.

"A bit of caution is always wise," she said diplomatically. "As Agatha Swanburne once said, 'Being careful costs nothing; being careless can cost everything.'"

"How true that is." Master Gogolev pressed a hand to his heart. "I am not familiar with this Agatha Swanburne. Is she a philosopher? A poet? A scholar?"

"She is a flounder," Cassiopeia said.

"A dead flounder, now," added Beowulf.

"She was the founder of my school," Penelope clarified. "The Swanburne Academy for Poor Bright Females. That is where I lived and studied before coming to work for the Ashtons."

"Yes, the elusive Ashtons! When shall we be introduced to your employers, Miss Lumley?" Madame Babushkinov's eyes glittered with interest. "I long to meet these Ashtons of yours, and find out what brings them to Brighton at this time of year, but they have hardly left their rooms. Is there some mystery afoot?"

"No, no! There is no mystery about the Ashtons," Penelope answered, perhaps a bit too quickly. "Lady Ashton is with child. She was sent here on doctor's orders, to take the sea air; perhaps she is still recovering from her travel."

Privately she marveled at how well the servants were managing to play along with Lady Constance's unfortunate misunderstanding about Italy. So far it seemed to be going well, according to Jasper. "We're all complaining about the cold and winking, and then we let m'lady overhear us talking about pasta recipes and sunburn remedies and so on," he had explained earlier when she had sought him out for an update. "This pretending to be pretending business is not so bad, once you get the hang of it!"

"If Lady Ashton is here to take the air, perhaps she ought to try going outside," Master Gogolev quipped.

His remark caused some unkind laughter at the

table, but Penelope hardly heard it, for she had spotted Margaret. The young housemaid stood in the entrance to the dining room, making wild gestures and exaggerated facial expressions. Luckily, Penelope had always been a whiz at charades, and even at a distance she could glean the gist of it: first, that Penelope's presence was needed at once, and second, that Margaret was much too terrified of the Babushkinovs to set even one foot the dining room.

"Excuse me. It appears I am being summoned." Penelope touched her napkin to her lips and placed it neatly on the table. "Children, come along. . . ." But all three Incorrigibles were deeply engaged. Alexander listened raptly as Veronika told the plots of all her favorite ballets, and Cassiopeia and Beowulf had just begun a four-way staring contest with the twins.

"Leave your charges with us, Miss Lumley," Madame Babushkinov urged. "They will be no trouble. Master Gogolev shall watch them as if they were our very own."

This was hardly reassuring, given Max's recent misadventure on the ice. Yet Margaret's performance in the doorway grew more urgent by the minute. Now she was squinting while holding her hands in front of her lips. If this were truly a game of charades, Penelope would have guessed the young housemaid was playing a flute in a darkened room. But what might that have to do with Penelope?

"Only if Master Gogolev does not mind," she said, rising from the table. She spoke in her most respectful tone, as befits one educator addressing another.

"It will be a pleasure to supervise your pupils," he replied. "Such well-behaved young people are a rarity in this ill-mannered world."

"No doubt they are a credit to their governess. Careful, Master Gogolev, or you will compliment yourself out of a job!" said Madame Babushkinov merrily.

"Ah. Ha. Hah!" laughed the captain, and took another helping of sausage and eggs.

"THANK GOODNESS YOU UNDERSTOOD WHAT I meant! One of the porters asked if I'd been stung by a bee, as if bees would be buzzing out and about in January! Even those wee creatures have the sense to stay in their hives until spring." Margaret sailed across the lobby like a skiff caught in a strong current. Penelope had to throw in a few skips and hops in order to keep up with her long-legged guide.

"Who is it that wants to speak with me?" she asked, breathless.

"Lord Fredrick, of course. Didn't you see me acting

out being nearsighted and smoking a cigar? Whoops! Good morning, Your Lordship." Margaret dropped seamlessly into a curtsy, for they had rounded a corner and nearly careened into the man himself, pacing in the hall. "Here's Miss Lumley, sir. Will there be anything else?"

He squinted until he got Penelope in view. "Ah, yes. There you are. That will be all, Margaret. Miss Lumley, come in."

The young maid slipped away, and Lord Fredrick ushered Penelope into the nearest room. On this, more expensive, side of the hotel, the view through the porthole-shaped windows overlooked the sea. The bed had been removed and replaced with a desk and a pair of wing chairs; the rest of the furniture had been arranged so that the room might serve as Lord Fredrick's private study for the duration of their stay.

He closed the door behind them but did not sit. "I understand you've given the servants some instructions regarding my wife," he said without preamble. "You've told them to humor her fantasy of a surprise trip to *bella Italia*, as it were. Bit complicated, but I think I follow it."

That Lord Fredrick might have an opinion about this plan had not occurred to her previously, and she wondered if she had made a grave mistake. "I did suggest that, sir. Given Lady Constance's delicate condition, I thought it would be best to avoid delivering any bad news, and as you know she is utterly convinced we are going to Italy. I ought to have asked your permission first, of course," she added hastily, "but it was quite unplanned. I only thought of it when I was in the midst of speaking to Jasper. I was speaking extempore, as one would say in Latin."

"Extempore, hmm? I never was much for Latin. Too many ipsums and whatsits and ex post factos." Lord Fredrick leaned on the back of a nearby chair, whose curved, wooden-spoked back resembled a ship's wheel. "As for your unplanned plan—good thinking, Miss Lumley! What a relief to see Constance happy and rosy-cheeked, with a hearty appetite! She's nearly stopped complaining altogether. Imagine that! But there's one problem with your scheme. Fairly significant. I imagine you've already thought it through." He paused. "By which I mean, the ship."

Penelope had been listening carefully, but somewhere along the way she had lost the thread of his meaning. "What ship, my lord?"

"The ship to Italy! The one my wife thinks we're about to board. She keeps dropping hints about her 'surprise.' I can't stand to disappoint her. Sooner or later we'll have to get her on a ship. Then there's Italy to think of. Hmm." He stood with his hands in his trouser pockets and rocked back and forth. "I haven't got a ship, mind you. Wondering what you planned to do about that. Since this was all your idea."

Where on earth was she going to get a ship to Italy? Penelope straightened her spine and forced a smile. Like every Swanburne girl, she knew that good posture and a calm demeanor were the greater part of what people call self-confidence. "I am . . . working on it, my lord."

"Very good. If not for this blasted affliction of mine, I'd happily take her to Italy myself and be done with it. But imagine me shipboard during a full moon, with no place to hide! It's not an option, I'm afraid." He gazed out the porthole window with a look of real melancholy, and Penelope could not help but feel sorry for him.

"Sir, if you are concerned about your privacy on Tuesday, there is one other hotel open in Brighton. I happen to know it is completely empty of guests," she offered.

"That's useful, thank you." His dark mood lifted as quickly as it had come. "Now I must run. I've convinced

172

Constance to let me take her for an after-breakfast walk along the esplanade. It's quite pleasant here by the sea, after all, even in winter. Dr. Veltschmerz was right." He inhaled and pounded himself on the chest. "A few deep breaths, and I expect I'll be feeling better about things myself. Babies aren't all bad, what?"

Penelope thought of little Max. "They come in a range, my lord," she said diplomatically.

"Ha! A range, yes. Like most things, I suppose. *Arrivederci*, then. Constance is teaching me Italian. Charming language, if a bit heavy on the vowels." He turned to Penelope, and for once his eyes seemed in perfect focus. "Miss Lumley, you've got to get to the bottom of this curse, quick. From the looks of my wife, the Barking Baby Ashton's growing bigger by the day."

THE ODDITIES MUSEUM WAS A brisk half hour's walk from the Right Foot Inn. Alexander and Veronika strolled side by side, Veronika talking, Alexander nodding. The twins and the two younger Incorrigibles were behind them, hopping on alternate legs and holding their noses for occasional seahorse races, but generally making forward progress. Over Julia's halfhearted objections, Max's carriage was pushed by

Master Gogolev, hatless and dour as ever. The captain and his wife had remained at the inn; they had some business affairs to attend to, or so they said.

Penelope did not mind walking alone, for it gave her time to think. "Taking dictation from doctors, undoing family curses, and now I am expected to acquire a ship! I know I am well paid as governesses go, but my duties have grown far beyond what was specified in the contract I signed when I was first hired by Lady Constance. Perhaps I ought to take Lord Fredrick at his word, and ask for an increase in salary."

The bell of a nearby church began to strike the hour, and her scattered thoughts fell naturally into the tune and rhythm of the famous Westminster Quarters: "Pirate costumes . . . Ahwoo-Ahwoo . . . Edward Ashton . . . barking babies. Pudge! Pudge! Pudge! Pudge! But I must have patience," she told herself as the bell continued to chime all the way to eleven. "There is nothing to be done about the curse upon the Ashtons until Simon arrives with the costume, so that he might impersonate the admiral and persuade old Pudge to tell his tale. Until then, I would be wise to not think of Simon at all—not once!—and simply enjoy our trip to the Oddities Museum."

Yet her resolve not to think of Simon splintered the

moment they walked by a mailbox. "O glorious postal service!" she thought, giving the mailbox a grateful pat. "Thanks to your brisk efficiency, Simon will receive my letter this very afternoon. If only I might see his face as he opens it and reads it! And how I wish I might hear his reply at once, without having to wait for the post! If only some clever inventor could build a device by which two people could speak to each other even while in distant cities . . . it is an absurd notion, of course. I might as well imagine that omnibuses could be made to fly—but truly, how complicated could it be?"

"Look, Lumawoo, a sign!" Beowulf said. Penelope's gaze flew skyward, as if the delivery of her letter to Simon might reasonably be heralded by the appearance of a celestial comet, but the boy simply meant that they had arrived at the museum. The sign on the door read:

MARTELL'S ODDITIES
WE SPECIALIZE IN CURIOSITIES, ANTIQUITIES,
RARITIES, AND MORE!
THE IMPLAUSIBLE AND UNBELIEVABLE!
THINGS IMPOSSIBLY OLD AND THAT WHICH IS
AHEAD OF ITS TIME

If you can see it anywhere else,
you won't find it here.

"Not very humble, is it?" Dr. Martell appeared at the door. "But science costs money, so we must keep the visitors coming. No, Master Gogolev, you are very kind, but put your rubles away. You are all my guests today."

With a smile he bid them enter. The Oddities Museum was not a grand building with a colonnaded front, like the British Museum in London. It was a rambling, many-roomed house, and in each room the walls were lined with bookshelves and glass-fronted cases. "My collection is organized according to chance, which is to say I put new acquisitions wherever there's a bit of space. But it's more fun that way, don't you think? A surprise at every turn," Dr. Martell explained. "Let's start with that basket on your left. There's something you've not likely seen before; at least, not at that size."

Inside the basket, on a nestlike bed of straw, was a smooth, cream-colored orb that looked very like an egg, except for the fact that it was the size of a cantaloupe.

"I'd scramble that giant egg for breakfast and eat the whole thing," one of the twins boasted.

"No, you wouldn't! Because I'd eat it first," his brother retorted. Then they pinched each other and argued about whose pinch was harder.

"It's an ostrich egg," said Dr. Martell.

The Incorrigible children blanched. "Is there a Baby Bertha inside?" Beowulf whispered. He touched one fingertip to the shell, gently, so as not to wake its inhabitant. Dr. Martell looked puzzled.

"At Ashton Place we have an ostrich named Bertha," Alexander explained. "She is not a pet, exactly. She is more like . . . an athlete."

"Liar!" the twins shrieked. "No one has an ostrich."

Master Gogolev glared and cuffed them each on the head, but Penelope felt a more educational response was called for. "It is true that most people do not have an ostrich. We, however, do," she said firmly. "There are important distinctions to be made between the unlikely and the impossible. Agatha Swanburne had several wise sayings on this topic, and I shall be glad to share them, if you are curious. But there is no need to call people names." She fixed her gaze on Boris and Constantin until their lower lips began to tremble and they looked shamefacedly at the floor.

"Apologize, savages!" Gogolev ordered. The two boys mumbled incoherent apologies, which Alexander graciously accepted by offering a handshake to each. Instead the twins wept and threw their arms around him and kissed him on both cheeks. They pinched each other again, hard, to atone for their rudeness, and everyone was friends once more.

"An ostrich! Remarkable!" Dr. Martell shook his head. "Sounds like you ought to have an oddities museum of your own. But this egg is too old for hatching. It's been on exhibit here for years." Even so, each of the Incorrigibles petted the egg fondly as they followed Dr. Martell to the next glass case.

"Sasha, you are amazing," Veronika cooed to Alexander. "I wish I could see this ostrich of yours!"

"Why do you call him Sasha?" Cassiopeia asked. She sounded annoyed; it may have been because Alexander had hardly paid attention to anyone but Veronika from the moment they left the hotel.

Veronika rose dreamily to her toes and floated down again. "In Russia, everyone has a nickname. Now we are like sisters, so you must call me Nikki."

Cassiopeia scowled. She had already learned three names for her new friend; was a fourth truly necessary? "All right," she conceded. "And you can call me Cassawoof."

"Woof? Like dog noise? You are too pretty for

dog-noise name." Veronika put one finger to pursed lips, as if posing for a portrait of someone thinking. "I know! You shall be Cassarina. That is a name for a Russian princess."

"Princess Cassarina," Cassiopeia repeated, testing it out. She made a face. "No. I like Cassawoof." She growled, to make her point, and for once Veronika had no answer.

"Gather 'round, children." Dr. Martell held up an object. "Can you guess what this is?"

It was piece of wood, they all agreed. But when Dr. Martell passed the item around, it was shockingly heavy.

"It's petrified wood," he said. "That means it was wood once, but over time, bit by bit, it's been transformed into rock."

Cassiopeia pressed her nose to the glass case. "Is that a comb?" she asked.

"That's a plate of baleen. It's what some types of whales have in their mouths instead of teeth," Dr. Martell explained.

There were many more peculiar and fascinating items in the Oddities Museum. There was a walnut shell whose interior had been carved to resemble two facing rooms, like a teeny-tiny dollhouse (which was, to put it in a nutshell, impressive). There were ancient Roman coins that bore the likeness of an emperor, although whether it was Julius Caesar or Claudius was unclear. There was an entire display case of fossilized ferns, which delighted Penelope no end.

"Look, a painting on a mirror!" Beowulf was mesmerized by the lifelike depiction of a Parisian street.

"Uncanny, isn't it? But it's not a painting. It's a real picture of a real place. It's called a daguerreotype. It's a new picture-taking method, invented by a Frenchman, Monsieur Louis Daguerre. He also creates what he calls 'panoramas.' Those are enormous paintings, designed to make you feel like you're inside whatever scene they depict." Dr. Martell paused at a doorway. "In this room I keep what I consider my greatest treasures. May I present—the bone room!"

Penelope gave the Incorrigibles a warning glance, for bones tended to bring out their urge to gnaw. But this was no ordinary bone.

"So big," Alexander was the first to observe. Indeed, it was much too big to fit in a case and was displayed openly on a large, felt-topped table.

"So bony," Cassiopeia said.

"So delicious," Beowulf muttered. A sheen of drool appeared on his chin.

Even in a storybook it would be hard to believe
such creatures could exist.

Luckily, Dr. Martell did not hear that last remark. "That," he said proudly, "is the thighbone of a megalosaurus."

The Incorrigibles had not yet studied much Greek, but between them they knew enough to figure out the word's meaning. "Big lizard?" Alexander ventured.

"Precisely, yes! At least, that is the current theory. The fellow who dug up this specimen thought it was the leg of a giant! Now we know better, of course." Giant or lizard, simply imagining a creature with a thighbone that big made the children shiver.

Dr. Martell circled the table, and his eager listeners crowded close around. "These bones are older than you can imagine. Possibly they're all from the same big lizard, but we can't know for sure. This is the jawbone, and these seem like pieces of the spine. This thing that looks like a horn is from a different beast, an Iguanodon. Imagine a world filled with such creatures!"

"Monsters!" Veronika trilled. "If I saw one, I would scream!"

Dr. Martell smiled. "No need to worry. They're all extinct. Bad luck for them, but good luck for anyone who'd prefer not to cross paths with one of these." He tapped the enormous jawbone, and everyone took a step back. "We call them dinosaurs."

"Dinosaurs," the children repeated in awe. Even in a storybook it would be hard to believe such creatures could exist, but here they were, as real as real could be. It was the sort of discovery that makes the whole world look a little different than it did before.

THEY ALL WERE ENTRANCED WITH the dinosaurs, but there was more to see, and the longer they stayed near the bones, the hungrier the Incorrigibles looked, so Penelope encouraged the group to move on. "Who knows what wonders may lie within the next room?" she playfully coaxed. "Flying carpets? Magic lanterns? A piece of cheese that once was part of the moon?"

"I hope it's cheese," said Beowulf. The others agreed that cheese would be best. Clearly all the children were ready for a snack. But the next room contained one object only, and a rather ordinary-seeming one at that. It stood on a simple pedestal, in the dead center of the room.

The twins looked scornful. "It's a seashell," one scoffed.

"We could find that on the beach," the other added.

"It is very pretty," Penelope said. It was a lovely shell, no question, but after fossilized ferns and dinosaur bones, even she found it disappointingly ordinary.

"Is it the kind that lets you hear the ocean if you press it to your ear?"

"It will do that, certainly. Any seashell would," said Dr. Martell. "But do not be deceived by its commonplace appearance! This shell came to me by way of an old sailor, who claimed to have found it on a strange tropical island, in the middle of an unmapped sea. It is an enchanted shell," he continued, in a marvelous storyteller's voice, "and there is no other like it, anywhere. At least, that is the story. This, my friends, is the Seashell of Love."

"Ugh! Does it make you fall in love with someone?" one of the twins asked in horror.

"Does it make someone fall in love with you?" Veronika inquired, clasping her hands to her heart.

Dr. Martell smiled. "Nothing so dramatic as that. But according to the story, if you lay so much as a fingertip on this seashell, you have no choice but to tell the truth about whom you love."

Julia gasped and grabbed Max so hard he spilled his milk bottle all over himself and the floor. Master Gogolev coughed violently into a handkerchief.

"I don't believe that for a minute!" the other twin exclaimed, yet they both hid their hands behind their backs.

"Quite understandable. I wouldn't believe it either, if I were you," Dr. Martell said. "Even so . . . would anyone like to touch it?"

Oh, the downcast eyes, the anxious glances! Dr. Martell nodded. "As I thought! Well, perhaps some of you will choose differently in private. That's it for the tour. Feel free to wander around the museum. If you have any questions, I won't be far off."

WITH THE SOLE EXCEPTION OF Penelope, who found the seashell a fine specimen in its own right and worthy of being sketched, everyone soon found a reason to leave the room. Julia excused herself to go clean up Max, whose pants were now soaked, while Master Gogolev went in search of a mop to clean the floor. The children asked permission to return to the dinosaur bones, which Penelope granted only after she had extracted a no-gnawing promise from the Incorrigibles.

None of them had touched the Seashell of Love; no one had come within six feet of it. And yet the very idea that their romantic secrets might be pried out of their hearts seemed to create, in each of them, an overwhelming desire to confess.

Master Gogolev was the first to crack. He returned with the mop, but instead of mopping, he stood near

Penelope and sighed like a broken pipe organ.

"Julia!" he wheezed. "Julia!"

Penelope looked up from her sketch pad. "Are you looking for the baby's nurse?" she inquired. "For I believe she is changing Max's pants."

"Julia is the one I love." He held up a hand. "I know what you are thinking, Miss Lumley. Julia, of all people! It is absurd—"

Penelope interrupted, for she had no wish to hear more. "I assure you, Master Gogolev, I have no opinion whatsoever on the matter—"

"She is no beauty, I know," he went on. "Her thoughts are trivial and uninformed. She is anxious. Selfish. Incompetent. Yet there is something . . . her sad look, her stooped shoulders, her nervous, darting glance. Ah! It pierces me to the core!"

It was hard to know what kind of response would be appropriate to such a revelation. Penelope had to think for a moment. "I wish you much happiness," she said at last.

Master Gogolev groaned and clenched his fists. "Happiness! That is the one thing I can never have." From somewhere not too far off, Max wailed like a siren. "I must go," he said abruptly, and left.

Penelope had only just returned to her sketching

when Julia herself entered, still holding Max's milk-sodden pants. Warily, she circled the Seashell of Love. Now that they had been pointed out to her, Penelope could not help but notice her stooped shoulders and darting glance.

"That shell! I'm afraid to touch it," Julia anxiously whispered.

"Those fossilized ferns were marvelous," Penelope remarked, trying to steer the conversation to safer territory. "Why, you could make out every fossilized frond—"

"For if I did touch it, I would confess that I love . . ." Julia's glance darted this way and that. "The captain!"

"Captain Babushkinov?" Penelope exclaimed, quite shocked.

Julia's shoulders stooped even more. "He knows nothing of how I feel! I avoid him as much as I can, for he is my employer, and he is married, and a military man of rank, and he would never in a thousand years think of me that way. But there is something about him . . . that deep, rumbling voice . . . those mountain-ous shoulders . . . those fantastic whiskers, like the end of a broom. . . ." Her eyes darted in Penelope's direction. "He must never know. Never! Promise me you will keep my secret!"

"I promise," Penelope said, and meant it, for she had every intention of pretending this conversation had never happened. Yet against her better judgment she found herself saying, "Still, I wonder if someone nearer your own age and station might be a more suitable object for your affection."

"Nearer my station . . . do you mean Master Gogolev? Karl Romanovich Gogolev? The penniless tutor?" Julia laughed shrilly. "The captain is strong, no-nonsense. Nothing worries him; nothing frightens him! Gogolev is the opposite. Injured, brooding, sad. I wonder what makes him so sad? Perhaps I shall go tease him for a while, to amuse myself." Then Julia left, and Penelope was left to ponder this new information alone.

THE SEASHELL OF LOVE GAVE the children something to think about, too. The boys gathered among the ancient bones to talk the matter over. They even included Max, now in dry pants, but they made Master Gogolev wait outside, for this was boys' business. The question of who each of them loved was passed around like a dare.

"We love dinosaurs," either Boris or Constantin announced.

"But our love is extinct," the other added.

"It is more romantic that way," Beowulf said approvingly. He clasped his hands to his heart. "Whereas: I am in love with art." The others nodded, for who could find fault with this?

"I need no enchanted shell to reveal the truth of my heart," Alexander proclaimed. "For your sister, Veronika Ivanovna Babushkinova, is my true love!"

The twins made gagging noises, but Alexander merely closed his eyes and smiled.

"Who does Maxie love, oojie-woojie-woo?" Beowulf asked, chucking the baby under one of his many chins.

"Mama!" the baby yelled. "Papa!"

Meanwhile, Veronika had pulled Cassiopeia to the far corner of the room. "Shhh!" she hissed, although she was the one speaking. "I have never told anyone, but I will tell you, Cassarina, for we are like sisters now. I am in love!"

"With Alexander?" Cassiopeia guessed, although the thought did not please her. "I mean, Sasha?"

Veronika laughed. "No. Sasha is a boy, a sweet little boy. Come closer and I will say it in your ear." Cassiopeia did as she was asked; she stretched up on her toes, and Veronika bent low. "I am in love with Master Gogolev," she whispered.

"Eww." Cassiopeia made a face.

Veronika straightened and gave a joyous twirl. "He does not know, of course! He thinks I am a silly girl, a bad student, a spoiled child. And I am! But is it not romantic to be in love with your tutor? When I am old enough to marry, he will be an old man, stooped and wrinkled, and so it can never be, for I will require a husband who is handsome and rich and able to fight duels in my name. Mama says so. But for now . . . oh, it is terrible, wonderful, to have such a secret!"

"I am not in love with anyone but me." Cassiopeia sounded relieved.

"That is because you are only a child, Princess Cassarina. Just wait till you are older," Veronika said, not unkindly. But Cassiopeia looked to be in no rush.

THE EIGHTH CHAPTER

*This time the postal service
truly outdoes itself.*

BABY NURSES IN LOVE WITH captains! Tutors in love
with baby nurses! The revelations of Julia and Master Gogolev had left Penelope grateful to be spared
this particular form of madness. "Still, the distraction of these lovesick Russians has worked wonders in
keeping me from thinking of Simon—whoops! Well,
until now, anyway," she thought, and took out a fresh
pencil with which to draw, for the first had already
grown dull.

Her sketch of the troublemaking seashell was soon

finished. She looked it over and was pleased; it would make a useful addition to her planned lesson on the difference between crustaceans and mollusks. "The Mollusk of Love," she thought, and chuckled at the absurdity of it all. "Family curses are one thing, but honestly—a magical mollusk? Impossible!"

Yes, impossible, and yet important distinctions could be made between the unlikely and the impossible, as she herself had recently noted. She was alone in the room, and unobserved. If anything, well . . . *unusual* . . . should transpire between Penelope and the mysterious Seashell of Love, no one would be the wiser. Ought she? Dare she?

(No doubt you are asking yourself: "What would *I* have done in such a situation?" Consider how such seemingly minor decisions can have life-changing consequences: A bowl of leftover soup carelessly poured down a sink causes a clogged drainpipe and a call to the plumber. The soup pourer is charmed by the plumber, and the plumber by the soup pourer. Love blossoms, marriage ensues, a new family is begun—"And that is why we named you Piper," your parents never grow tired of saying. All because of the soup!)

But with so much on her mind already, Penelope

was in no mood for an unexpected plot twist. "What would Agatha Swanburne do?" she asked herself, and chose the path of reason with a spoonful of caution thrown in. "As the wise founder herself once advised, 'If you wish to resist temptation, put it in a locked safe.' Since I have no intention of touching that seashell—none whatsoever, not a smidge!—best to leave the room at once."

To that end, she packed up her drawing supplies and returned to the bone room. Julia and Master Gogolev were nowhere to be seen, but the children were happily engaged. Boris and Constantin squabbled about what was admittedly a hypothetical situation—in a fight between a megalosaurus and Captain Babushkinov, who would win?—and the Incorrigibles staged a shadow-puppet show for a delighted Baby Max, based on their favorite plots from the Giddy-Yap, Rainbow! books. Veronika was unfamiliar with the tales of Edith-Anne Pevington and her pet pony, Rainbow, but the interpretive dances she made up on the spot were full of graceful gallops and much prancing.

Penelope discreetly checked the dinosaur bones for signs of tooth marks; there were none. Satisfied that all was well, she allowed herself to wander farther, past the daguerreotypes and fern fossils and nutshells, past the ostrich egg and the whale baleen. Soon she found herself at the door of a small, out-of-the-way room that had not been included on their tour. As she stepped inside, she felt a flutter of anticipation—what sort of remarkable oddity might this room contain? A walrus tusk, perhaps? A quill pen that had once belonged to Shakespeare?

No such luck. Before her were shelves of junk: old glass bottles by the dozen, haphazardly arranged, their cork stoppers still in place. They were filthy with mud and crusted over with barnacles, and the whole room smelled faintly of rum.

"Mysterious, don't you think?" Dr. Martell said, startling her. She turned. The doctor stood by the window, near a pile of wooden crates.

"It is a collection of old bottles," she said, once her heart had slowed. "I see no mystery about it."

"On the contrary; these bottles pose quite a puzzle. They've been washing up on the beach for months. Where do they come from? I wish I knew. I haven't had time to examine them thoroughly yet. The latest ones are still in these crates." He checked his watch. "Now you must excuse me; I only came in here to collect the dead flies from the windowsills. It's time to feed the carnivorous plants."

"Mysterious, don't you think?" Dr. Martell said, startling her.

The doctor left her alone with the mysterious bottles. Idly, she picked one up. The pale green glass was too dirty to see through. She tipped the bottle and something rattled inside.

Now curious, she tugged at the cork. After several hard twists, it came out with a loud *pop*. She wrinkled her nose at the strong whiff of rum and seaweed and other smells of the briny deep. The bottle's contents remained wedged inside.

"A hairpin will do the trick," she thought, and slipped one loose from her bun. She turned the bottle upside down and used the pin to pry out the treasure within. It was a small scroll of paper, crinkled and smudged, but still readable, once she unfurled it and smoothed it flat with both hands. "Dear Miss Lumley," it began. "How goes the war? Hard to believe I'm still at sea, the captive of these pirate rogues . . ."

"Simon!" She looked around to share her amazement, but she was alone, save for the bottles and whatever dead flies Dr. Martell had missed. Frantically she took more bottles off the shelves, popped their corks, and extracted the notes from each.

. . . two weeks have passed, or three, it's hard to keep count. The ship is lost, I'm locked in the brig

and there's no navigator above decks. A frustrating situation, for sure!

. . . finally my captors have let me out for a look at the stars. Thank goodness for my sextant! We're far off course, but I think I can steer us safe home, if they'll let me. . . .

Still becalmed, with no sign of wind. Only hard-tack and salted beef to eat. On the bright side, I've learned some rousing sea chanteys. . . .

Months late, sea stained, and delivered to the wrong address by the notoriously unreliable Tidal Post, but there they were at last: the notes from Simon Harley-Dickinson, written and tossed overboard during his captivity at sea, as often as he could find a scrap to write upon.

Stunned, she sat on the crate and spread the notes before her. "That they should wash up in Brighton, of all places!" she thought. "Surely this is the oddest thing in the whole museum of oddities."

Eager to share her discovery, she went in search of Dr. Martell. She found him near the Seashell of Love, wielding the mop that Master Gogolev had carelessly left there. "Dr. Martell, I have solved your mystery," she cried, rushing in. "I can tell you where the bottles came from. Unlikely as it seems, they are addressed to me. They were tossed in the sea by an acquaintance of mine. His name is—"

"Miss Lumley, careful!"

In her haste she did not notice the puddle of milk, which the good doctor was about to mop up. She stepped in it and slipped; her arms flew into the air and she seized the nearest object to prevent herself from falling.

"Simon! Simon Harley-Dickinson!" she finished, breathless. Then she looked at her hands. Both of them were firmly planted on the Seashell of Love.

"Simon Harley-Dickinson," she said again, in a whisper. Slowly she peeled her hands off the shell. What was this strange feeling that washed over her? Had the floor shifted beneath her feet? All at once her heart seemed too big for her rib cage.

The mop clattered to the floor as Dr. Martell rushed to her side. "Miss Lumley, are you all right?"

"Quite all right, thank you." The late-afternoon sunbeams that streamed through the window positively glittered in the air. The sweet winter birdsong of a distant robin—or was it a wren?—could not have been more vivid if the bird itself had perched on her shoulder. Even her skin had changed: It felt sheer as a veil, as if what was inside of her and outside of her was all one and the same.

Was it possible, after all? Was the Seashell of Love no ordinary mollusk?

Could she be in love with Simon?

THE WALK BACK TO THE hotel was a quiet and pensive one, for all of them. Each head was full of new thoughts and new ideas, and none of the intrepid museumgoers—not even Baby Max, who could now whinny like a pony and move his chubby arms up and down with a dancer's grace—saw the world in quite the same way as they had before.

This is the whole purpose of museums, of course. One does not go merely to collect facts and souvenirs and picture postcards, but to enlarge one's notion of all that has been, and all that is, and all that might be. In this way we begin to understand what part each of us was born to play in the marvelous tale of existence. Put another way: We enter museums to look at the exhibits, but when we come out, it is ourselves we see more clearly. (Remember this the next time some well-intended adult suggests you spend a rainy afternoon reorganizing your sock drawer. "No!" you must loudly protest. "I wish to go to the mew-eezum, and enlarge my sense of life's possibilities." Remarkable adventures have blossomed from just such a request!)

As for Penelope, she felt so changed by her adventure in the mew-eezum that she doubted she would recognize herself in a looking glass. On the way there, she had resolved not to think of Simon at all; now she could think of nothing but Simon. "No doubt he is reading my letter at this very moment," she fretted, "which means he will soon arrive in Brighton. And when he does . . . oh, what shall I do?"

What *should* she do? Tell him about her epiphany and hope for the best? Or pretend she had never laid eyes, or hands, on the Seashell of Love, and try to carry on as before?

"I beg your pardon, Miss Lumley." It was Master Gogolev, walking alone. Julia was doing her own carriage pushing now. Since the two of them had resurfaced at the museum, they had given each other a wide berth, which is a sailor's way of describing two ships that are trying not to sail too close to one another.

"Forgive my boldness," he went on, "but there is something I have been wishing to say to you. It struck me like a thunderbolt, the first moment I saw you! But it is personal, and I hope you do not take offense."

Something personal? Thunderbolts? Penelope did not like the sound of this one bit. "You—you may say whatever you wish," she stammered, "but really, Master Gogolev, there is no need . . ."

"I wish to compliment you," he said, "on the shade of your tresses."

"My dresses?" Nearly all of Penelope's dresses were brown, more or less, including the one she had on. It was a practical garment, clean and mended, but the color was hardly one to attract compliments. Or so she had thought.

"Your *tresses*. By which I mean, your hair. The children's, too. Your four heads are like four oak trees in autumn, their russet leaves dancing in the wind." His own dark hair whipped across his face in the brisk ocean breeze, but he made no move to push it away. "How sad and beautiful are the words I just spoke! They fill my heart with joy and despair, for my dancing days are over. No doubt you have been wondering about my limp."

In fact, he had no limp, at least not that Penelope had noticed, but his train of thought did seem to be running along several tracks at once. She wondered if Julia had upset him somehow at the museum.

Perhaps he had confessed his feelings to her, and been rebuffed, and now he was half mad with a broken heart? Was this what lay in store for her, too, now that she had entered the perilous terrain of love? Would she too end up prattling nonsense to near-strangers, and going out in the cold without the sense to put on a hat?

"In my youth, I was a dancer," he went on. "How ambitious I was, and how foolish! One day, though I was warned against it, I attempted the legendary double-quintuple pirouette: five pirouettes on my left foot, followed immediately by five more on my right. It is a very difficult spin," he added. "Almost impossible."

"I should think so." Personally she could not imagine such a feat. Then again, she had been known to get dizzy playing ring-around-the-rosy.

"Luck was not with me that day. I spun out of control, and fell. I broke the bone. The leg did not heal straight, as you see." Roughly, he slapped his thigh, which seemed perfectly straight to Penelope. "Most days it is fine. But when I exert myself, as I did last night, ice-skating . . ." He slapped his leg again, this time in anger. "Ow!" he yelped.

"Perhaps you ought not to strike it so, if it hurts,"

Penelope suggested, but Master Gogolev had not finished his tale.

"After that, no more ballet for me. Unable to dance, with a temperament too, too—what is the word?—*magnificent* for regular employment, I grew lost. I grew bitter. I was near death from hunger, but I spent my last ruble on a poem, for what is life without poetry? Now I am employed as a tutor to this family, this crazy, angry, terrible family. Pity the Babushkinovs! They are mad, all of them, and yet beautiful in their anger and misery."

This was all a great deal of information to take in. Penelope tried to focus on the parts of his tale that she could most easily understand. "I am sorry to hear about your leg," she offered. "That is a misfortune."

He ran his hands through his wild hair. "Yet misfortune is still a kind of fortune, no? The leg, the arm, the head, what does it matter? The soul is what matters. I act the role of tutor, but in my soul I am a poet. I hear the silence in the crash of the waves. The music in the hideous cry of the gulls, screeching. *Caw! Caw!*"

His gull cry was so lifelike that the children looked up, expecting to see birds. *"Caw!"* he said again. "Terrible and beautiful, all of it. And your hair! Never have

I seen such a color. So red, so brown, so light, so dark. It is a symphony of color and light and hair. If I were a painter, I would insist on painting your portrait."

"You are very kind to say so." Penelope fell in step with the Incorrigibles; the tutor's remarks made her uneasy, and she was eager for this strange conversation to end. "But I am not the sort of person whose portrait gets painted, I assure you. I am only the children's governess."

"You may be the governess." He looked down at the children's hair, and back at her. "But perhaps you are not *only* the governess."

THAT EVENING THE BABUSHKINOVS AGAIN invited Penelope and her pupils to join them for dinner at the hotel. Penelope said they would, for the Incorrigibles and the Babushkawoos were quickly becoming inseparable; in any case, she was so distracted she hardly knew what to do with herself. A governess in love with a pirate playwright! It was like something out of a play Simon himself might write.

"I *so* am disappointed not to meet Lord and Lady Ashton." Madame Babushkinov gestured toward the two empty seats at the long table. "I think they are avoiding us."

"Don't take everything personally, dear wife," the captain said lightly.

"We are the only other guests here, dear husband. How else am I to take it?" Sharply, she bit into a breadstick. It snapped in her mouth like a bone.

"Papa, we have a question for you!" one of the twins blurted, and elbowed his brother. "*You* say it," he hissed.

Obligingly, the other one asked, "Papa, would you challenge a megalosaurus to a duel?"

"Of course," the captain said. "I challenge anyone."

This made the Babushkawoos laugh, for of course their father had no idea what a megalosaurus was. To be laughed at made the captain scowl, but the children quickly explained about giant extinct lizards from countless years ago, with thighbones the size of the axles on a hay wagon.

"I do not understand," he said when they were done, but at least he was not angry.

"Nor do I. And I see no point in a museum devoted to strange objects. Surely life is strange enough!" Madame Babushkinov turned to Penelope. "What did you think of the place, Miss Lumley?"

"It was . . . like life, just as you say. Strange and terrible," she offered, remembering her talk with

Master Gogolev, which she felt had provided valuable insight into the Russian temperament. "Full of happiness and woe."

Madame Babushkinov lifted a glass. "So wise for one so young! Is that what you learned at the Swanburne Academy?"

Briefly Penelope imagined a small pillow embroidered with the words *Happiness and Woe,* and how it might look tucked in the window seat of Miss Charlotte Mortimer's office at Swanburne. "Not exactly," she replied. "But there is more to life than what one learns at school."

"Also true," the captain said approvingly, and raised his drink as well. As they clinked the glasses together, he and his wife exchanged a look full of meaning.

The doors to the dining room swung open, and a butler announced, "May I present . . . Lord and Lady Ashton."

Lord Fredrick entered the room with Lady Constance on his arm and led her to the table. "Good evening! Sorry we're late for dinner. Busy afternoon, what?" Waving away a servant, Lord Fredrick himself pulled out a chair for his wife, and introductions were made all around.

"Buona sera!" Lady Constance chirped, and placed her napkin in her lap.

The Babushkinovs exchanged puzzled looks. "Does your wife speak English?" Madame Babushkinov inquired.

Lord Fredrick gave an embarrassed chuckle. "Yes, certainly! Constance, dear, will you *parlare* in *inglese*, just for tonight?"

"If you insist, Fredrick, but I am keen to practice my Italian!" Lady Constance smiled sweetly at the captain. "Hello, signor! *Dove si trova il negozio di souvenir?* That means, 'Where is the gift shop?'"

"We are Russian," the captain said, frowning. "I don't know about gift shop."

"How nice," she answered, not paying attention. "Fredrick, *dove si trova* my dinner? I am simply starving!"

"Right away, my dear," he said, and jumped up to summon the waiter.

IT WAS A PLEASANT ENOUGH dinner, at first. Lady Constance's frequent references to Italy puzzled the Babushkinovs, but soon they accepted her preoccupation with that warm, sunny Mediterranean country as just another affectation of the peculiar English. After the food was served, Lord Fredrick asked the captain polite questions about his business affairs, his land holdings, and so on. The captain shook his head.

"I will be frank, Lord Ashton. My estate in Plinkst is troubled. My crops do not grow. My serfs are unhappy."

Beowulf, who had guessed that serfs were something like a cross between a servant and a peasant, asked, "Why are they unhappy?"

"Because they are serfs," the captain said. "Is that not reason enough?"

"What kind of crops?" Lord Fredrick inquired.

"The kind that are failing."

His wife interjected. "He means beets, Lord Ashton. Beets, beets, and nothing but beets."

"I tasted some borscht once," said Lady Constance, naming a type of soup made largely out of beets. "Blech! Dreadful. It is a wonder anyone bothers to grow them at all."

"Plinkst is beet capital of Russia. But still, they are hard to grow," the captain explained. "In winter, ground is frozen. Too cold to grow beets. In summer, no rain. Too dry to grow beets."

"What about spring and fall?" Lord Fredrick asked.

The captain sighed. "Too quick. No time to grow beets."

Alexander leaned over to Penelope and remarked, "It sounds like beets will go extinct."

Lord Fredrick offered some noises of sympathy. The captain shrugged. "Life is a struggle; why should mine be different? I sell pieces of land here and there. My estate shrinks, my debt grows. . . ."

His wife put down her fork. "Ivan Victorovich, enough. If you cared so much about the estate, you would spend more time there." She turned to Lady Constance. "My husband is away with the army half the year. When he is gone, I am unhappy—a woman alone, four children to raise, my inheritance squandered. . . ."

"Let no head go uncovered!" the twins cried on cue. Self-consciously, Master Gogolev ran his hands through his hair.

Madame Babushkinov's lips curled into a sad, rueful smile. "Now we are supposed to be on holiday, and look where we are! Brighton! Who comes to England on holiday, Ivan Victorovich? I ask you, who?"

The captain shoved a chunk of meat in his mouth. "It was cheap," he said, chewing.

"One tenth of one ruble would still be too much," she retorted. "Close your mouth when you eat, Ivan. This is not a barracks."

"The Black Sea," his mother mumbled from her wheelchair, eyes closed. "Now, that's a nice beach."

"I like Brighton!" Lady Constance said gaily, buttering her third piece of bread. "It's not Rome, of course, but what is?"

"I for one am glad you came to England, madame," said Alexander, full of charm. "If you had not, we would not have met the Babushkawoos."

"The Babushka—whats?" Madame asked, puzzled.

"Yes, why *do* you call us the Babushkawoos?" one of the twins demanded, suddenly cross (perhaps his parents' bad mood was contagious). "Are you mocking us?"

"Mocking us! This insult cannot go unanswered!" the other twin agreed. They had no gloves to throw down as a challenge, and were about to take off their socks and use those, but the Incorrigibles quickly explained that they meant no offense; they had simply been raised by wolves during their early years and had picked up a howling sort of accent along the way.

"Wolves!" Veronika trilled, deliciously afraid. The twins forgot their anger at once and peppered the Incorrigibles with questions: "Did the wolves bite you? Did you have fleas?" and so on.

The Princess Popkinova had dozed off again in her wheelchair. Now she raised her head, her half-opened eyes hooded as an eagle's.

"Did you say wolves?" she asked.

"Yes, Princess," Penelope replied, for the children looked too frightened of the old woman to answer. "They were very unusual wolves, of course."

Slowly the princess's eyes opened wide. "There is old Russian story about wolves," she said tantalizingly. "It is gruesome story, too horrible to repeat. About a bride and groom, on their way home from the wedding . . ."

Madame Babushkinov leaned over to interrupt. "Grandmamma, no! That is a terrible story to tell at the dinner table, with our new friend Lady Ashton in her delicate condition, and so many innocent children present!"

Now all the children wanted to hear the story, of course. They looked to Lady Constance for permission.

"Tell whatever tales you like! I am eating, not listening," Lady Constance said gaily, and the children turned eagerly to the princess, who tented her gnarled fingers in her lap.

"Are you sure?" she teased. "Bride and groom is only one way to tell story. Could be a teacher and her students instead." She gave Penelope a sideways glance. "Could be about an unhappy family, with their crazy old grandmamma!" The old woman laughed, darkly, the way her son did—"Ah, ha, hah!"—but each syllable was no more than a breathy creak, like the sound of wind through dead branches.

"Tell it, tell it!" the children begged.

And so the Princess Popkinova began her tale. "Not so long ago, near a small Russian village, there was a beautiful wedding. Afterward, the groom, the bride, the best man, and some of the guests traveled home together through the woods. They rode on a sleigh, pulled by a good horse, fast and strong. Everyone was singing, happy, full of good food and drink from the wedding feast."

"Something bad is going to happen," said one twin to the other.

"How did you know?" said his brother, and punched him in the arm.

"Ow!"

"Shh!" hissed Julia, who wanted to hear the story.

The princess waited for silence, and went on. "Then, out of the dark forest came a pack of wolves. Eyes, yellow. Teeth, like this." She snarled, demonstrating. "The wolves chase! The horse runs fast, very fast—what is the word in English?"

"Galloping, my lady," Master Gogolev said.

"Galloping, yes. The horse, galloping. The wolves galloping more. The wolves biting, like this." She snapped her jaws. "The mouths are wet. Hungry, you understand? They wish to eat the people!"

"Yum, yum!" Boris and Constantin rubbed their bellies. This time their mother shushed them, for she, too, wanted to hear the tale.

"The wolves are close. Too close! The best man says to the groom, 'If the wolves catch us, they will kill us all. We must throw someone to the wolves, so the rest can escape.'"

"No!" the Babushkawoos screamed, loving it.

"The groom says, fine. They grab one of the guests and throw him to the wolves. The wolves eat the guest! The people get away! For a while." She paused for effect. "But then . . . the wolves come again. Closer, closer, snapping, biting . . ."

"Throw someone else!" the Babushkinov children cried. Wide-eyed and white knuckled, the Incorrigibles remained silent.

The princess nodded. "That is what they did. They threw another guest. And another. Each time the wolves ate, they wanted more. One by one, all the guests were eaten. Now there are only three people left in the sleigh: the groom, the bride, and the best man. Again, the wolves chase! The best man turns to the groom. 'Throw your bride to the wolves!' he says. Can you imagine it? His beautiful new bride!"

The princess peered through her monocle and pointed a clawlike finger at each of the children in turn. When she got to Alexander, she stopped. "What do *you* think the groom did?"

"Did the groom throw the best man to the wolves?" Alexander guessed uneasily.

"Yes! He grabs his friend and throws him to his death!" she crowed. "But do you think that satisfied the wolves?"

"No!" yelled the Babushkawoos.

"You are right." She leaned back in her wheelchair and paused, for telling such a tale was hard work. "Now the bride and groom are alone on the sleigh. The horse is tired, his breath like this—" She made a sound like a broken bellows, to demonstrate the wheezing pant of the exhausted animal. "Behind them, the wolves keep running, running. Closer and closer. Still hungry."

Alexander and Beowulf looked pale. Cassiopeia clutched Penelope's hand under the table. The eyes of the Babushkinovs, young and old, glittered with anticipation. The table fell silent, save for some excited gurgles from Max.

"What happened next?" Cassiopeia squeaked.

The princess raised one crooked finger. The milky jewel of her moonstone ring caught the candlelight and shone like a tiny pale planet. "To save himself, the groom throws his bride to the wolves. And finally, he gets away."

"The groom lives, yay! Happy ending!" Veronika clapped Max's chubby hands together for him while the twins cheered. Alexander, Beowulf, and Cassiopeia sat in silence, their mouths hanging open in shock.

The princess laughed. "Fools! Is not happy ending. When the groom reaches the village, and the people learn what he has done, they call him monster, monster! They cast him out. He lives out his days alone, weeping. That is how my story ends. With guilt and misery and loneliness."

She stabbed a piece of meat with a fork and ate it with deep satisfaction.

"Good story," the captain said, after a while. "In the end, most are dead; the rest, unhappy. Just like life."

"Thrilling, yes," Lord Fredrick agreed, although he did not sound terribly thrilled. "Bit of a dark message in there. Not sure what it is, though."

Lady Constance smiled angelically. "Pass the bread basket, please!"

AFTER DINNER, ADULTS AND CHILDREN alike rose from the table and gathered in chairs near the fire for coffee and after-dinner biscuits. The Incorrigibles were strangely subdued after hearing the princess's tale about the wolves (although the wolves were hardly the worst thing in it, as some of you will surely agree). But Boris, Constantin, and Veronika now proudly referred to themselves as the Savage Babushkawoos, and begged the Incorrigibles to teach them to howl, which of course they were glad to do. Even little Max attempted some piping baby howls. His parents found it endearing. It was certainly no worse a noise than hearing their children whine and fight.

Penelope could not wait for the evening to be over. She was utterly worn out from love-struck epiphanies and gruesome tales, and more than anything she wanted to have a bath and go to bed. Perhaps by morning she would no longer be in love with Simon, and circumstances would return to normal. Although, to be frank, Penelope hardly knew what normal circumstances were anymore. Were grooms throwing their brides to the wolves normal? Were family curses? And what about the strange similarity in hair color between her and the Incorrigible children, which even the self-absorbed Master Gogolev had noticed? Surely that kind of coincidence was not the least bit normal; in fact, it seemed highly unlikely, although perhaps not impossible—

"Excuse me," said one of the hotel staff. "There is a strange old woman in the lobby who claims to tell fortunes. Shall I send her in? Sometimes our guests find such persons amusing."

"Oh, do!" cried Madame Babushkinov, before anyone could protest. "I don't believe a word any fortune-teller says, but her nonsense will cheer us up, after sitting through that terrible story."

"Yes, spooky nonsense. It's all poppycock," Lord Fredrick said. He stood abruptly, as if possessed by the urge to bolt, but Lady Constance dozed in her fireside chair with her feet on a cushion and a contented smile on her lips, and could not easily be moved. He stood near her, cracking his knuckles and glancing nervously at the door.

Moments later the fortune-teller came in, hunched and shuffling, and swaddled in countless layers of colorful scarves. "Good evening, good people," she croaked.

"At least she has the sense to keep her head covered," Madame Babushkinov said to Gogolev, who jumped up from his chair as if pinched.

"We don't believe in you, soothsayer, but sit and be comfortable," the tutor said, and gestured for the woman to take his seat.

"But you *do* believe in me," the crone replied in her rasping voice. "All of you do, except one." She closed her eyes and swayed like a charmed cobra. "Yes, I see it clearly. Even now, one of you wishes to speak to me in private, and is wondering how it might be arranged."

At that, Julia started to cry. Gogolev went over to assist, but she shook him off and fled the room, weeping.

"Oops," said the fortune-teller with a shrug. "Sorry about that."

"Never mind that foolish girl; she would cry all day if she could," Madame Babushkinov said. "But I think you have already told a false fortune, soothsayer. Who is the one person among us who does not believe in you?"

The fortune-teller slowly turned. "Him," she said. She was pointing at Baby Max.

"Ahwoo," the baby howled, clapping his hands. Lord Fredrick flinched, but the fortune-teller grinned.

Approximately half of her teeth were missing.

The many scarves, the spooky pronouncements, the hunched posture, the missing teeth . . . "She gives an *impression* of Madame Ionesco, but this woman is not Madame Ionesco," Penelope thought. For one thing, even hunched over, she was much too tall.

The Incorrigibles looked suspicious as well. All three sniffed deeply. "Our friend Madame Ionesco smells of Gypsy cakes," Alexander said, cocking his head to the side. "This lady smells of . . . greasepaint."

"And pirates, but nice ones," said Cassiopeia, puzzled.

"And iambic pentameter," added Beowulf.

"Clever children," the fortune-teller cooed. "Such clever wolf babies!"

Penelope was on her feet in a heartbeat. Greasepaint and pirates and iambic pentameter? She approached the fortune-teller until she was close enough to see the gleam of genius in her—that is to say, his—eye.

"That is no soothsayer!" she yelped. "It is Simon Harley-Dickinson!"

And then, most uncharacteristically for a Swanburne girl, Penelope fainted dead away.

The Ninth Chapter

*A trip to the HAM gets
sandwiched in.*

"CALL FOR THE DOCTOR," MASTER Gogolev barked to one of the hotel staff. "Martell was his name; he was here last night."

"Yes, someone call for Dr. Martell!" Madame Babushkinov repeated the order, although she herself made no attempt to be useful. She spoke to her husband in a low voice. "It was that awful story your mother told at dinner that must have upset the girl so! Why must the old woman always be so unpleasant? In the future we must remember to keep her far away from the young governess—"

She stopped midsentence when she saw the Ashtons standing nearby. "Poor thing!" she cooed to Lady Constance, in quite a different tone. "Your Miss Lumley must be one of those delicate English roses one hears about. Does she often collapse?"

"I'm sure I wouldn't know." Lady Constance stretched and yawned. "But my goodness, Miss Lumley looks so comfortable lying down on the carpet like that! The sight of her is making me sleepy. Fredrick, take me to my room, if you please. It was a lovely dinner, except for all the talking, but I scarcely listened, so no harm was done. Good night to you all, or should I say, *Buona notte a tutti!*"

Her husband was quick to obey, but he spoke a few words in the ear of the hotel manager on the way out. "Yes, fetch the doctor for Miss Lumley and do as he advises, what? I'll cover the expense, just add it to my bill."

Meanwhile, the Incorrigible children and Simon had rushed to Penelope's side (for, yes, beneath his costume and stage makeup, the newcomer was, in fact, Simon!). The children patted her hands and cheeks and made soothing cooing sounds, while Simon tore the scarves off his head and put his ear to her chest.

"Her heart seems steady enough," he said, though he sounded worried. "Halloo! Are you in there, Miss L?"

"Fortune-tellers always frighten me! I nearly fainted, too." Veronika fanned herself dramatically. "It is unnatural! The future is supposed to be a mystery."

The princess laughed bitterly. "What mystery? Future is same for everyone. We are born, we live, we die. Simple."

"And all the rest is poetry," Gogolev exclaimed with fervor. He pressed his fingertips to his temples, so that he might think deeply about what he had just said.

At last Penelope's eyes fluttered open. She struggled to sit up. "Simon!" she said, and then, "What happened to your teeth?"

He grimaced and rubbed off the tooth black with a pocket handkerchief. "Bit of stagecraft, that's all. Part of my fortune-teller act. Sorry for the fright! If I'd know my little performance would upset you so, I'd have sung a few harmless sea chanteys instead."

"Did you hear that? He is an impostor! Someone call the police," Madame Babushkinov demanded. At her words, the twins clenched their fists, eager for an excuse to start punching.

The captain held up his beefy hands. "My dear Natasha, calm yourself! This is my fault. Let the actor explain." He gave a nod to Simon, who, after receiving a reassuring look from Penelope, began.

"It's a tale of theatrical adventure gone wrong, I'm afraid. I arrived in Brighton this afternoon. On my way from the station, I stopped at the post office, where I happened to meet the captain. We struck up a conversation about his whiskers, which I admired greatly. Still do!" He grinned. "I thought they'd be just the thing for a costume of Lord Nelson. I'm thinking of writing a play about the Battle of Trafalgar, wouldn't that be a thrill? Though I haven't yet figured out how to get the Spanish fleet on stage."

"Admiral Nelson, enemy of Napoleon!" the captain roared, then spat on the ground in disgust (as you may recall, the mere mention of the name Napoleon was enough to set the captain off).

"That he was, sir! Anyway, about the whiskers . . . I said, 'Are they real?' and the captain said, '*Da!*' and invited me to give a pull. In this way, a friendship was born! After that, we got to talking. When he found out I was a man of the theater, he asked me to provide a bit of entertainment tonight, after dinner."

The captain shrugged. "My wife gets bored. I thought she would like."

Madame Babushkinov rolled her eyes but nevertheless

seemed pleased to have somehow been the cause of all the trouble.

Simon sat back on his heels. "The fortune-teller act was my idea, inspired by an acquaintance in London."

"Madame Ionesco!" the Incorrigible children guessed.

"Correct! I improvised a costume, found my way to the hotel, and you know the rest. But imagine my shock at seeing my good friends, Miss Penelope Lumley and the Incorrigible children, right here in the front row! That's an unlikely plot twist, even by my standards." With fresh concern he added, "And now I've frightened Miss Lumley half to death, too. I hope you can forgive me! I knew better than to break character during a performance, but rest assured, I was just as surprised to see you as you were to see me."

"But I asked you to come!" she said, still groggy. "I sent you a letter!"

He reached into his shirt pocket and produced a familiar envelope. "I know. I'm looking forward to reading it, too. I picked it up today, in Brighton." At her bewildered look, he explained. "My life in London is a bit footloose at present, but as long as my great-uncle Pudge lives in the Home for Ancient Mariners, Brighton's the one place I can count on returning to now and again. I've had all my mail forwarded to the Brighton General Post Office; it's always my first stop when I arrive." He held the envelope up to the light and read, "'Theatrical Firmament.' Say, that's a nice touch."

He looked at her with the trace of an easy smile still on his lips, and carelessly pushed that poetic lock of hair off his forehead. The room spun 'round, and Penelope sagged once more. Luckily, someone had had the sense to fetch Mrs. Clarke, who had just arrived in her nightgown and slippers. She was armed with smelling salts, which she now waved under Penelope's nose.

"I smell . . . seashells . . . by the seashore . . . ," Penelope mumbled, slowly coming to. Then, "Simon!" she exclaimed when she saw him bending over her, and she closed her eyes, for she had just remembered that she was in love with him.

Alarmed, Simon gestured for Mrs. Clarke to give another wave of the smelling salts. "I'm Simon, we've established that, yes. Say, are you going to keep fainting?"

"The doctor's here, the doctor's here!" the twins chanted, and everyone stood back to make room for Dr. Martell, who quickly took charge. "The girl needs some air, that's it. All of you, please go about your

225

business," he ordered, and promptly sent the Babush-kinovs and all the curious, hovering servants away. He asked the Incorrigible children to find an empty luggage cart and bring it right back. They dashed off to do as they were told, as it was all for the good of their beloved Lumawoo.

Dr. Martell was a man of great experience and wisdom, of course. And, as you no doubt recall, he had been the sole witness to Penelope's unplanned skid into the Seashell of Love. Something about the way this earnest young man with the unruly forelock refused to budge from Penelope's side made the good doctor put two and two together.

"Your name's not Simon, is it?" he asked. "Simon Harley-something?"

"Why, yes! How'd you know?" Simon answered.

"A little seashell told me." He chuckled. "No wonder she fainted! Stay right here; I'll need you to help me get Miss Lumley onto the luggage cart so we can wheel her to her room. Tomorrow, when she's awake, I expect the two of you will have a matter of importance to discuss."

THE NEXT MORNING PENELOPE AWOKE in a buoyant mood, like a happy seabird floating effortlessly over

226

the waves. "What a remarkable dream," she thought, and smiled at the sheer absurdity of it. Imagine, Simon dressed in costume as Madame Ionesco! And Dr. Martell giving her a ride on a luggage cart, as if she were a little girl!

It was only after she rolled onto her side and saw Cassiopeia tangled in the sheets, still in her clothes from the previous day and deep in the openmouthed sleep of a child who has gone to bed hours past her bedtime, that a pulse of suspicion began to throb. She sat up and swung her legs over the side of the bed. The boys were also asleep in their clothes, and she could not for the life of her remember putting them to bed that way, or putting them to bed at all. The morning light streamed in brightly through the porthole window. It must already be nine o'clock, well after their usual breakfast time.

Penelope sniffed. There was a faint smell of ammonia in the room. She followed her nose to a small table near the door. Upon it was a stoppered bottle of smelling salts, next to a handwritten note that read: *Just in case! From your friend Simon, the Very Sorry Soothsayer.*

"It was no dream!" she whispered as the disjointed events of the previous night came galloping back to mind. Parts of her memory were lost in a fog, and she hoped nothing dreadfully embarrassing had taken place, but of one thing she was certain: Simon was here, in Brighton, already!

Her sentiments began hopping willy-nilly from one emotion to its opposite. Simon's arrival was the best—and worst—and best—thing that could have happened! She wanted to see him and hide from him, and tell him and not tell him what was in her heart. But she was a Swanburne girl, after all, and her pluck and common sense had been largely restored by a good night's sleep.

Still, it was not easy to settle herself. What she most needed, she decided, was a nice restorative cup of tea. That would put to rest any remaining flutters of her heart and mind, and then she could get on calmly with the tasks of the day.

"I expect it will be a busy day, too," she thought as she washed her face, dressed, and pinned her hair into a smooth, tidy bun, with not a stray hair to be seen. It was the bun of a young lady who would not be easily flustered, by romance, family curses, or other super-natural events. "It is certainly convenient that Simon has arrived ahead of schedule. Now that he is here, we can go to the HAM, visit Great-Uncle Pudge, and learn the secrets of Ahwoo-Ahwoo. Then I can see about procuring a ship for Lady Constance. Clearly, I have much too much to do to allow myself the distraction of lovesick poppycock!"

Out of the room she stepped—and almost tripped over the luggage cart parked directly in front of her door, upon which reclined Simon Harley-Dickinson.

"Simon! Oh, my!" she exclaimed. Her hand flew to her bun, which suddenly seemed in danger of springing loose. "That is to say, good morning."

He leaped up at the sound of her voice and narrowly missed hitting his head on the cart. "Yes, it's me, the man himself. Good morning! You're just the person I was hoping to see." He grinned, and rubbed his head. "I suppose that's clear by the way I've set up camp outside your room."

"I was expecting—that is to say, hoping—to see you as well." In a desperate act of self-preservation, she added, "The children are still asleep, and I am on my way to the lobby to get some tea. Would you care to join me?"

"That is a fine suggestion," he said, and off they went.

IN SILENCE THEY MADE THEIR way to the lobby. They poured cups of tea from the tea station, added lumps of sugar and splashes of cream, and found adjoining seats near the fire. Only after Penelope had taken a few calming sips did she dare sneak a look at her friend. Had he changed, since last they met? Or was all the change in her? "I am glad to see him," she decided, "but I must not let myself be *too* glad, or I shall not be able to maintain my composure," and so she found herself glancing away from him every thirty seconds or so, by redirecting her gaze at the carpet, or the wallpaper, or the ceiling.

Simon drained his tea in a gulp and gave her a warm smile. "Well, you're up and talking, at least. That's good news. Did you sleep well?"

"Perfectly well, and you?" She took another sip, with her eyes fixed on her shoe.

"Well enough. I've never spent the night on a luggage cart before." He set down his cup and leaned toward her, hands clasped, with his elbows perched on his knees. It brought his face nearer to her, which made it more difficult to look away. "Say, it's awfully good to see you. I apologize again about giving you such a scare! I never took you for the fainting type, to be honest."

"I cannot explain it myself; it has never happened before," she said, which was true. Then again, she had never been in love before! "I am sure it was not your fault," she went on hurriedly. "No doubt it was all this sea air."

He frowned. "I thought the sea air was good for you."

"Exactly, quite right; taking deep breaths by the sea has put me in such vibrant good health, I have grown lightheaded from it!" She smiled at him as long as she dared, then lifted her eyes and gazed intently at some hairline cracks in the wall plaster.

"What are you looking at? Is there a fly buzzing about?" Simon glanced around, puzzled. "I don't see one. Anyway, now I've read your letter from start to finish. So what's this about pirate costumes and boyhood adventures?"

Relieved to slip into their familiar roles as co-conspirators, Penelope explained her scheme about having Simon impersonate Admiral Percival Racine Ashton in order to get Pudge to tell his tale. "But you will need a costume," she said. "What a pity you did not get my letter before leaving London!"

"It wouldn't have mattered. *Pirates on Holiday* sank faster than an anchor hitched to another anchor. The producers sold everything but the actors to make back some of the money they'd lost. Those costumes are scattered to the four winds by now. But there's no shortage of old sailor outfits at the HAM. I know where the storage lockers are. I'm sure we could find something suitable."

Penelope's optimism swelled like a wave, and for the first time she grinned at her friend in her old, easy way. "Will you do it, then?"

He stroked his chin. "Me as the long-dead admiral, eh? Pudge knows the cut of my jib very well, but with plenty of stagecraft and a bit of inspired acting, it just might work." He paused. "But is it right to try to trick old Pudge into breaking his oath, even if it is for a worthy cause? It feels like an ethical dilemma to me."

(Ethical dilemmas are like the sevens and eights of the multiplication tables, which is to say, they are a particularly tricky kind of problem. They occur when the difference between right and wrong is shrouded in mist. For example: Is it wrong to steal a loaf of bread to save the life of a starving child? Is telling a friend that his appalling new haircut looks fantastic a dreadful lie, or simply good manners? Is it ever right to throw one person to the wolves so that others might escape harm? Such questions keep philosophers in business, and the rest of us scratching our heads.)

Penelope and Simon talked it over. They decided that Pudge's loyalty to the admiral was praiseworthy, but the admiral's true intentions ought to be considered as well. "No doubt he swore Pudge to secrecy to protect his family, but surely his purpose would be better served by undoing the curse itself. We must think of the Barking Baby Ashton," Penelope observed, and Simon agreed.

But would their scheme work? Together they stared at the cracks in the wall plaster and considered the odds. "How is your great-uncle's eyesight?" Penelope asked, thoughtfully swirling the last sip of tea 'round the bottom of her teacup.

Simon leaned back in his chair. "Not bad for an old bird who spent his boyhood staring into the sun from the crow's nest. This will be the greatest acting challenge of my career so far!"

AFTER THAT THEY PARTED, FOR Penelope had the children to attend to, and Simon wanted to practice swaggering and speaking like an admiral. They agreed to arrive at the HAM at one o'clock, when Pudge would be fresh from his after-lunch nap. Simon felt his great-uncle would be in good spirits then, and as likely to tell tales of his boyhood adventures to long-dead admirals as they could reasonably expect. How likely that was remained to be seen, of course.

Penelope found the Incorrigibles already up and planning their own lesson for the morning. They were fascinated by the "panorama" mentioned by

Dr. Martell, and had decided to draw one called *The Secret World of Hermit Crabs*, which they hoped would give the viewer the experience of actually living inside a shell.

Penelope thought it was a fine idea, and arranged to have their breakfast brought in so they could get straight to work. Privately she hoped it would keep them occupied while she put her mind to the vexing problem of how to find a ship for Lady Constance to board. A ship! Perhaps a local fisherman might be willing to lend her one. "But even Lady Constance is likely to notice the difference between a fishing skiff and a square-rigger of the type that might reasonably sail across the sea," she thought. "I could ask Simon for advice, for he is well versed in all things nautical. . . ."

In a flash her mind scampered in his direction, like a spaniel helplessly bounding after a squirrel. "Simon, and nothing but Simon!" she inwardly lamented, as a lovelorn sigh escaped her. "This business of being in love is terribly inconvenient. In the first place, it is distracting beyond reason, and in the second place—well, so far it is comically one-sided! How on earth is one person supposed to have any notion of how another person feels? Though I suppose that is what poetry is for."

Unfortunately, the poems Penelope knew and liked best were about shipwrecks, tygers, gloomy supernatural birds, and similar topics that were of little help to her now. "If only I had read a love poem or two along the way," she thought with regret. "Then I might have some idea about how to proceed."

Her thoughts were interrupted by a knock at the door. The children were so absorbed in creating their panorama that they did not even hear the knock, so Penelope rose and answered the door herself.

It was one of the hotel stewards. "A package arrived for you, Miss Lumley," he said, and handed her a small parcel. This puzzled her, for Simon had been the only person from whom she had expected to receive mail in Brighton. Who else knew she was here?

"Is this from the post office?" she inquired.

"I don't know, miss. Someone left it at the front desk for you," he replied. He clicked his heels sharply before leaving, a gesture doubtless picked up from Captain Babushkinov.

Mystified, Penelope took the parcel and let the door close behind her. It was wrapped in brown paper, with some words scrawled upon it. " 'Delivered to the Wrong

Shore by Mistake: Please Forward to Miss Lumley, Right Foot Inn, Brighton,'" she read.

She held the parcel to her face and sniffed, for the whiff of rum was unmistakable. Her heart raced as she tore it open. Inside, flattened and tied in a neat bundle with a piece of twine, were the letters (no longer in bottles) from Simon, along with a note: *I believe these belong to you. Regards, Martell,* it read.

The letters! She grabbed the bottle of smelling salts, just in case, and decamped to the chair by the window. "First I shall put them in order," she thought, shuffling the letters according to the date, "for a story is best told from beginning to end, and not the other way 'round. I am sure Simon would agree." Finally, after taking a deep, calming breath, she began to read.

The first letters described what it was like being locked up belowdecks, the rudeness of his captors, and the poor quality of the food. Later he told of how he slowly befriended the pirates, and learned of their despair at having lost their navigator (the poor fellow had taken dramatically ill during a raid on a beautiful tropical island, and insisted on being left behind to meet his gruesome end among the palm trees and coconuts and kindly native peoples there).

Then came a clearly difficult letter, filled with blotches and crossed-out words, in which Simon confessed that he had been sworn in as part of the crew. "I don't mind it so much myself," he wrote. "Call it an adventure! But I worry that you might not think well of me being a pirate. Perhaps you've forgotten about me anyway, but I have to be honest, my dear Miss L, and say your opinion weighs on my mind."

Penelope began to read more slowly after that. A few letters later, she found this:

I do think of you every day, Penelope (may I call you that?). It helps keep my spirits up, although sometimes I wonder if I'll ever get back to England and see you and those dear Incorrigible children again.

And, later, this:

Nobody but our old friend Madame Ionesco knows the future, of course! Life with a playwright would be scandalous enough, but a playwright pirate? Surely you could do better. Still, I like to think we're cut of the same sailcloth, you and I. . . .

And this:

I know it's my business to be good with words,
but I seem to be sailing in circles trying to say what's
really on my mind. Perhaps, Penny dear (if I may
be so familiar!), if this letter ever finds you, you'll be
able to figure it out.

Penelope put down the letters and sat quite still.
She was shocked. Shaken. Overjoyed! Dismayed!
And above all, thoroughly confused.

"Perhaps he was just lonely at sea," she thought, not
daring to hope. Even so, he had felt that way about her,
once. Might he still?

It was possible, she decided. Yet if he did, why on
earth had he not said anything? "Yet I have not said
anything either," she thought, and drummed her fingers on the table. "Blast! If only I might get him to the
Oddities Museum to lay hands on the Seashell of Love!
Then it would all come tumbling out. But there is no
time for that today." Indeed, the clock showed that it
was already quarter past twelve. Soon it would be time
to make their way to the HAM.

"To discover Simon's true feelings, I will have to
use my powers of deduction and stay on the lookout

238

for clues," she decided. Carefully she put away the letters. "But these letters are surely cause for optimism, if anything ever was!"

THE INCORRIGIBLES WANTED TO MEET Simon's great-uncle, about whom they had heard so much, but the HAM had limited visiting hours for children. Apparently, the ancient mariners were prone to using salty language, and found it tiring to stop when young people were present.

It was just as well, for even in costume Penelope did not think the children would make plausible sailors, given their small size and childlike voices. She arranged for them to stay behind at the Right Foot Inn, studying hermit crabs with the Babushkawoos under the supervision of Master Gogolev. This idea was met with enthusiasm, for a variety of reasons: Veronika was glad to spend time with "her brilliant Sasha," the twins liked the idea of pinching Baby Max with imaginary crab claws, while Master Gogolev felt that the forced migration of the hermit crab from its borrowed shell was a tragic commentary on the relationship between the serfs and the land they worked but did not own.

With the children's afternoon accounted for, Penelope and Simon headed off. His fortune-teller costume slowed their progress, since his gait was hampered by all the long skirts. Still, they agreed it was best for him to travel in disguise, as his many visits to his great-uncle over the years had made him a familiar face at the HAM.

Penelope was glad of the costume for another reason, too. With his handsome head wrapped in scarves, his physique concealed by shawls, and that charming hint of a sailor's swagger hidden beneath the skirts, it was, if not easy, at least easier to put the question of romantic feelings aside temporarily.

They walked in silence, for the wind was too blustery for easy conversation. "There it is," Simon said at last. The Home for Ancient Mariners was a long, low structure, with rows of windows facing the sea. From the rooftop widow's walk, a proud flagpole stretched skyward, and the Union Jack and the flag of the Royal Navy tautly fluttered and snapped in the wind. A stone path, neatly swept, led them from the street to the main gate.

Simon lifted a hand to ring the bell, then paused and turned to her. "Say, I wanted to ask you something. Dr. Martell said you and I would have a matter of importance to discuss today. What do you suppose he meant?"

"Dinosaurs, I expect," Penelope replied, not missing a beat. "Giant lizards, long extinct. You might write an interesting play about them, although it would be a challenge to depict such creatures on the stage, as they were shockingly large, here, let me." She leaned across him and rang the bell. Then she made a great show of waiting, tapping her fingertips together and listening at the lock.

"Giant lizards! Really?" Simon scratched his veiled head.

"Enormous! The size of an omnibus! Shh, someone is coming."

Simon hunched over and drew the scarves close 'round his face. The gate swung open to reveal a man in a nautically styled uniform with the initials HAM embroidered on the chest pocket. Below it was the image of a sunset at the ocean's horizon.

Penelope stood straight as a bowling pin and spoke in her most confident, Swanburnian tone. "Good afternoon, sir. My dear grandmamma and I are here to visit Captain Ahab. May we enter?"

"Captain Ahab?" The man frowned. "We don't have a resident by that name." Penelope had plucked the name from a long American novel she had heard of, having to do with a whale. She had not read the book, but a great stack of them had once nearly fallen on her in a bookshop window display. Naturally, the experience made an impression.

"Captain Ahab is an old family friend," she said with brisk authority. "Perhaps you have him listed under an alternate spelling. Do not trouble yourself! We shall simply go inside and see for ourselves."

Smiling and nodding, she and Simon swept past the poor fellow, who was left puzzling over how else one might spell Ahab. Once they were inside and unobserved, Simon steered them to a stairwell that led downstairs to the residents' storage lockers.

"What did I tell you?" he said, opening the trunks. "Old uniforms everywhere. Sailors are a sentimental lot, indeed." As an expert on stagecraft, he was able to quickly assemble costumes out of these treasures. Penelope dressed as a cabin boy, with her hair tucked up beneath a cap. For himself, Simon fashioned an admiral's uniform out of dark trousers, a brass-buttoned jacket with fringed epaulettes, and a jaunty two-cornered hat. (Such a hat is often called a "bicorne," which means it has two corners, just as a bicycle has two wheels and a bivalve mollusk—such as a clam or an oyster—has two shells.)

"Now for the face." Simon had brought his kit of

stage makeup. Expertly he applied spirit gum and fake whiskers, nose putty, a bit of greasepaint and pencil, and some loose powder to blend it all together. When he was done, he turned to Penelope.

"Ahoy there, lad! How do I look?" His voice was gruff, older, perfectly admiral-like, she thought. And truly, with his long, sloping nose made of putty, thick side whiskers, and drawn-on wrinkles, he hardly looked like himself at all, save for the unruly lock of hair that had escaped from his hat and tumbled poetically over his forehead.

"The nose is pure Ashton. But the hair is Simon Harley-Dickinson, through and through," she replied. Without thinking, she reached out and tucked the stray lock beneath the brim of his hat. The two of them stood there and gazed at each other, and for a moment Penelope was sure she was about to get the clue she was looking for.

But Simon was already in character. "Come along, then, my boy!" he said, in his admiral's voice. "It's time to go talk to my old friend Pudge."

IN HIS UNIFORM SIMON CUT a dashing figure, and the residents of the HAM saluted sharply and greeted him with nods of respect as he and Penelope walked to

Pudge's room. One old salt gave Penelope a sour look. "It's bad luck to have a woman aboard ship," he said, addressing Simon.

"Mind your manners, sailor," Simon replied. "This is Pete, the cabin boy."

The man glared at her. "Like I said. It's bad luck, *miss.*"

"Bad luck for you, maybe!" Penelope spoke with all the growl she could muster. She shoved a fisted hand on each hip and stood wide legged, as she imagined a sailor might. "One more word and I'll have no choice but to challenge you to a—"

"Mind your temper there, young Pete!" Simon interrupted, stepping between them. "Hot heads sink ships, how many times must I tell you?" He clapped the old sailor on the back. "As for you, my good man, better get those eyes checked!"

"If you say so, Admiral," the man muttered, and slunk off.

Penelope was disappointed, for she had thought her disguise was quite convincing. "Do I really look so much like a girl?" she whispered.

"It's nothing to complain about. But maybe this'll help." In a flash he drew a mustache on her lip with one of his grease pencils. "Much better! You're still Pete

"Do I really look so much like a girl?" she whispered.

the cabin boy, only a few years older. Here's Pudge's room. Ready?"

"Aye aye, sir!" She saluted and nearly knocked off her cap.

Simon gave a rap on the door, but there was no answer. "His hearing's not what you'd call shipshape," he explained. He listened at the door for a moment, and slowly pushed it open. Pudge was in his rocking chair, gazing out the window.

"Ahoy, lad!" Simon bellowed, swaggering in. "Why, if it isn't my favorite cabin boy, Pudge!"

The old man turned his head. Without question, he was the oldest person Penelope had ever seen. His leathery skin, nearly bald pate, and thin, wide smile reminded her of a tortoise. Even so, there was something familiar about the gleam in his eye, not to mention the remaining shock of pure white hair that tumbled over his creased, permanently sun-browned forehead.

"Don't you recognize me, Pudge?" Simon went on. "It's me! Your old friend and commander, Admiral Percival Racine Ashton. It's been a few years since our last voyage, but I'd know you anywhere. Why, you haven't changed a bit."

The shadow of some kind of understanding passed over the old man's face, and a smile broke out across his wizened features "Why, so it is!" he exclaimed. "Admiral Ashton, as I live and breathe. You look well, sir. Very well. And who's the young lad?"

It took Penelope a moment to realize he meant her. "Pete the cabin boy, at your service!" she said huskily.

"Aye, Pete the cabin boy! Fancy that. Looks like you could use a bit of a shave, son." Pudge struggled to stand up, and Simon quickly caught his elbow.

"No need to get up, Pudge. We've just come for a visit. I thought it would be amusing to sit and talk about the old days. Spin a few yarns, as it were."

"The old days, yes! Nothing beats looking back on the old days." Pudge settled back in his chair. It made a rhythmic squeaking sound as he rocked.

Simon sat on the edge of Pudge's cot. "I'll bet you remember them better than I do. You always were a sharp one, Pudge, my lad!"

"That's what you always said, Admiral!"

The two men chuckled fondly. There was nowhere else to sit, so Penelope stood near the door. She could hardly believe how well it was going.

"Remember when we were shipwreck'd, Pudge, my boy? That was our greatest adventure together!"

Pudge cackled. "Do you mean, on the island of Ahwoo-Ahwoo?"

"I do indeed. Do you remember?"

"Like it was yesterday." The old man closed his eyes and rocked faster in his squeaking chair.

"What a shipwreck it was!" Simon went on, trying to draw him out. "It was—quite a wreck, wasn't it?"

"Aye, that it was. It was a miracle we made it to that curséd island! And a tragedy so few of us escaped," Pudge said with relish. "Meaning, only two. You and me." He rocked and squeaked, clearly enjoying himself.

"That's right! We were the only ones to escape. How did that happen, Pudge, my boy?"

"Surely you remember, Admiral!"

"Not as well as you do, Pudge! Your memory's sharp as a tack!"

"That it is. But even if it weren't, I'd still know the tale. For I wrote it all down in my cabin boy's diary." He paused and looked at them both. "I wrote it in the form of a poem."

Simon snuck a look at Penelope. "A poem, you say? That's impressive! Pete, next time you set sail, try to be as clever as Pudge, here, will you?"

"Aye aye, sir!" Penelope barked. "I'd like to hear that poem, sir!"

"Me, too," Simon said, and smiled. Penelope smiled. Pudge smiled too.

"It's a long one," the old man warned. "Any particular part you'd like to hear?"

"We'd like to hear the part about—" Simon caught himself. "I mean to say . . . well, I do recall, vaguely, something about a curse."

"A curse! Yes. A dreadful curse!" The old salt cackled merrily.

Simon slapped his knee. "Let's hear that part, then. What say you, Pete?"

"I'd like to hear the part about the curse, too, sir!" Penelope piped up.

"I bet you would, boy." Pudge cackled and rocked. "But the curse is not in the poem."

"Wait. The curse is not in the poem?" Simon asked in disbelief.

"That's just what I said, Admiral. The curse is not in the poem. I tried to put it in, but it wouldn't fit the poetic meter."

Simon was momentarily stumped. "Ah! Well." He looked at Penelope for help.

She cleared her throat. "Bad luck about the poetic meter, Mister Pudge, sir! Could you just *tell* us what the curse was, then? The exact words of it? In prose?"

Pudge cocked his head to the side, as if to listen with his other ear. "Crows? I heard a poem about crows once. By a Mr. Poe. 'Nevermore!' That's what it was called."

"Actually, it is called 'The Raven,'" Penelope corrected, for she knew the poem quite well.

"Not crows, my boy! Prose!" Simon said. "Prose with a P. Could you tell us the curse in prose?"

Pudge's thin, close-lipped smile spread from ear to ear. "Ah, prose with a P! P as in pirate. Well, I don't know anything about prose, but I could tell you in plain speech. *If* you were the admiral."

Simon faltered, but only for a moment. He scowled and puffed up his chest. "I beg your pardon, lad! I *am* the admiral!"

Pudge rocked and laughed until he had to wipe a tear of mirth from his eye. "Oh, come on, Simon! I'm old, and one of my ears is worse than the other, but I'm not blind, and I've more wits than most. I've played along with your little game. But now I'm thirsty, so that's enough. Let's go to the mess hall and have a wee glass of punch." He squinted at Penelope. "And who's the young lady, eh?"

Blast! The ruse had failed, and there was no need to go on pretending. Penelope summoned what dignity she could. "I am Miss Penelope Lumley," she replied. "It is a pleasure to make your acquaintance." She had no idea how to curtsy in trousers, so she gave a small bow instead.

Simon took off his hat and ran his hands through his hair. "All right, Uncle. You found us out. We shouldn't have tried to trick you. You're too sharp for that."

"You shouldn't try to flatter me, either," Pudge said, sounding annoyed.

"Sorry! You're right as ever." Simon perched on the edge of the cot, a hand on each knee. "Here's the plain truth, on my honor as a Harley-Dickinson: Miss Lumley and I need to know what happened on Ahwoo-Ahwoo. We're asking you, please, to tell us."

"I swore an oath to the admiral. I'll discuss it with no one but him."

"I know you swore an oath, Uncle. But it's important. The fates of—well, quite a few people depend on it."

"Including the admiral's own great-great-great-great-grandchild, who is soon to be born," Penelope added.

Pudge was unmoved. "Like I said. Bring me the admiral, and we'll have a nice chat all about it."

Simon looked at Penelope, who gave a regretful nod. There was no other way. He placed a hand on the old man's knee.

"Uncle, I'm sorry to be blunt, but the admiral's dead."

Pudge tipped his head to the other side, making the question of which ear was his good one difficult to answer. "Fled, you say? Of course he fled! If you were being chased by cannibals, you'd flee, too."

Simon leaned forward and his voice rose. "Listen here, Pudge. Admiral Ashton is no longer among us. He has passed through the realm of the living and now dwells Beyond the Veil!" Penelope could not help but admire how, even in dire straits, Simon surely had a way with words.

"No need to shout, lad! I'm right here." Pudge's thin lips grew thinner still. "The admiral's dead, I know that. Dead as a dodo. Why'd you think I put 'sole survivor' in the name of my book? Sole means only! If the admiral was alive, I'd not be the sole survivor, would I?"

His logic on this point was hard to refute. "But how can you insist on speaking to him when you know it is impossible?" Simon asked, exasperated.

Pudge stilled his chair. The squeaking stopped, and silence blanketed the room like snow. "Simon, my boy, I'm an ancient mariner. I spent my whole life aboard ship. There's much I've seen, and much I wish I hadn't seen. My word is my bond, an oath is an oath, and the older I get, the less your sort of logic means to me.

Impossible things happen all the time. If you were as old as me, you'd know that."

His rocking resumed, back and forth, and so did the piercing, rhythmic squeak of wood on wood. "When the admiral comes, I'll talk a blue streak. Until then, I'm silent as a clam. I'm waiting for the admiral, and that, my boy, is that!"

The Tenth Chapter

The reading of difficult poetry
gives Penelope an idea.

DEFEATED, SIMON AND PENELOPE HELPED Pudge into his invalid chair and wheeled him to the sitting room for a glass of punch. All the ancient mariners looked forward to this afternoon refreshment, which was a daily ritual at the HAM. They stood in a long, bow-legged line, elbowing one another and making sly remarks about waiting their turn to "walk the plank." (The old sailors were joking, of course, for to "walk the plank" was the most drastic punishment that could be doled out on a ship. Even the tastiest glass of punch

254

would hardly be worth such a gruesome end.)

The drinks were ladled out by a jolly serving woman in an apron made of patched sailcloth. She was tall and rotund, with a bulbous nose, round eyeglasses, and circles of red blush painted on her cheeks. She indulged the sailors' good humor by pouring imaginary spirits from an empty rum bottle into each glass before handing it over, all while singing in a deep alto voice.

"What do you do with a drunken sailor,
What do you do with a drunken sailor
What do you do with a drunken sailor
Earl-eye in the morning?"

The sailors found this hilarious, but the rum bottle made Penelope think of Simon's letters. Oh, the letters! Thank goodness she was still dressed as Pete the cabin boy. It made it easier to swagger about and wipe her mouth with the back of her hand and swear mild sailor oaths, like "Pickled herring, that's good punch!" instead of sitting morosely in a corner, wondering whether Simon was or was not in love with her. "Pickled herring!" she thought, losing patience. "If he is, he ought to say so, oughtn't he?"

The wind blew cold by the water, but Pudge insisted on being wheeled outside to drink his punch on the wide, sea-facing porch. He longed to hear the waves, gaze at the horizon, and take a few deep breaths of the frigid ocean air. "That's why there are so many ancient mariners, you know," he said, as Simon and Penelope shivered in their sailor suits. "A life spent breathing that fine salt air! If you don't fall overboard, or die of scurvy, or get eaten by a shark, or slain by pirates, or killed in a mutiny or . . . well, any number of things . . . a sailor's life is bound to be a long one, yes sirree!"

Soon their visit was over. Simon and Penelope returned Pudge to his room and their costumes to the trunks in the storage area downstairs. "Talk about a knack for the theatrical! Old Pudge put on quite a show for us. I'd say his performance put mine to shame," Simon groused as they trudged along the boardwalk back to the hotel. He was again dressed in his fortune-teller outfit but made no attempt to walk or talk "in character." As the saying goes, that ship had sailed.

"No, Simon. The failure of our scheme was my fault, not yours. I was being optoomuchstic to think you could fool your own great-uncle, despite your consid-erable talent and skill with stagecraft," Penelope said, just as unhappy. The day had been a double failure as far as she was concerned: Not only had they not learned the exact words of the curse upon the Ashtons, but she had not discovered a single clue one way or the other regarding Simon's feelings toward her! It was all quite disheartening.

Simon handed her a pocket handkerchief and tapped a finger to his upper lip. "Not that you don't look good in a mustache," he said with a grin.

"Oh!" she blurted, embarrassed. She turned her head to hide her blush as she wiped off the grease pencil, and wondered if the compliment "You look good in a mustache" could be considered a reliable sign of a love-struck suitor. If only the rules of love were as simple and straightforward as, say, the rules of poetic meter. . . .

"Poetic meter!" she exclaimed. She stopped walking and turned to her friend. "Simon, surely you remember how badly Edward Ashton wanted to read Pudge's diary? So much so that he stole it away from us before we could read it ourselves?"

"Do I! That was a dark day. After all the work we'd done to visibilize the invisible ink that rascal Pudge had used to write down his tale! Sorry. I shouldn't call him a rascal, but I'm a bit cross with the old man at present."

"Understandably so," she said, though she was

impatient to get to her point, "but do you recall *why* Edward Ashton was so desperate to read it?"

"Sure I do. To end the curse on his family, he had to know exactly what happened on Ahwoo-Ahwoo. . . ." He looked at her, realizing. "I think I see what you're driving at here! Thanks to the rules of poetic meter, the curse—"

"—is not in the poem. The curse is not in the poem," she muttered, thinking it through. "Which means that Edward Ashton must still be trying to find out what happened on Ahwoo-Ahwoo, just as we are. He, too, must discover the exact words of the curse. And your great-uncle Pudge remains the only living person, on land or at sea, who knows the answer."

She gazed up at him, her eyes gray as a storm. "Simon, it is only a matter of time before Edward Ashton turns up in Brighton. When he does, he will use all his trickery to persuade Pudge to reveal to him what we were unable to learn."

"Good luck to Edward Ashton, then! At least we know for sure that that stubborn old man will only talk to the admiral."

"Whom Edward Ashton resembles far more than you do, I am afraid." She resumed walking, so determined that Simon had to hop to keep up with her. "Nor is he a stranger to costumes and disguises. Recall how he adopted the guise of 'Judge Quinzy,' by the use of black hair dye and thick glasses to conceal his striking dark eyes, and was thus able to go unrecognized by Lord Fredrick, his own son."

"Who's blind as a mole, but still . . ." Simon hoisted up his skirt in annoyance. "If only I looked less like a Harley-Dickinson and more like an Ashton. Edward Ashton fits the bill perfectly."

"But so does his son." Even in her familiar brown dress and warm winter cloak, there was no mistaking the confident swagger in Penelope's walk. "No hopeless case is truly without hope, Simon! Today our show flopped, but with a slight change of casting, I believe we can turn the ship around, so to speak. We simply have to beat Edward Ashton to the Pudge."

PENELOPE STOOD BEFORE HER EMPLOYER, her hands clasped before her like a soloist in a choir. Lord Fredrick played with his unlit cigar and considered her proposal.

"So let's see if I've got this right," he said. "You want me to put on an admiral suit, pretend to be my own great-grandfather, and chat with an antique sailor named Pudge who knows more about the curse on my family than I do."

"That is correct." She paused. "There is a strong family resemblance among the men in your family, sir."

"I was never much for acting at school," he muttered, unconvinced. "Kept bumping into the scenery. My father had the knack, though! He could have gone on the professional stage. He liked to fool with putty noses and funny accents and so on."

"You did ask me to discover how to undo the curse on your family," she said, gently prodding. "If we can learn the exact wording of it, there may be a way to unravel it."

He chewed the end of his cigar. "It's all in the wording, eh? Like a contract. Sounds like I need a lawyer. Or a judge!" He let out a sharp, rueful bark of a laugh. "Very well. We'll put on a little show for this Pudge character. Someplace private, if you please. The staff already thinks I'm an odd duck; no need to risk getting caught running around in a sailor suit. But I can't do it tomorrow. I promised Constance I'd take her sightseeing for the day. It'll have to be Monday. Tuesday will be . . . inconvenient."

At the mention of Tuesday, they both glanced out the window. The pale disk of the waxing gibbous moon shone faintly in the late afternoon sky. It was only slightly less than full.

"Too bad about the full moon," he said. "Bad timing, what? It's been pleasant here at the hotel, with Constance in a good mood. She won't be pleased when I disappear for a day. But I'd rather she not see me carrying on like a hound with a bellyache. . . ." He looked up, his eyes uncharacteristically bright. "Miss Lumley! Where are the wolf children now?"

"In our room, sir, doing their lessons." As far as she knew, they were still working on the panorama with Simon.

He sprang from his chair. "I'd like to see them. Take me to them, please."

Startled, Penelope jumped up to follow. "Of course, sir, but if I may ask . . . why?"

"Call it an impulse." He was already at the door. "Unlike most people, they've seen me in the worst of my full-moon fit. I'd like them to know what I'm really like. Just an ordinary fellow in most respects, despite this blasted curse and being absurdly rich, of course. Not sure which is more of a burden, frankly! Unless you think I'd frighten them?" He stopped, concerned. "Perhaps they only like me doggish? I realize I've hardly spent any time with them otherwise."

"That is considerate of you to think of, my lord." In fact, she was surprised by how considerate it was, but

261

Lord Fredrick was full of surprises lately. "I am certain the children would be pleased if you paid them a visit. All children thrive on attention."

"Wives, too, so I've discovered," he said, more to himself than her. "Curious! That I might frighten the wolf children never would have occurred to me before. Perhaps it's because I'm soon to be a father myself." Abruptly, he toughened up. "Still, they are my wards, and I am their guardian, so they have to do what I say, no matter what. Finders keepers, eh? Now take me to them, if you please, Miss Lumley!"

PENELOPE GAVE A WARNING KNOCK on the door of room fourteen before entering. At once she regretted not preparing Lord Fredrick for the strange scene within.

"Welcome to *The Secret World of Hermit Crabs*," Simon announced, beaming. The panorama was coming along nicely. Floor-to-ceiling-sized illustrations had been tacked up on the walls to dry. The children's leaping imaginations had conceived all sorts of thrilling underwater vistas, and Simon's knack for theatrical scene painting and the use of perspective had added real verisimilitude to their efforts. (As the Latin scholars among you know, "verisimilitude" means "the appearance of truth," which is not the same thing as actually being true. The boldest lie can possess verisimilitude, if it is told well, while something that is true but highly unlikely might have no verisimilitude at all. Magicians know this, as do certain types of criminals and storytellers of all kinds.)

Lord Fredrick's blurry eyesight must have rendered the illusion even more convincing. He turned 'round slowly, to get the full effect. "Marvelous!" he exclaimed. "I feel quite underwater in here."

"Veronika is seaweed," Cassiopeia pointed out. The older girl was wrapped in a dark green sheet and stood swaying in a corner. "And Boris and Constantin are barnacles." This happy choice had been made by Simon; it meant the twins had to stay silent and still and cling to one side of the wardrobe, which represented the hull of a sunken schooner.

Penelope took two steps into the room and tripped over a lump on the floor. "Master Gogolev, are you unwell?" she asked, for it was the tutor, on his back on the carpet, his eyes closed.

"I am a coral reef," Gogolev answered serenely. Julia had gone to care for the princess Popkinova. In her absence, a kind of peace had descended over the tormented tutor. Alas, the mere sound of his voice prompted the barnacles to come loose from their

"Marvelous!" he exclaimed. "I feel quite underwater in here."

moorings; soon they were attempting to bind themselves to the coral by jumping on it, over the forceful protests of the reef.

"Careful, lads, the paint's still wet! And look, I've taught the children how to make papier-mâché," Simon said with pride. "That's French for 'chewed paper.' It's an easy way to create small props, models, masks, and so on. A few three-dimensional effects will make any painted backdrop more convincing." Beowulf, in particular, had taken the idea of chewed-up paper to heart (as you know, he loved to gnaw) and had created an ample supply. It was a messy business, but thanks to his efforts *The Secret World of Hermit Crabs* had gained in complexity, with the addition of underwater iguanodons and other fanciful creatures.

"Remarkable," Penelope said as the Incorrigibles showed off their creations. "Are there really dinosaurs in the secret world of hermit crabs?"

Probably not, the children conceded, although secret dinosaurs could not be ruled out.

Lord Fredrick picked up a papier-mâché skull of a megalosaurus. "'Alas, poor Yorick!'" he said, in a deep, theatrical tone.

"Shakespeare!" Alexander cried in recognition.

"Right you are, wolf boy. It's from *Hamlet*. We acted

it out at school when I was no older than you. 'To be, or not to be!' I've forgotten most of it by now, but that line I remember. It was good fun being someone else for a change, as I recall. Bit of a relief, to be honest."

"Now, now, lordawoo. Don't be *weltschmerz*." Cassiopeia had spent more time with Lord Fredrick than her brothers had, and felt more familiar with him. Without shyness, she took him by the hand and led him to a chair. "Sit, relax, and enjoy the seaweed," she advised as Veronika continued her nearly imperceptible Dance of the Fronds.

Lord Fredrick watched for a while, but soon grew distracted and gazed out the porthole window. "Wish I could remember more. There was a nice bit about 'a sea of troubles,'" he said, still quoting *Hamlet*. "That's what I've got, a sea of troubles. Poor Constance! I do wish I could take her to Italy. It's not so much to ask, really."

His face clouded with sadness, and the kindhearted Incorrigibles besieged him with offers of entertainment. Would he like a short lesson about mollusks? A rousing sea chantey? Perhaps he would like to make something out of papier-mâché?

"I know! Let's hear a poem from Lumawoo," Beowulf suggested, and his siblings agreed readily, for with all the distractions of their holiday they had not yet heard the poem their governess brought with her from Ashton Place.

The Babushkinov children were less eager, until Penelope announced that the poem she had chosen included a gloomy supernatural bird.

"It is not a raven, this time, but an albatross," she explained.

"Gloomy birds make the best poems," Beowulf assured the twins, and they grudgingly agreed to give it a try.

Lord Fredrick was still adrift on his sea of troubles, but he pulled up his chair to join the others. Someone even put Max on his knee, for who is not cheered by holding a baby? He did his best to prop up the child, and groaned comically at the boy's heft and damp diaper, but he did not give him up, even when Veronika offered to take him away.

Penelope took out the poetry book and opened it to the correct page. "This mysterious poem is by Mr. Samuel Coleridge. It is called 'The Rime of the Ancient Mariner.'" She had not given much thought to the title before, but now it struck her as a coincidence, for had she not recently met an ancient mariner with a taste for poetry?

She began to read it aloud, and although it was

not an easy poem to follow, the hypnotic beat of the poetic meter soon captured the attention of her listeners. Verse by verse, the ancient mariner of the title unfurled his tale of a long-ago sea voyage that went horribly, spookily wrong. By the time she reached the part where the doomed ship and its desperate crew were becalmed in some haunted, unmapped sea, with not even a breath of wind to move them along, even the Babushkawoos were wide-eyed.

"Down dropt the breeze, the sails dropt down,
'Twas sad as sad could be;
And we did speak only to break
The silence of the sea!

All in a hot and copper sky,
The bloody Sun, at noon,
Right up above the mast did stand,
No bigger than the Moon."

"Eureka!" she cried, though it was not part of the poem. She turned to Lord Fredrick. "Never fear, my lord. Lady Constance will have her ship. It is all quite simple, really; I cannot imagine why I did not think of it before."

Lord Fredrick nodded, but his eyes were closed and he waved at her to continue, for by now he, too, had become lost in the strange tale penned by Mr. Coleridge, and wished to hear the end. Simon looked at her with intense curiosity, but that discussion would have to wait until later. Calmly, on the outside at least, she continued to read.

> *"Day after day, day after day,*
> *We stuck, nor breath nor motion;*
> *As idle as a painted ship*
> *Upon a painted ocean."*

THE DEEP THOUGHTS AND HYPNOTIC rhythm of the poem had left the children in a state of dazed contemplation. Master Gogolev snored philosophically from the floor. Lord Fredrick was in no hurry to relinquish his role as Max's babysitter; the enormous infant had fallen asleep in his lap, and he was loath to disturb the child by getting up.

Penelope's new and excellent idea required certain arrangements to be made, and there was no time to waste. She instructed the others to ponder the meaning of "The Rime of the Ancient Mariner" on their own, and invited Simon to join her for a walk down

Front Street. By the time they arrived at their destination, she had explained her idea.

"It is a simple question of verisimilitude. . . . Where on earth is this fellow?" Insistently, and for the third time, Penelope rang the bell. "It is private here," she remarked to Simon as they waited. "I believe it will do quite nicely, for our purposes."

Simon looked around. "I'll say it's private. There's no one here."

Impatient, Penelope called through cupped hands. "Hello! Is anyone minding the front desk?"

"Yes, yes; just a moment, please!" The desk clerk at the Left Foot Inn came stumbling out of the office, yawning and rubbing his eyes as if he had been roused from a deep sleep. "Who's ringing the bell in January? Only a madman would turn up here in the off-season—Oh! You again." He gave Penelope a knowing look. "Well, you can't say I didn't warn you about the Babushkinovs. They must have done something unspeakable to send you running back." He propped his elbows on the desk and put his chin on his hands. "What was it? Start at the beginning, and don't leave anything out."

Penelope raised a disapproving eyebrow. "My good sir, gossip has no place in polite conversation. As a wise person named Agatha Swanburne once said, 'Inform, praise, thank, or amuse—or be quiet and listen, that works, too.'" She gestured at Simon. "My colleague and I are here to inquire if the Left Foot Inn is still empty of guests."

The clerk pursed his lips. "Completely empty, I am overjoyed to report."

"Excellent!" Penelope turned to Simon. "Just as I had hoped."

"What she means is, we'll take it," Simon added. The two of them stood smiling at the clerk, as if the whole business were already settled.

He gaped at them, uncomprehending. "You'll take—what?"

"Why, the hotel. What else?" Penelope said, with Simon cheerfully nodding along. "For Monday, please."

The clerk looked appalled. "You wish to reserve the *entire* hotel?"

"From stem to stern. Fore and aft. And from port to starboard, too." Simon elbowed Penelope as if he had made a hilarious joke.

"Monday? But that's the day after tomorrow!"

"Correct. But we shall not arrive until the afternoon, so you will have more than enough time to get the hotel shipshape, as it were." Penelope paused as Simon snorted with mirth at her pun. "Please instruct the kitchen: At five o'clock we will host a formal dinner for a party of, say, twenty people." She tallied up the guest list in her head: the Ashton household, the Babushkinovs, the Incorrigibles, Dr. Martell, and possibly a few others, too, for a real ship would be full of passengers, and verisimilitude was the goal. "Best make it twenty-five," she said. "There is no need to order flowers or decorations, for we have our own . . ." She stopped, unsure of how to describe it.

"Artistic consultants," Simon interjected.

"Yes! The artistic consultants will prepare the hotel prior to the arrival of the dinner guests. Please give them your full cooperation. Lastly, you must make sure that all of your employees speak only Italian for the duration of our stay. A few basic, socially useful phrases will suffice."

"Dinner? Decorations? Speaking Italian?" The clerk closed his eyes and shivered, as if trying to shake off a bad dream. "This is a mammoth undertaking. Unprecedented! I am not sure we can oblige—but *if* we can, I must warn you, it will be enormously expensive."

Penelope knew that Lord Fredrick could afford any expense, but *A Swanburne Girl Is Thrifty*, as one of the embroidered pillows in Miss Mortimer's office read. "Nonsense," she answered firmly. "It is a themed dinner party, plain and simple. You may certainly charge extra for speaking Italian, but otherwise there is nothing unusual about it. The theme is *Bella Italia*. Do keep that in mind when you plan the menu." Meaningfully she added, "You may send the bill to Lord Fredrick Ashton, care of the Right Foot Inn."

Even the hotel clerk at the Left Foot Inn in Brighton had heard of the richer-than-Midas Ashtons. He harrumphed and frowned, and slammed his hand on the brass service bell a few times out of sheer frustration until the ringing drove him mad and he stuffed the bell in a drawer. "All right," he said. "We'll do it."

AFTER THEIR BUSINESS AT THE Left Foot Inn was settled, Simon walked Penelope back to the Right Foot Inn. After that he intended to make a beeline to the HAM to keep an eye on his great-uncle. "I'll stay with the old salt until he's tucked in bed and the gates are locked for the night," he assured her. "Trust me, there's no chance that Edward Ashton will get to him before we do! Anyway, not-so-dead Edward's been quiet for so long; perhaps he's given up."

Penelope wished she could be so sure. She bid Simon farewell and watched him go, with the tiniest ache in her heart that she quickly and firmly put out of her mind. Overall, she felt quite pleased with how she had managed things. The day after tomorrow Lord Fredrick would pose as the admiral, and the Left Foot Inn would pose as a ship. Pudge and Lady Constance would be fooled, the exact words of the curse discovered, and that troublemaking Edward Ashton was still nowhere in sight. Best of all, the children had been introduced to the poetry of Coleridge and the life cycle of the hermit crab, and would soon become expert in the finer points of Italian culture and cuisine. Why, a whole term at Oxford could hardly be more educational than this trip to Brighton in the off-season!

She had not forgotten about Lord Fredrick's full moon needs, either. Before leaving the Left Foot Inn, she had asked that one room be reserved for Tuesday "in the most soundproof part of the hotel," she was careful to specify.

"As for Lady Constance, I will simply suggest that she spend Tuesday having me write picture postcards to all her friends," she thought. "I will go slowly and make many mistakes and inkblots, she will grow cross and distracted and will keep starting over. The day will fly, she will hardly notice her husband's absence, and by Wednesday, all the troubles in our sea of troubles will be over. . . ."

All except one, that is. The ache in her heart came back doubled. Did Simon Harley-Dickinson love her, or did he not? All day Penelope had been on the lookout for evidence as to which way the wind blew, so to speak, but overall he seemed the same cheerful, kind, clever, and thoroughly loyal Simon she had known for more than a year.

"Compared to the horrible throes of lovesickness suffered by Master Gogolev, Simon shows no sign at all of romantic torment," she thought. "I suppose that answers my question, and I ought not to think of it anymore. Blast that Seashell of Love! I have been caught in a whirlpool because of it, but I expect in time I will find calm waters once more."

It would be dishonest to say she was not disappointed, but she was also relieved. She liked—well, loved—Simon just the way he was, and she did not think she would enjoy seeing him in a state of love-struck agony, even if she herself were the cause. However, she did resolve to ask Master Gogolev to recommend some love poems to her, ones he thought captured the authentic feel of it, the storm-tossed nerves and woeful *weltschmerz* of the whole experience. They were bound to make educational reading, at least.

THE INCORRIGIBLE CHILDREN WERE DELIGHTED to be given the important responsibility of creating the decorations for the *Bella Italia* dinner at the Left Foot Inn. They worked on the project after supper and all the next morning. Ideas flowed, brushes were dipped in paint, and a great deal of papier-mâché was chewed up and spit out. By early afternoon on Sunday, they were done. The pieces were set aside to dry for the next day.

"Wonderful work all around, children," Penelope said after all the art supplies were put away and lunch was finally eaten. "Because you have worked so hard, we now have a free afternoon. How would you care to spend it?"

"We want to play with the Babushkawoos!" the children declared. While painting they had made two name signs for the twins to wear 'round their necks, one that said BORIS and one that said CONSTANTIN, for even the Incorrigibles had grown weary of not being able to tell the boys apart.

But where *were* the Babushkawoos? After some careful sniffing, the Incorrigibles caught the scent of toe shoes and black eyes, and followed their noses to the dining room. Veronika, Boris, and Constantin were there, tired and cranky and picking at a late lunch. They had spent a long morning with their parents, being dragged along on some tedious grown-up errand. "At a dreadful, boring old bank," Veronika complained in a melodious whine. "So much talking and signing of papers! I never want to grow up if it means such dull business."

"On my honor, Veronika Ivanovna Babushkinova," Alexander said gallantly, "you shall never have to grow up and sign papers! I swear it!" Veronika twirled and giggled.

Meanwhile, the others tried to agree on what sort of game to play. Beowulf proposed a chess tournament. But the hotel had only one chess set, and Boris and Constantin sheepishly admitted that chess was not their strong suit; they would simply fight over who would play the white pieces and who the black, accuse each other of cheating, and so forth.

"We could play at being Eskimaux," Cassiopeia suggested. But the Babushkawoos said that snow and ice made them think of Siberia, an especially cold and sad part of Russia to which people were sent as a punishment for crimes, or sometimes merely for having unpopular opinions. (For those of you who have never heard of it, rest assured that Siberia was a brutal place. The people sent there were likely to freeze or starve to death, or perish out of sheer boredom and misery. If *weltschmerz* were a place one could find on a map, it would doubtless be Siberia.)

Then Constantin had an idea. "Let us play at being judges," he said. "We could sentence people to hang!"

"Yes! We could send them to jail for stealing loaves of bread," said Boris.

"Or for no reason at all," his brother proposed.

Penelope held up a hand. "How do you know so much about judges?" she asked, deeply unsettled. The twins stared at the floor and shrugged and would not answer, and turned their name signs around, too, as if that somehow rendered them invisible.

"Naughty savages! If you ask them a question about anything, they think they are about to be punished, for they have always done something to deserve it. Papa has a friend who is a judge," Veronika explained. "What a frightening man! His eyes are black as lumps of coal, and he wears thick blurry glasses, so you can never be sure where he is looking."

Penelope's heart lurched in her chest. That could only be Edward Ashton, posing as Judge Quinzy!

"Veronika, this friend of your father's . . . what is his name?"

The girl shrugged. "I don't remember. He is a new friend. Papa met him here, in Brighton. He was at the bank this morning, too. Papa said he needed to do something with money and sign some papers, and his friend the judge was there to open the bank on a Sunday and advise him on important business."

"It was *sooo* uninteresting! It took *sooo* long!" the twins complained.

"Stop whining, please!" Penelope's tone was uncharacteristically sharp. To Veronika, she said, more gently, "What kind of business?"

"I don't know, but Papa said he was using the money to get us something we would like very, very much." Veronika hugged herself in excitement. "I hope it is a pony! A snow-white pony to match my coat. Or a sable pony to match my other coat. Or an inky-black pony to match my other coat. . . ."

Under normal circumstances Penelope would rather talk about ponies than about nearly any other topic, but not now. A slow chill crackled its way up her spine, like a skin of ice forming over a pond. So Edward Ashton *was* in Brighton! Thank goodness Simon was with Great-Uncle Pudge at the HAM;

279

she need not worry about the old man's safety—but what business could Edward Ashton have with the Babushkinovs?

Her brow furrowed as it always did when she was deep in thought, for this unexpected new piece threatened to upend the whole puzzle. "If Edward Ashton has befriended the captain, as Veronika says, he must have been here in Brighton for some days already. In that time he has not revealed himself to us, or to Great-Uncle Pudge—but he *has* sought out the Babushkinovs! Why? Dear me! I fear I may have underestimated him. Perhaps he has not come to Brighton to see Pudge at all, but for some other, unknown reason. . . ."

Clearly, she needed time to think.

"Playing at judges is an unpleasant game, best saved for never," she said to the children. "Upon reflection, I believe the afternoon ought to be spent in educational pursuits. Who would like to recite the multiplication tables? Boris, Constantin, surely you are able to count by twos?"

The twins looked at her in disbelief. Fortunately, Cassiopeia was always eager for a math lesson. She clambered upon a chair in the middle of the dining room, stood straight and tall, and cheerfully began:

"One times Boris and Constantin is two Babush-kawoos, two times Boris and Constantin is four Babushkawoos, three times Boris and Constantin is six Babushkawoos . . ."

THE ELEVENTH CHAPTER

A long-awaited tale is told.

PENELOPE SLEPT FITFULLY THAT NIGHT. "Seven sevens is forty-nine Edward Ashtons . . . ," she mumbled, dreaming. "Seven eights is fifty-four—no!—fifty-six Edward Ashtons. . . ."

But the hours of the long night passed, as hours always do, and soon enough it was morning. Monday, at last! A cold rain fell, and the sky was thick with clouds. It would have been a good day to stay under the covers, snug as a hermit crab in its cozy shell, but a great many things had to happen before the sun set, the dinner guests arrived, and Tuesday's full moon rose in the sky.

The Incorrigible children were more well rested than their governess, and jumped out of bed with purpose. They inspected their artwork, now dry, and added whatever finishing touches they deemed necessary. Then they inquired if they might ask the Babushkawoos to help with the decorating.

Penelope had already thought about this, given the Babushkinovs' unhappy history at the Left Foot Inn. She had briefly considered not inviting them at all, but with Edward Ashton up to no good, she thought it best to keep the Babushkinovs in her own sights for the evening. In any case, it would have been frightfully rude to exclude them from the party, after the children had sworn bonds of eternal friendship.

"Let us not spoil the surprise," she replied. "After the Babushkinovs arrive, you may find other ways for your friends to be helpful. But look, it is nearly nine o'clock already, and we have breakfast to think of, and all these invitations to address, after which we must meet Lord Fredrick and Old Timothy downstairs for a, well . . . *unusual* adventure. Now, who would like to help me seal these envelopes with wax?"

MEANWHILE, AT THE HAM, A metaphorical boatload of ancient mariners and one dashing, perfectly nice young playwright were having their morning meal of hardtack, salt beef, and sauerkraut. The sauerkraut was meant to prevent scurvy, which was a problem during long sea voyages but hardly a risk at the HAM. However, old habits die hard, and the men liked the taste of it. As they ate, they drank black coffee out of tin cups and spoke, as sailors often do, about the weather.

"Awful rain out there, eh, lads?"

"Aye, and howling winds, too! It's not fit for man nor beast."

"Only a fool would put out to sea on a blustery day like this!"

Simon's conversation took a different tack, which is a sailor's way of saying he followed a different course. "Come, dear Pudge!" he said, pushing away his untouched plate. "It's not healthy to sit inside. Let's go for a stroll on the boardwalk."

"It's raining cats and dogs, nephew," Pudge answered. "Now, are you going to eat your sauerkraut, or not?"

"I'm more of a bacon-and-egg man myself, Uncle," he answered. Poor Simon had eaten enough hardtack, salt beef, and sauerkraut for a lifetime while he was a pirate. "Let's go outside. You know how you like the fresh sea air."

In fact, Pudge did like it, and was not seriously opposed to bad weather, as he had seen his share of it. He shrugged and let Simon help him into his invalid chair. In the closets, Simon found each of them a hooded oilcloth slicker to wear against the rain. The other sailors laughed and called them loony for putting out to sea in a storm, but Simon ignored them and wheeled the old man outside. The sky was a cold, dark gray, the color of crucible steel.

The empty boardwalk unspooled like a ribbon that lay between the shore and road. The sea's low roar and the occasional gull cry were the only sounds, at first. As they rounded a curve that took them out of sight of the HAM, a luxurious clarence carriage pulled by two fine gray horses came clattering down the road. As it neared them, it slowed.

"Hey-ah, hey-oh!" Old Timothy called from the driver's seat.

"Ahoy, did you say? Ahoy! Pirates! Scurvy knaves!" Pudge shouted, and clambered out of his chair. "Out of my way, Simon! This time I won't let those ruffians take you without a fight!"

Simon held back the old man without difficulty. "Easy, Uncle. I don't think these are pirates. For one thing, pirates don't travel by horse and carriage."

"Yes, you're right about that," the old sailor conceded.

The carriage stopped. Old Timothy jumped to the ground and opened the door. Inside sat a tall, lanky seaman, dressed in an admiral's uniform that smelled faintly of mothballs. A bicorne hat straddled his head, only partially concealing his gently but unmistakably pointed ears.

The uniform, the ears, the long, sloped, typically Ashton nose—even a person with superb eyesight might easily have mistaken him for Admiral Percival Racine Ashton. Or (to be precise) a somewhat younger version of the same long-dead admiral who gazed coldly from the ancestral portrait that hung in his great-grandson's study, unblinking among the taxidermy.

"Get in, Pudge!" cried Lord Fredrick, patting the seat. "It's been a long time, what?"

Pudge's eyes grew wide. "Admiral?" he cried. "Bless my barnacles, Admiral! It's you!"

SIMON HELPED PUDGE INTO THE seat next to Lord Fredrick and sat across from them. But these three men were not the only passengers of this carriage. Hidden in the luggage compartment were Penelope and the Incorrigible children. To learn the exact wording of the curse was their goal, which meant that Penelope had to be within earshot to take notes with her pencil and pad. But with Edward Ashton lurking around Brighton for nefarious reasons yet unknown, she dare not leave the Incorrigibles behind.

The children did not mind the close quarters, especially when Penelope suggested they pretend to be hermit crabs trapped in a shell that had grown too tight. Crammed into their hiding spot beneath the seat, they could hear every word spoken between Lord Fredrick and Pudge. Such shameless eavesdropping would previously have posed an ethical dilemma for Miss Penelope Lumley, who, as a schoolgirl, had once stitched *A Swanburne Girl Minds Her Business* onto a pillow, but no more. The stakes were too high.

Old Timothy moved the horses along at a lazy walk. "I'd nearly despaired of seeing you ever again, Admiral," said Pudge, wiping a tear from one crinkled eye.

"Well, it's good to see you, too, Mr. Pudge!" There had been no time for even a brief acting lesson with Simon, but Lord Fredrick was clearly doing his best. He spoke in a bold, deep voice and slapped Pudge on the knee in a friendly fashion. "I was hoping we might reminisce, what? About a particular voyage. Our final voyage, in fact! You know the one."

Pudge nodded. "Indeed I do, Admiral. I've waited a long time to be able to relive this tale with you, sir! I'll never forget it. There we were, in the easternmost part of the westernmost Indies, when came that terrible storm that smashed our boat to splinters on the shore of an island that was nowhere shown on any of our maps. It was a pretty place, and a peaceful one—or so we thought. The inhabitants called it Ahwoo-Ahwoo."

"Ahwoo, ahwoo!" The Incorrigibles softly howled in echo from their hiding spot. Penelope shushed them at once and hoped that Pudge had not heard.

"Yes, Ahwoo-Ahwoo! The sound of it tolls like a church bell in my ear, to this very day," Pudge went on. "The natives were kind to us at first, we strange fair-haired men who came from the sea. They shared their papaya fruits freely, and taught us the lilting songs of their tribe. I think I remember a bit of one. Raise your voice with me, sir!" He threw back his head and sang: "Ahwoo, ahwoo-ah! Ahwoo, ahwoo-ah!"

Penelope clapped her hands over the boys' mouths and shot a warning glance at their sister. Cassiopeia managed only a tiny squeak before covering her own mouth.

"You're in fine voice as ever, Pudge," Lord Fredrick

said. "But I'm not much for singing these days. Let's stick to the tale."

"As you wish, Admiral! The weeks passed sweetly on Ahwoo-Ahwoo. It was a peaceful, tuneful, papaya-ful time. Until that dreadful day." Pudge's face grew dark. "The day when you—well, you know what you did, sir."

"Haven't a clue! My memory's not what it was, I'm afraid. Do go on, Pudge, my old friend!" Lord Fredrick slapped the old sailor's knee once more.

"You went hunting, Admiral."

In the dark of the luggage compartment, the children yelped, and their eyes grew round as six full moons. Penelope had the sinking feeling that it may have been a mistake to bring them after all, but now it was too late.

Even Lord Fredrick seemed taken by surprise. "Did I? Blast!"

"Sure you did, Admiral! You arranged a hunting expedition for the whole crew. You thought it would cheer them up." Pudge shook his head. "Those poor cubs."

"Cubs?" Lord Fredrick exclaimed. "Surely he—I mean, I—didn't go around shooting cubs? That's not very sporting, what?"

"Five little wolf cubs, cute as can be. As I recall, you thought their pelts would make a nice soft lining for a new buckle-back vest you had in mind. Oh, if only you'd known!"

Lord Fredrick glanced at Simon. "Known, yes—known what?"

"That the wolf was the sacred animal of Ahwoo-Ahwoo! These were highly unusual wolves, Admiral. I mean, how many tropical islands have wolves on 'em to begin with, am I right?"

"Good point, Uncle," Simon interjected, to give Lord Fredrick a moment to compose himself. "This story is giving me goose bumps!"

"It's no story, lad. It's what happened." Old and frail as he was, Pudge seemed to gain energy in the telling. "The mother wolf came roaring down from the hills like a flood. She chased the admiral back to the village and howled a fearful curse upon his head! We couldn't understand it, of course, as we didn't speak her sacred wolf tongue, but the leader of the tribe was more than happy to translate." Pudge paused. "What a dreadful, horrible curse it was. Oh, she was mad, that wolf!"

"Quite understandable." Lord Fredrick scratched at his head; it seemed his bicorne hat was beginning to itch. "Remind me, old friend. What did she say?"

Pudge nodded. "First, I'd like to recite a poem."

Simon interrupted. "I thought you said the curse was not in the poem, Uncle."

"It builds up to it! Just listen." Pudge closed his eyes and recited.

"The wolf threw back its head, and howled!
And then the monster said,
'I lay this curse that I will curse
Upon the admiral's head.'

The wolf pronounced the curse, and lo!
The clouds ran o'er the moon.
Then darkness fell, too thick and deep
To cut it with a spoon."

Pudge paused. "I never liked that bit, 'cut it with a spoon.' Should be knife. No one cuts with a spoon. But I couldn't think of another rhyme for moon."

From the luggage compartment came suggestions: "June, spoon, macaroon . . ."

"Hey!" Pudge knocked hard on the compartment. "Who's hiding in there? Come above deck, knaves!"

Guiltily, Penelope and the three children climbed out.

Pudge peered at Penelope. "Why, it's Pete the cabin boy, freshly shaved and dressed in a skirt. You aren't trying to get in a lifeboat by posing as a girl, are you? Men have been hanged for less." He turned to the children. "And what do you three stowaways have to say for yourselves?"

"Loon, pontoon, gold doubloon," they helpfully offered.

"Blast, that's enough poetry for one day." Lord Fredrick scratched furiously at his ears. "Never mind the stowaways, I'll deal with them later."

"Will we have to walk the plank?" Beowulf yelped in fear.

"Maybe!" Lord Fredrick bellowed. He was very much in character now, or perhaps the itching was making him cross. "Now finish telling us what happened, old man. Just the highlights, please."

"Aye aye, Admiral! Well, the wolf had barely done cursing her curse when our former friends from Ahwoo-Ahwoo revealed themselves to be cannibals! They'd been fattening us up with those papaya fruits the whole blessed time! Our crew raced back to the ship, but it was naught but a splintered wreck. The cannibals arrived, laughing and rubbing their bellies! Some of the crew got caught, more's the pity. The rest jumped into the ocean and swam; they decided they'd rather drown than be eaten."

"At least they didn't throw the bride to the cannibals," Alexander observed, and his siblings nodded.

"Let me finish, if you don't mind, lad! I'm just at the best part." Pudge paused, clearly relishing the tale. "But all along, brave young Pudge, the cabin boy—the hero of our story, you might say!—had been secretly building a raft out of the ship's wreckage. A beauty it was, too. Some planks of wood, a coat of tar, a sack of fresh papayas to prevent scurvy . . ." He closed his eyes, lost in the memory. "This way, Admiral!" he cried, in a boy's soprano voice. "It's our only chance!"

Simon nudged Lord Fredrick with his foot. "Ahem! I'm on my way, Pudge!" Lord Fredrick cried, playing along. Pudge smiled his tortoiselike smile, which spread from his right ear all the way to his left, and opened his eyes once more.

"So me and the admiral made our escape, on the raft I built myself. The full moon lit our way, but oh, what a moon it was! Twice the size of the fullest full moon you ever saw, and bloodred, and instead of the man in the moon, it had the face of a wolf on it, too, like this: *Ahwoo! Ahwoo!*" He howled to demonstrate.

"I'll never forget that wolf moon, no sirree!"

Simon could take it no more. "Blast, Uncle! What about the curse?"

"Didn't I say it already?"

"No!" they all yelled together.

Pudge laughed. "Ah! Well, I'll never forget that, either. The strangest night of my life, that was!"

Penelope readied her pencil as Pudge leaned forward and swept his gaze around, lingering on each one of them in turn. She could have sworn his eyes glinted yellow in the dark interior of the carriage. "Listen, now! For here's what the wolf mother said.

" *'You killed my cubs with no more compassion than a hungry wolf shows for its prey. And so I place a wolf's curse upon you:*

As the wolf has two eyes and two ears, so shall your family be split in two. One side will do evil in the world. One side will do good.

The evil ones will outwardly prosper, but the full moon reveals their true nature—violent, selfish, and cruel. They will die unusual, gruesome deaths.

The good ones will suffer misfortunes, but their nature is plain for all to see—generous, compassionate, and kind. They will live long and die in peace.

As my five cubs were cruelly hunted, so shall it be for you. The hunter must vanquish his prey, or the prey must vanquish the hunter.

As the wolf has four paws, four generations must pass under this curse. In the fourth generation, the hunt begins—and ends.

As the wolf has one tail, only one line of your descendants can remain.

When that comes to pass, the curse is finished. Otherwise, the house of Ashton, all it has been and all it might ever be, shall be destroyed, forever.'"

"That's nonsense," Lord Fredrick cried. "Poppycock!"

Pudge gave him a curious look. "Funny, Admiral, that's just what you said at the time. The mother wolf didn't like it, either. The mad beast snarled a bloodcurdling snarl, and her eyes gleamed yellow as paraffin lamps. These were the last words she spoke:

"'Wait till the full moon comes, sailor. Then we'll see what's poppycock. Ahwooooo!'"

IN THE WAKE OF THIS terrible tale, the passengers of the carriage fell silent. Only the *clip-clop, clip-clop* of hooves kept time, slow and uneven, like a dying heart. Soon Pudge asked the admiral to join him in singing their favorite sea chanteys from the old days. Lord Fredrick cleared his throat and bum-bum-bummed along, for he did not know the tunes, but Simon pitched in to cover.

"What can you do with a curséd Ashton,
What can you do with a curséd Ashton,
What can you do with a curséd Ashton
When the moon is full, oh!"

That is how Penelope heard it, anyway. And cursed by a wolf, no less! She had taken notes during Pudge's story, but there was no need to look at them; every word was stamped in her memory. "'The hunter must vanquish his prey; or the prey must vanquish the hunter,'" she thought. "Edward Ashton fancies himself the hunter, and I fear he has made us his prey. But what is meant by the family split in two?"

She thought of the ancestral portraits in Lord Fredrick's study at Ashton Place. Father and son, father and son. It was a strange and unlovable lineage, perhaps, but as far as Penelope could see, the Ashtons descended in a straight, unbroken line.

The mournful singing and the slow rocking movement of the carriage soon lulled the children to sleep.

Lord Fredrick was sweating now, and scratched his arms and legs. "This antique uniform must have fleas in it," he muttered. He looked so uncomfortable that Penelope instructed Old Timothy to return to the Right Foot Inn at once. The old coachman had not spoken a word during the long and eventful ride, but never had there been a more enigmatic look on his face than there was now, as he held open the carriage door for his twitching, unhappy master.

"So long then, Pudge!" said Lord Fredrick, climbing out. "Lovely to catch up. Don't know when we'll meet again. All the best, fair winds to you, and so on."

Pudge, too, had dozed off. Simon gave him a poke. "Say good-bye to the admiral, Uncle."

The old man roused and clutched at his heart. "Ah, my admiral! Why must you go so soon?"

Lord Fredrick tipped his head to the side and scratched behind his neck. "Ah, Pudge! I've got a ship to catch. Such is a sailor's life; you know how it is. I'd best be off—wait, what's this?"

Penelope had quickly written and passed a note to Simon, who now handed it to Lord Fredrick. She had written it in large letters, so Lord Fredrick could read it. He looked it over and stuck his head back in the carriage.

"One more thing, Pudge! About that curse. Were

those the *exact* words of it?"

Pudge gave a sly look. "Why does it matter?"

Lord Fredrick turned to Penelope, who mimed signing something. "Ah, yes!" he said. "Well, a curse is like a contract. It's all in the wording, so I'm told."

Pudge leaned back and crossed his arms. "Those were the exact words spoken to the admiral, never you fear. You look just like him, too."

"Like who?" Lord Fredrick batted behind his ear with a cupped hand, like a dog after a flea.

"The admiral! He came to see me last night, at the HAM. It was just past my bedtime. At first I was sure I was dreaming."

"But I thought *I* was the admiral?" Lord Fredrick looked at Penelope and Simon in confusion.

"No, lad! You're Fredrick, his great-grandson. You're a good boy, from what he told me last night. Not the most watertight ship in the fleet, mind you, but a decent lad. He wanted me to talk about the curse, too. Isn't that peculiar?" Pudge smiled his wide tortoise smile. "Everybody wants to talk about the curse. . . ."

"Edward Ashton!" Penelope said under her breath, to Simon. "Blast! He *did* beat us to the Pudge!"

Pudge leaned back in his seat. "Here's a funny thing, too: Last night after we talked, the admiral

298

released me from my oath! He said I'd done a fine job keeping my promise all these years, and now it wasn't a secret anymore. Lucky, eh? Just in time to have a bit of fun with you, Freddy!" The old sailor laughed. "And you, too, nephew! Fooled you again, didn't I, Simon? A knack for the theatrical runs in the blood of us Harley-Dickinsons, sure as the compass points north!"

IT HAD BEEN A LONG, effortful morning for Pudge, and he was ready for a nap. Young Jasper was summoned to escort him to a room at the Right Foot Inn. Along with the room key, Simon delivered stern instructions to put the old fellow to bed and stand guard by the door. "Let no one in, and don't let Pudge get out, either," he said. "He's old but full of mischief." Once they had gone, Simon kicked the side of a carriage wheel in fury. "Ouch!" he yelped, rubbing his sore toes. "I'm in high dudgeon for sure! Edward Ashton slipped by me once already. I'll not risk him getting to my great-uncle again."

Meanwhile, Lord Fredrick frantically undid his costume. "There! Now this blasted itching will stop," he said, wriggling out of the brass-buttoned jacket. "That was quite a story the old sailor told. Poor little cubs! It's enough to make a man lose his taste for hunting."

He turned to Penelope. "Now that we've heard the exact words of the curse, I must say, I don't understand them one bit. Family tree split down the middle? What does it mean? And that bit about 'fourth generation'—that's me, I suppose? And who was this other admiral the old man spoke of? The whole thing is—*woof!*—peculiar, if you ask me." He scratched behind his neck and glanced up at the inscrutable sky. "That's odd. I'm starting to feel a bit—*bark!*—barky. But no worries. Tuesday's not until—*yap!*—tomorrow. And we've got a trip to Italy to get through yet, what? It's going to mean the world to Constance. Don't want anything to go wrong. Not tonight. *Woof!*" Gnawing on the edge of his hat, he loped inside the hotel.

Old Timothy chuckled from the driver's seat.

"Say, Timmy, what's so funny?" Simon called to him.

"The full moon's tomorrow, he says. Oh, that's rich!"

Penelope had come to trust the old coachman somewhat more than she used to, but his enigmatic behavior still rankled her; why was it so difficult to speak plainly about things, and leave out all the mysteriousness? "Lord Fredrick checked his almanac," she said. "Double- and triple-checked."

The coachman turned to her with a smirk. "And which do you believe? An almanac that won't stay put,

300

or the proof of your own two eyes?" He looked up at the sky. The cool blue glow of a hundred full moons could not cut through that impenetrable gloom.

Penelope looked up, too. "Do you mean to say . . . ?"

"Unlike most people, I *mean* to say nothing. I say, or I don't say. If you want answers, governess, look at the sky! Look at what's above you, behind you, and ahead of you. It's all as plain as the nose on your face . . . or the hair beneath your hat . . ."

Without thinking, Penelope raised a hand to smooth her hair. Answers were precisely what she wanted, and she, too, was puzzled by the curse. What *was* the split in the Ashton family tree? Who was on one side, and who was on the other, and what did she and the children have to do with it all? The only explanation she could come up with seemed so wildly implausible, so utterly improbable, so completely lacking in verisimilitude—it could not possibly be true, could it?

"Yet there are important distinctions to be made between the unlikely and the impossible," she thought, and inhaled sharply, as if the cold salt air itself was eager to rush in and remove the last tendrils of mist from her mind. *Could* the Incorrigible children occupy some distant twig on the Ashton family tree? And could Miss Penelope Lumley, she of the long-lost parents, with not one scrap of family left in all the wide and lonely world, somehow be related to the three people she loved best?

Honestly, what were the odds?

The horses were restless, stamping and snorting. Old Timothy hopped down from his seat and scurried to their heads, to speak to them quietly in whatever language man and beast shared.

Simon shook his head. Under his breath he said, "Enigmatic chap, that Tim! We'd best start loading the carriage; there's a heap of decorating to do at the other hotel, and the clock is ticking."

But Penelope kept looking at the sky.

SIMON WAS QUITE RIGHT: THERE was no time to waste.

Old Timothy waited outside while Simon and the children took a luggage cart to gather all the decorations. Meanwhile, Penelope went to see Mrs. Clarke. "Here are the invitations for tonight. Make sure they are delivered promptly, and that my instructions are followed to the letter," she cautioned, giving the housekeeper the handwritten envelopes she and the children had earlier sealed with wax.

Mrs. Clarke opened hers at once and peered at it through a pair of reading glasses that hung on a length of ribbon around her neck. "My, my! What an imagination you have, Miss Lumley!" she said in wonder. "Never you fear. I'll have everyone shipshape for tonight."

By the time Penelope returned to the carriage, Simon and the children had finished loading it with the decorations. Some were quite large, leaving no room for passengers. It was decided that Simon would travel with Old Timothy, riding next to him in the driver's seat, and Penelope and the children would proceed to the Left Foot Inn on whatever foot they pleased.

The Incorrigible children were strangely quiet as they walked. They said nothing to their governess, but every now and then they put their heads together to exchange a few words in private. Penelope feared that Pudge's gruesome tale had upset them, especially the part about those poor wolf cubs. After a while she asked what was on their minds.

"Time," Alexander said simply. "We want to understand how it works."

"We know there are three kinds," said Beowulf. "What was, what is, and what is yet to come."

Cassiopeia hopped idly from foot to foot. "But in Great-Uncle Pudge's story, they are all mixed up. How can cursing people who are not yet born fix what happened in the past?"

Beowulf drew in the air with his hands as he walked. "Unless time is shaped like a circle?"

"Or maybe a curse is like a time machine?" his sister suggested.

Now Penelope understood. "I cannot tell you more about time than you already know," she said. "But the admiral is long dead, my dear children. So are the wolf cubs, I am sorry to say, and no doubt their mama wolf is, too. If only their troubles had died with them! But terrible deeds and terrible hurts often outlive their original owners, as any number of tragic plays will tell you."

"Shakespeare," said Alexander knowingly, and all three children nodded in sad understanding.

"Now let us turn our minds to happier things. We have a highly unusual dinner party to organize, and your marvelous decorations are the key to the success of the whole affair. Look, there is the Left Foot Inn, just ahead." At the sight of the inn, the children began to hop, happy once more.

Penelope wished she could feel so light of spirit, but now the words of the curse weighed fresh upon her heart. To think that a family could be asked to sacrifice some of its own members in order to survive! "It is like Princess Popkinova's tale about throwing the bride to the wolves," she thought. "A tale that does not end well for anyone in it. Except the wolves, of course. They were rather well fed by the end!"

THE FRONT DESK CLERK AT the Left Foot Inn was already in a dreadful state of anxiety. He soon excused himself to lie down, complaining of a vicious headache brought on by "the presence of guests," as he explained.

Penelope was sorry for his headache but deeply relieved that he would not be on hand to greet the Babushkinovs. "As Agatha Swanburne once said, 'When an unstoppable force meets an immovable post, it is bound to create quite a ruckus,'" she remarked to Simon. (As the philosophers among you know, a collision between an unstoppable force and an immovable post is an example of a "paradox," which simply means an idea that contradicts itself: a hotel clerk who cannot abide guests, for example, or a doctor who cares nothing for the sick. Paradoxes are great fun to ponder and even more fun to invent: What if a shoelace that could never be untied met up with a scissor that could cut any shoelace? What if a dessert so delicious it could never be eaten met up with a hungry Incorrigible? And so on.)

Happily, the Left Foot Inn had been made ready

exactly as Penelope had requested, with plenty of extra staff hired for the day. The tallest of these were assigned to help the Incorrigibles with the decorations, while Penelope checked the dinner menu. It was a good thing she did, for they had planned to serve Napoleon pastries for dessert. Penelope liked Napoleons very much (as any sensible person would, for they are delicious), but given Captain Babushkinov's strong feelings about the name, she thought it best to have the kitchen prepare a tasty tiramisu instead.

By half past four, the preparations were complete. There was even time for a relaxing cup of tea before dinner, as well as a few biscuits for the hardworking children. Penelope regretted not having a dress more appropriate for the evening's event, but alas, she had not packed any sunbonnets or summer gowns suitable for the Italian Riviera. "Ah, well," she thought as she took a soothing sip of her tea. "It is Lady Constance who must be convinced, and she is unlikely to notice what anyone is wearing other than herself. I do hope Lord Fredrick holds up for the evening! *Can* he have misread his almanac, I wonder?"

At five o'clock, the guests began to arrive. When they had all gathered beneath the sign of the foot, Penelope gave a brief welcoming speech reminding them of the rules for the evening. "In order for our masquerade to succeed, from this moment on, you must not think it is a masquerade at all, but entirely real. Let your imaginations leap! It ought not to be difficult, for I think you will find the 'vessel' you are about to board quite convincing. One last point: No party is complete without a dance. Tonight we shall be doing the Sea Sway. It is a simple step, which I shall now demonstrate." She did so. "Now, your turn."

On her signal, all the guests swayed to the left.

"Well done. Now, one to the right!"

They obeyed. Truly, when everyone swayed at the same time it was hard not to believe that the ground itself was a ship's deck, rolling from side to side with the waves.

"Superb. Are there any questions?"

"Are there lifeboats aboard?" Jasper joked.

Penelope lifted an eyebrow. "We expect fair winds tonight, and following seas. However, in the event of a shipwreck, women and children first. Now, smooth sailing to you all, and welcome aboard the good ship *Riviera!*" she concluded, and stepped aside to let them proceed into the hotel.

What they saw was a tribute to the power of the imagination, for through the skillful application of

"No party is complete without a dance. Tonight we shall be doing the Sea Sway."

stagecraft, the Left Foot Inn had been transformed. Rope ladders and complicated rigging was strung here and there. A tall mainsail hung from the ceiling, and the farthest walls of the lobby had been covered with panoramic paintings of the sea.

"Why, I could swear I hear the crash of the waves!" Mrs. Clarke exclaimed. This was thanks to the use of what Simon called an ocean drum, which was simply a large quantity of dried beans swirled rhythmically inside a box. The Incorrigibles had made one according to Simon's specifications and hidden themselves behind the rigging to contribute this sound effect as the guests arrived. This, too, was Simon's suggestion. "If you hook the audience right away with something that has a bit of truth in it, their imaginations will do the rest," he had explained. "They'll follow you anywhere!" (Interestingly, the idea that the imagination of the audience can be relied upon to accept even highly unlikely plots was invented by the same Mr. Coleridge who wrote "The Rime of the Ancient Mariner." He called it "the willing suspension of disbelief." To this very day, most of us are more than willing to suspend our disbelief if it means we can enjoy a rollicking tale about gloomy supernatural birds, angry wolves that spew curses, seashells with romantic insight, or other, well . . . *unusual* topics.)

"Naturally, you can hear the sea. After all, we are aboard ship," Penelope said with conviction.

"Whoops! Of course, Miss Lumley, you are quite right," Mrs. Clarke said quickly, and that was the one and only time any of the guests slipped up that evening.

With the stage set, so to speak, it was time to bring in Lady Constance. At Penelope's nod, Jasper went out to the carriage to signal to Lord Fredrick. Moments later, the lady was brought in. She wore a blindfold and was led by her husband. He was still twitching and scratching, but not so severely that he could not play his part.

"Forgive all the cloak-and-dagger, my dear," he said, patting her arm. "But I know how you love a good surprise. Watch your step, now, we're about to come on board—"

Obediently Lady Constance raised her feet extra high as she walked, like a pony trained to prance. "Did you say 'on board'? And is that the roar of the ocean I hear? Why, Fredrick, aren't you clever! I *do* love a surprise, and I assure you I have absolutely no idea what you have planned!"

"That's a relief! It's not easy keeping a secret in a busy household, believe me. You can take off your blindfold now," said Lord Fredrick, with a nod to Penelope.

As the blindfold fell, Penelope signaled a Double Sea Sway: first to the right, and then to the left. The ocean drum played its low roar. For someone as passionately inclined to suspend her disbelief as Lady Constance, the illusion of being at sea was already complete.

"Welcome to the good ship *Riviera*, my dear," Lord Fredrick said, tugging at one ear. "Tonight we sail for Italy."

"Italy!" Lady Constance brought both hands to her heart, and her mouth fell open in a wide O of surprise. Truly, it was a performance worthy of the West End. "Italy! Why, Fredrick, I am shocked! Shocked as a person could be!"

"Thought you'd like it, what?" Lord Fredrick rocked on his heels and grinned. Like nearly everyone else in the room, he knew her surprise was an act, yet there he stood, blushing with delight.

Lady Constance slipped her arm through his and broke into a radiant smile. *"Bella Italia,* here we come! And to think, all this time I have been *utterly* convinced that we were staying in Brighton!"

THE TWELFTH CHAPTER

The full you-know-what
makes itself known.

PENELOPE LINGERED NEAR THE DOOR and marveled at how well her scheme had worked. "It seems that a knack for suspending one's disbelief may be the true key to happiness in this world," she thought. "To judge from the example of Lady Constance, it is not what happens, but what we believe to be happening that governs our mood. A topic that surely deserves further study—but not now."

She turned to Simon, who was dressed in a snappy first mate's uniform that suited him distractingly well. With effort, she kept her thoughts on the task at hand.

"Dinner will be served in a quarter of an hour. Is the captain ready?"

"He's all dressed and raring to go," he answered, tugging his cap to a jaunty angle. "But I hope he sticks to the script! Speaking of captains, where do you suppose the Babushkinovs are? They're likely to miss the boat."

She frowned, for her instructions had specifically said to be punctual. Once the imaginary ship had left the imaginary dock, latecomers would not be easy to explain. "If they arrive during dinner, I suppose we can say they sailed to sea on a different ship, and came over in rowboats to join us for dessert. . . ."

"Or to borrow some rope," Simon suggested. "You can never have too much rope on a ship."

Luckily, the Babushkinovs arrived moments later, just as Simon took the brass bell from the front desk and began to ring it.

Clang clang! Clang clang! "All ashore that's going ashore!" he shouted, which meant the ship was about to sail. Madame Babushkinov dropped her fur cloak into the waiting arms of a footman and tossed her head like an impatient horse. "The customs of the English are so strange. Imagine, making such a performance out of dinner!"

"All customs are strange. Every dinner is a

performance," the princess Popkinova said darkly. She was being wheeled by Master Gogolev. He was all in black except for a scarlet cravat tied loosely around his neck, but his hair was as wild and wind tossed as ever.

"Indeed, Princess. 'All the world's a stage,'" he said.

"'And all the men and women merely players.' Shakespeare!" finished Alexander with a bow. The Incorrigibles had run to greet their friends the moment they smelled the captain's bearskin cape. Alexander took Veronika by the fingertips and led her daintily inside. Tonight she wore a dress of ocean-blue silk, with a diamond brooch in the shape of a whale pinned to the collar of her matching coat.

"Shakespeare! Did you hear that, Ivan Victorovich?" Madame said confidentially to her husband, in Russian. "And the way that strange English boy bowed to our Nikki! How well mannered and well educated these Incorrigible children are. I am bursting with our news; I can hardly stand the wait!"

The captain put a finger to her lips. "Not yet, my love. We shall tell her tomorrow morning, as we planned. No need to spoil the party! Ah. Ha. Hah!"

PENELOPE INSTRUCTED THE INCORRIGIBLES TO quickly teach the Sea Sway to the Babushkinovs, who had missed the earlier demonstration. As first mate of the good ship *Riviera*, Simon then gave a brief safety talk about how to use the lifeboats if needed. This made Margaret squeak with fear, until Jasper whispered to her. Her face went blank; then she giggled, stopped herself, and abruptly looked far more frightened than before, but in a fake and overwrought way, like a bad actor in a play.

At last the guests were ushered to the dining room. Here the windows offered a different view than the ones on "deck." Miraculously, it appeared that the ship had already sailed far out to sea, and there was water, water, everywhere. If one looked carefully, faint out-lines of mermaids could be seen in the waves, and a smiling walrus with whiskers that perfectly resembled those of Captain Babushkinov did the backstroke over a distant swell.

Everyone *ooh*ed and *aah*ed over the absurdly swift rate of travel, and Penelope threw in a few Sea Sways for verisimilitude. "That was a powerful big wave that just hit the ship, my, my!" Mrs. Clarke exclaimed each time they leaned to the side. Mar-garet used these episodes as an excuse to hang on to Jasper's arm, which seemed to please them both. By now it seemed as if even the guests half believed that they were, in fact, at sea.

The Ashtons' table included Dr. Martell, Captain Babushkinov and his wife, and the princess Popkinova. Two chairs remained empty. "Those must be for the captain and first mate," Lady Constance said gaily to Madame Babushkinov. "Then we shall have two captains at the table. I hope it does not spark a mutiny! Look, here he comes."

Madame Babushkinov turned to look, as did everyone else within earshot. The old fellow wore a crisp white uniform with a broad scarlet border around the collar and cuffs, and rows of shiny gold buttons down the front. He leaned on Simon's arm as they walked, but there was still plenty of swagger in his rolling sailor's gait.

"Good evening, honored guests!" Simon announced. "Allow me to present the captain of the good ship *Riviera*—"

"*Capitano* Giuseppe Pomodoro!" Pudge interrupted. He waved and blew kisses to all the guests, and bowed to each of his tablemates in turn. Finally, he sat down, and Simon took the chair beside his.

Penelope and the children were at the next table. The Incorrigibles recognized "Capitano" Pudge right away, but happily suspended their disbelief.

Penelope had to hold back a smile. Clearly the old sailor's knack for things theatrical had prompted him to embellish his role, but as long as he did nothing to spoil the evening's illusion, she saw no harm in him enjoying himself. "It is the captain's dinner, after all," she thought.

And what a dinner it was! There was antipasto, which simply means the food that comes before the pasta. Then the pasta course was brought out, followed by a main course of meat and fish dishes. The guests ate and drank and laughed and enjoyed themselves thoroughly, especially the staff from Ashton Place, for it was a rare treat for them to have an excellent meal that they did not have to prepare and serve and clean up after themselves.

The waiters made heroic efforts to speak in Italian, as they had been told to do. In practice this meant a lot of nodding and saying *"Bellissima!"* and *"Magnifico!"* and making enthusiastic gestures with their hands. Their pronunciation was poor and the accents were dreadful. However, Lady Constance knew only a few words of Italian herself and had never heard the language spoken by a native, so it was all the same to her.

"Hold on, everyone!" Mrs. Clarke bellowed, clutching the table edge. Penelope had just signaled a Sea

Sway to keep the illusion going during the meal.

"Rough seas, *woof!*" Lord Fredrick remarked. His itching and barking seemed to be getting worse. During the main course of a tender osso buco, he gnawed helplessly on the bone of his veal shank.

"I have heard it said that impending fatherhood can make men as hungry as their expectant wives, but Fredrick, you are attacking your dinner like a hungry wolf!" Lady Constance observed.

"Sorry, my dear, *woof!* It's just all very—*woof!*—tasty," he mumbled as he continued to gnaw.

Dr. Martell put down his fork. "Are you feeling all right, Lord Ashton? It sounds like you've got a nasty whooping cough coming on, or something of that ilk."

"*Woof*ing cough? Nonsense. Just a bit of—*ahem! Ahwoo!*—phlegm." Lord Fredrick cleared his throat loudly, to demonstrate, and promptly picked up another bone to chew.

AFTER THE MAIN COURSE CAME a salad course, and then a fruit and cheese course. As the dishes were cleared, the headwaiter came by the Ashtons' table. "Sig-nora," he said, mistakenly pronouncing the G in "signora" so that it rhymed with "ignore-ah." *"Dolce? Dolce, si?"*

"Yes, bring on the *dolce*, please!" Lady Constance

turned to her husband. "That means cake, hoorah! It must be time for dessert." *Dolce* (cake) and *cioccolato* (chocolate) were two of the Italian words Lady Constance had managed to learn. The others included *spaghetti, Colosseo, regali* (which means "presents"), and, of course, *bambino.* She also recognized but could not yet pronounce the sentence *"Il vestito ti sta benissimo,"* which means "That dress fits you perfectly." She had thought it might come in useful while shopping.

The *dolce* was served, along with tiny cups of very strong Italian coffee. Pudge downed his in a single shot and babbled joyfully in vowel-heavy gibberish while waving his hands for emphasis.

"Such a lovely language," Lady Constance remarked to Madame Babushkinov. "I believe he is complaining about the high cost of cheese."

When Pudge stopped to catch his breath, Simon jumped to his feet and struck the brass bell to get everyone's attention. *Clang clang! Clang clang!* "First Mate Harley-Dickinson here, with an update as to our course and bearing. Thanks to some exceedingly fair winds, I am pleased to announce that we have already arrived at the port of—

"Rome?" Lady Constance cried in hope. Rome was hundreds of miles from the Italian Riviera and nearly fifty miles inland from the nearest port, but such minor details no longer mattered. "Port of Rome! Port of Rome!" the guests shouted merrily, and clinked their coffee cups in the air.

Simon shrugged. "I was going to say Genoa, but I stand corrected. The port of Rome it is. *Benvenuti,* everyone! Welcome to Italy!"

AND SO THE *SOSPENSIONE DELL' INCREDULITÀ* continued. That the good ship *Riviera* could set sail from England just before dinner and arrive in Italy by the time the *dolce* was cleared was impossible, navigationally speaking, but no one cared. The guests were well fed and enjoying themselves, and Lady Constance was over the moon with delight.

"I am utterly, totally, completely surprised! By everything!" No doubt she had convinced herself of that, too. "Fredrick, you are the best husband a woman could wish for! And this is the most wonderful night of our lives, so far, at least."

Lord Fredrick scratched behind his ears and beamed with pleasure. The mood of affection that swirled around these two was so genuine, and so unexpected, that many were deeply touched by it. Mrs. Clarke wiped away a tear, and Margaret and Jasper exchanged shy, tender smiles across the table. Veronika closed her eyes and clasped her hands to her heart, as if imagining the most romantic ballet ever devised, while Alexander gaped at her in ardent wonder. Poor Julia kept stealing looks at Captain Babushkinov as she wept quietly into her napkin, while Master Gogolev ran his hands through his hair, muttering, "Julia, Julia!" Then he gritted his teeth until the muscle in his jaw twitched.

Without meaning to, Penelope found herself glancing at Simon, only to catch him looking at her at the same time. Embarrassed, she tore her gaze away—that unruly hair! that gleam of genius! and, oh, that uniform!—and fixed it on her employers instead. No magical mollusk was needed to pry the truth from their hearts, for it was plain to see. Despite Lord Fredrick's uncontrollable woofing, and his wife's immeasurable foolishness, and the fact that everything around them was made of paint and papier-mâché, they looked, in a word, happy. Happy, and in love! This imaginary voyage had served its purpose so well that Penelope found herself wishing real, true contentment for this mooncrossed couple, and for the Barking Baby Ashton, too.

"But not at the expense of anyone else," she thought stubbornly. "I know what the curse said, but no one ought to be thrown to the wolves to assure the happiness of others. No true happiness can be purchased at such a terrible price."

"Bella Italia!" Pudge crowed. In the absence of rum, he had drunk several glasses of *vino* with dinner, and was ready to start singing. *"O sole mio!"* he bellowed, one hand upon his heart.

"Ahwoo, ahwoo!" Lord Fredrick howled in answer.

Lady Constance clapped her hands. "Fredrick, your Italian is much improved! 'Ahwoo-ahwoo.' Hmm! I know that word, let me think. Has it got something to do with olive oil?"

Penelope discreetly signaled a Double Sea Sway, to indicate the boat taking its berth at the port. In unquestioning imitation of the others, Lady Constance leaned first one way, then the other. "Hold on, everyone!" she sang out. "We have crossed a whole ocean, and I was not seasick once! I must be a natural-born sailor."

The party proceeded through a hallway that had been made to look like a gangplank connecting ship to shore. The painted ocean behind them gave way to vistas of the Italian countryside. Within these panoramas, the squirrels of Italy perched in the olive groves, squinting against the bright Mediterranean sun.

"How remarkable that it is still daylight," Lady Constance observed. "Why has the sun not set?"

Whoops! Penelope had not thought of this. Hours had passed since they set sail, time enough for a five-course meal and the *dolce*, and now it was after nine o'clock. Still the painted Mediterranean sun shone over the painted Italian hills, just as it had before.

"We are too far south," Alexander promptly explained, for he too realized their mistake. "At the South Pole, the sun does not set at all this time of year." Beowulf nodded forcefully, as if Italy being near the South Pole was a well-known fact of geography, and Cassiopeia gave Penelope a look that said, "Ought I quickly add some penguins to the panorama to make this tale more convincing?" But there was no need, for the good ship *Suspension of Disbelief* still had plenty of wind in its sails.

"Fredrick, did you hear that? He thinks the sun does not set at the South Pole in summer!" Lady Constance giggled and took her husband's arm. "What an absurd idea! I will not correct him, for he is only a child. We have had fair winds, as Capitano Pomodoro said, and have thus made very good time. That is the simplest explanation, and therefore it must be true." (Here Lady Constance unwittingly echoed the famous

323

William of Ockham, who lived in the fourteenth century and who died, alas, of the plague, but not before saying this: When there is more than one explanation at hand, the simplest one is best. His idea has come to be known as Occam's Razor, a sharp blade that shaves away the stubble of needless complexity. Also, note that Occam is the Latin spelling of Ockham. If you think that having two spellings for the same name is precisely the type of needless complexity that could do with a nice, close shave, congratulations; you have clearly understood the meaning of Occam's Razor.)

"Yes, fair winds, *woof!* Full speed ahead, *ahwoo!*" Lord Fredrick threw Penelope a desperate look. She had kept a close eye on him during dinner. With every passing hour, his condition had worsened; now he could hardly speak a sentence without barking. Quickly she found Dr. Martell and whispered a suggestion in his ear.

Before long, Dr. Martell offered to walk with Lady Ashton so that he might inquire privately as to her health. Soon they were deep in conversation. "I had the most awful experience with a doctor at home, at Ashton Place," the lady told him. "Such an unpleasant man. How I wish he could see me now, feeling so well and cheerful! A trip to the sea was all I needed, not a grumpy old doctor who smelled of stale bread pudding!"

Lord Fredrick hung back and panted as he leaned against the painted olive trees. "Look at her, smiling and laughing," he said as Penelope approached. "Happy as a lark, *bark!* It's going well. *Woof!* This pretending is hard work, though. Not sure how actors, *yap*! Manage it."

"Lord Ashton," she said quietly. "Regarding Tuesday, and the full you-know-what, I wonder if there may have been an unfortunate misunderstanding. . . ."

He wiped his brow with his pocket handkerchief, which was monogrammed with an ornate capital A. "I'm wondering, too, *yap!* I could have sworn the full you-know-what was tomorrow. But, *grr!* I think I may have—*woof!*—miscalculated." Desperately he patted his pockets. "Blasted almanac! It's gone again. *Ahwoo!* But now we're aboard this imaginary ship. I can't simply jump overboard and—*woof!*—disappear. What shall I do, *ahwoo*?"

Quickly and quietly, Penelope told him her idea. He nodded and made his way to where his wife stood with Dr. Martell. "I must leave you in the good doctor's care for a little while, Constance, *grr!*" He shoved his knuckles into his mouth to stop the growling.

"Why? Where are you going?" Lady Constance asked, with a twinge of her old nervousness.

"Another surprise, my dear. Another—*yap! Woof!*— surprise." Overcome, he dropped to all fours and loped out of the room.

THE INCORRIGIBLES HAD DONE A marvelous job transforming the lobby of the hotel into a ship's deck, and its dining room into an elegant restaurant at sea. But it was here, in their strange and fascinating portrayal of the Eternal City, as Rome has often been called, that their imaginations had truly taken flight. (To say Rome is eternal is hyperbole, of course, but as cities go, it has certainly been around a long time, far longer than most. Hence, the nickname.)

The panorama included several notable examples of ancient Roman architecture, including the Colosseum, the Pantheon (a superb example of Corinthian columns at work), and the spectacular Roman baths. They had no model to draw from, so for the Roman baths they had simply painted a collection of the sorts of bathtubs they were used to, rather than the large and magnificent bathhouse the ancient Romans built. However, the tubs were nicely drawn and had plenty of soap bubbles. One could easily imagine taking a relaxing hot soak at the end of a long day delivering orations in the senate.

Papier-mâché seashells were scattered along the banks of the River Tiber, ready to be collected. The terrifying volcano Mount Vesuvius belched smoke on the horizon. Careful observation revealed the tail of a megalosaurus peeking out between the columns of the Pantheon. Cassiopeia had insisted upon this detail, as she felt it lent an air of drama to the scene, and who could argue?

Alexander jumped to Lady Constance's side and pretended to snap open a parasol. "The sun in Italy is stronger than what you are accustomed to in England, my lady," he said gallantly.

"So it is." She ventured one pale hand outside the imagined shade and quickly snatched it back. "Yes, it is very strong!" Something on the ground caught her attention. "Look, Fredrick, a seashell! And there are more, over there. I will have to start a collection." Happy as the proverbial clam, she began to gather the papier-mâché shells.

Simon leaned over to Penelope. "This is a madcap situation, to be sure. If it were an operetta on the West End, we could call it *Ashtons on Holiday.*"

"Just wait; we are about to have the *tableaux vivants*," she said, amused in spite of herself. (*Tableaux vivants* are very brief plays in which the actors do not move or speak. In Miss Penelope Lumley's day, they were thought to be highly entertaining. As you see, progress does occasionally take a step in the right direction.)

"Our first *tableau* is called 'The Birth of the Hermit Crab,'" Beowulf announced. The tableau featured Veronika standing in a bathtub-sized seashell, with her hair hanging loose and wild. On one hand she wore a large papier-mâché claw.

"She is a hermit crab who has outgrown her shell," Cassiopeia explained. "The tableau is Italian because . . ." She paused, forgetting the reason. Beowulf whispered in her ear. "Because her name is Botticelli," she finished proudly.

This was not quite right, as Botticelli was the name of the Italian artist whose famous painting called *The Birth of Venus* had inspired the tableau. But Lady Constance had already moved on, after expressing regret that the seashell in which Veronika stood was too big to collect and take home to Ashton Place.

"Our next tableau: Romulus and Remus!" said Alexander. These were the twin brothers who were said to be the founders of Rome. They were portrayed by Boris and Constantin, both clad in Max's oversized diapers (according to legend, the brothers had been abandoned as infants). Their matching black eyes added a further touch of verisimilitude, for Romulus and Remus had fought bitterly over who got to be in charge. (If you have forgotten who won the fight, a clue can found within the name of the Eternal City itself.)

"After being left in a basket and set adrift on the Tiber, Romulus and Remus were rescued by a friendly wolf," said Alexander. By now the twins had become ace howlers, thanks to their friendship with the Incorrigibles. They threw back their heads and gave it their all.

"Ahwoo!"

"Ahwoo!"

From somewhere close by came a full-throated, manly howl, so convincing it might have been made by a real wolf.

"Ahwoooooooooo!"

Lady Constance pointed. "Look! That must be the wolf that raised them. I must say, he looks a great deal like my husband."

It was Lord Fredrick, of course. Following Penelope's instruction, he had found a fur cloak to use as a costume and hidden himself behind the tail of the megalosaurus. Now he stood beside the twins, howling with abandon and, it must be said, enjoyment.

"Ahwoooooooooo!"

"Ahwooooooooooo!"

His wife clapped her hands in delight. "Fredrick, I had no idea you possessed such talent! If you ever tire of being a wealthy lord, you could easily join an acting troupe, like Leed's Thespians on Demand—"

"That looks like my cape!" Captain Babushkinov said, with rising fury. "Who gave you that cape?"

Lord Fredrick blanched. "It was in the—*bark!*—closet, *woof!* The hotel clerk—*yap! Grr!* That is to say, the ship's mate—*ahwoo!*—said I could—*bark!*—borrow it."

"Napoleon! I knew it!" Captain Babushkinov roared, and snatched the cloak away from Lord Fredrick.

"Oh, dear!" Penelope said, to Simon. "If the clerk's name is Napoleon, no wonder the captain dislikes him so!"

The captain shook his fist. "Napoleon, Napoleon! This insult cannot go unanswered. I will challenge him to a duel! To the death!"

Everyone froze in alarm except Lady Constance, who had seashells pressed to both ears and missed the whole incident. In the silence, Great-Uncle Pudge began to cry. Great salty tears rolled down his cheeks, one after another, like waves lapping at the shore.

Simon put his arm around the old fellow. "Easy

there, *capitano*! There'll be no duels to the death on my watch, never you fear."

"What do I care about dueling? Let them have at each other, that's two less fools in the world." The teary old man pointed at the tableau. "It's the twins, lad! Those poor twins! Oh, those poor, poor children!"

Boris and Constantin hitched up their diapers and flexed their muscles in a display of good health. "We are not hurt, see? We were only pretending to be raised by wolves!"

"And we *were* raised by wolves, but it was not bad," Alexander said consolingly. "We liked it! Nice wolves! Do not cry, Capitano."

"Not you, you brainless barnacles," Pudge roared. "It's the admiral's children I weep for!"

Penelope frowned. "The admiral's children? You mean his son, Pax Ashton?"

"Pax was one of 'em, yes. But the admiral had *two* children. He spoke of them often during our days at sea. His pride and his joy, that's what he called them."

Dumbstruck, Penelope thought of the paintings in Lord Fredrick's study. Admiral Percival Racine Ashton, the Honorable Pax Ashton, Edward Ashton . . . where was this mysterious missing Ashton?

Simon must have had the same thought. "Uncle—I

mean, Capitano—are you saying that Pax Ashton had a brother?"

"I am not saying that, no." Pudge smiled through his tears, relishing the moment. "What I *am* saying is that Pax Ashton had a *sister*. They were twins, just like these two scalawags in the droopy diapers."

Embarrassed, Boris and Constantin blushed and ran to their father. This was fortunate, as it meant the captain had to put aside the idea of a duel and help the boys put their clothes back on.

"Those poor twins!" Pudge went on. "Oh, it's a tragic tale. That's what caused this salty flood upon my cheeks! These hot, unmanly tears!" He turned to Simon. "Salty flood, not bad, eh, Simon?"

"We'll discuss the use of metaphor later, Uncle! What about the twins?" Simon answered, and indeed, everyone wanted to hear the tale.

"Twins, aye!" the old man went on. "The best of friends, they were. Thick as thieves! Inseparable! But after the admiral and his wife were killed in that hunting accident, everything changed." He sniffed loudly and wiped his nose on his sleeve, despite the three clean pocket handkerchiefs that were promptly offered by the Incorrigibles. "Imagine surviving a shipwreck and cannibals and days spent floating on a raft at sea, only to meet a gruesome end on your own property, on the first full moon after being rescued and returned to dry land! It's a shame Pax's wife joined the hunting party that day, but after he'd been away so long, it's no wonder she wanted to keep him in sight. The coroner couldn't tell what kind of ravenous beast did them in. Something vicious, it was! After it was done feasting on the admiral and his wife, there was scarcely enough left to tell them apart."

Someone brought over a papier-mâché chunk of Corinthian column so that the old salt could sit down. Those who liked a gruesome tale—meaning, nearly everyone present—hung on Pudge's every word. Only Lady Constance remained indifferent to the tale, for she was too busy gathering seashells.

"But what happened to the admiral's children?" Penelope urged.

Pudge clutched his heart. "Pax had always been a sweet and tender boy. A sensitive lad, and talented, too. He liked to paint pictures; his father always said he'd grow up to be an artist, if he didn't watch out! But after his parents were killed, he turned mean as a rabid hyena. His sister was the prime target of his wrath. Before, they'd been the best of friends. Thick as thieves! Inseparable!"

"You said that already, Capitano," Beowulf help-fully remarked.

"But no more!" Pudge gave the boy a sharp look and went on. "Pax was the son and heir, which left him in charge. Soon enough, he cast his sister out. Trimmed her from the family tree, you might say. He ripped her portraits off the walls—portraits he'd painted himself! He went through the house, the library, the family papers, and burned all trace of her existence. None of the servants were allowed to speak of her, ever again."

Simon knew how to spin a yarn as well as any-one, but even he could no longer stand the suspense. "Don't beat around the bush, Uncle! What was the girl's name?"

Pudge closed his eyes, remembering. "Agatha!" he said. "That was her name. Agatha Ashton."

AT THIS MOMENT MISS PENELOPE Lumley had what is known as an epiphany, which is a way of saying that she understood something extremely complicated all at once, as if a puzzle with many pieces had suddenly flown into the air and assembled itself. The force of it hit her broadside, and she found herself leaning first port, then starboard, until she toppled into Simon's arms.

"Whoa, there!" He put her back on her feet. "That's quite a Sea Sway. Must be a storm brewing."

"The split in the Ashton family was between Pax Ashton and his twin sister, Agatha," she said in a rush. "And somehow, Agatha Ashton grew up to be Agatha Swanburne!"

Simon rubbed his chin. "So, on one side of the curse are Pax's descendants—first Edward, then Fredrick, and soon, the wee woofing baby of Ashton Place. But who are Agatha's descendants?"

"Miss Charlotte Mortimer is one. She told me so herself; Agatha Swanburne was her grandmother." Penelope felt suddenly groundless, as if she were falling headlong through the air, but at the same time it felt like flight, like joy. "I—I am not sure. I think there may be others. In fact . . . I think . . . that is to say, I have come to suspect—"

Dr. Martell sniffed. "Does anyone else smell smoke?"

Lady Constance sneezed. "*Ah-choo!* Fredrick dear, this is no time for a cigar. I fear you have set your pelt on fire."

But it was not the pelt. Now everyone began to sniff.

"Smoke? Yes!"

"I smell it, too!"

"It's smoke, but from where?"

"Lumawoo," Cassiopeia said, her voice trembling. "Something spooky. Look." She pointed at the madcap panorama of ancient Rome. There, in the shadows of Mount Vesuvius and the Colosseum, between the tail of a megalosaurus and the olive trees full of stylish Italian squirrels, stood a man in a toga, his back to them. In one hand he held a violin.

His body shook with laughter, until he threw back his head and howled with it. He raised the violin to his shoulder, and the bow to his violin, and then he began to play.

THE THIRTEENTH CHAPTER

*A Roman holiday goes up
in smoke.*

THE INCORRIGIBLES WERE AMAZED. HAD their panorama achieved such verisimilitude that one of its inhabitants had sprung to life, complete with the knowledge of how to play the fiddle? Yet none of them could remember drawing Emperor Nero, the famously tyrannical Roman emperor who was said to have set fire to the city and fiddled while it burned.

"That is no painted emperor, but I fear it may be Edward Ashton," Penelope said urgently to Simon.

Lord Fredrick overheard her, for his hearing grew

wolfishly keen during the full moon (alas, his vision remained blurry as ever). At the mention of his father's name, his ears twitched, for of course he believed the man to be dead. *"Woof!"* he exclaimed in disbelief. *"Yap! Ahwoo!"* By now, these were the only sounds he could utter. Whatever else he longed to say about his long-lost father miraculously turning up in Brighton during the off-season, wearing a toga and playing the violin, would have to wait until later.

Dr. Martell took Lady Constance firmly by the arm. "This fire is too realistic for my taste. I suggest we all leave, at once."

Penelope was of the same mind. As she had sometimes seen Mrs. Clarke do, she held her fingers to her lips and let out a long, piercing whistle, like a Bloomer steam engine pulling into the station. "Attention, please! It seems the tide has turned. To catch the current, we must sail at once. Back to the ship, if you please!"

Simon handed the brass bell to Alexander. "Second Mate Alexander, you and the Incorrigible crew must get everyone out, lickety-split. Can you do it?"

"Aye aye, sir!" Alexander ran around clanging the bell, and took the opportunity to give a pithy but informative lecture. "The Great Fire of Rome burned for six days and six nights!" *Clang!* "Emperor Nero was

338

rumored to have started the fire." *Clang!* "But that was only rumor, so until someone invents a time machine, we may never know what truly happened!" *Clang!* "Also, historically speaking, he would have been playing a lyre, not a fiddle, as the violin had not yet been invented." *Clang! Clang!* "To the ship! To the ship!"

Beowulf and Cassiopeia herded the guests like sheepdogs. The Babushkawoos were terrified and clung to their parents, coughing and complaining. Tendrils of smoke curled from beneath the backdrop. In the confusion, Emperor Nero slipped behind the painted hills and disappeared.

"Edward Ashton!" Penelope cried. "He must not get away."

"Right you are." Simon turned to Captain Babushkinov, who was still spoiling for a fight. "There's your Napoleon, sir! Come with me. That fire-setting scoundrel with the fiddle has a lot to answer for."

The captain stood red-faced, with clenched fists. "Napoleon! In the name of the Tsar and Mother Russia, I come for you!" he roared. The two men took off after the violinist.

THE HOTEL WAS NOT THE only thing that burned. Penelope's mind was ablaze with Pudge's revelation about

Agatha Ashton, and all that it suggested about the Ashton family tree, and perhaps, her own. . . . "But there is no time for that now," she thought, "for we must get Lady Constance off the premises before the illusion of *bella Italia* goes up in smoke, so to speak."

Luckily, Lady Constance was preoccupied with her seashell collection, which she insisted on carrying herself. She kept dropping the shells and then squealing with delight at the chance to gather them up again. Once back aboard ship—that is to say, in the lobby of the Left Foot Inn—Penelope quickly fashioned a blindfold of pocket handkerchiefs and offered it to Lady Constance, to wear during the voyage home.

Of course, the "voyage" would be nothing more than several circumnavigations of Brighton in the clarence carriage, with Jasper playing the ocean drum in the backseat and Old Timothy making the occasional screechy gull cry for verisimilitude—*caw, caw!*—but as long as Lady Constance saw none of it, all would be well, Penelope was certain.

"It will shield your eyes against the harsh lights of the aurora borealis," she explained as she secured the blindfold around the lady's face.

"The northern lights, at the South Pole? How unusual! Well, it is too bad that Italy caught fire so soon after we arrived," Lady Constance remarked as Jasper led her to the carriage. "But short holidays are best. Now I see that looking forward to a trip abroad is far more pleasant than the bother of actually taking one. Don't you agree, Fredrick? Fredrick?" She waved her arms until she located her husband, who trotted along beside her on all fours like a well-trained dog. "Silly Fredrick, get up! Your performance is over; there is no need to stay 'in character.'"

"Yap!" said Lord Fredrick. *"Woof!"* The cursèd heir to the cursèd Ashtons was in the grip of his full-moon madness, but for the first time in his life there was nowhere to hide. He jumped into the carriage after his wife and curled himself on the seat.

Lady Constance adjusted her blindfold and patted him on the head. "Very well, if you insist on acting like a precious pet poodle, I shall simply pretend that is what you are! Do you know, Fredrick, as a girl I always secretly wanted a pony, but I knew my brothers would torment it horribly the minute they saw I was fond of it. So I refused to get one. I told everyone ponies frightened me and made me sneeze! Isn't that funny?"

"All ashore that's going ashore. Hey, yah!" Old Timothy called to the horses, and the "ship" began to move. Idly Lady Constance scratched her husband behind his ears. Once he was over his surprise, Lord Fredrick panted with contentment.

ONCE BACK AT THE LEFT Foot Inn the seven children refused to be separated (actually it was the Babushka-woos who refused, as they were being rather dramatic about the fire; one would have thought they had barely escaped the eruption of Mount Vesuvius with their lives). They were all put to bed in room fourteen, under the supervision of Master Gogolev.

Everyone tried to convince the princess Popkinova that she, too, ought to retire for the evening, but the old woman swore she would not close her eyes until her son came back from his pursuit of the arsonist.

They waited together, in the lobby. Pudge fell asleep in an armchair next to a grandfather clock, and his snores kept time in a duet with the clockworks. Dr. Martell stayed with them also, "in case any medical attention is needed," he said to Penelope. "Your friend Simon seems like a level-headed fellow, but the captain has a temper, and a taste for dueling. Who was that strange Emperor Nero, I wonder? I know my oddities, and there was surely something odd about him. I wish we had seen his face."

"With any luck, we soon shall," Penelope said. She

was glad the doctor was there, for she felt ill at ease with the others. Madame Babushkinov paced the lobby like a tigress and would not look at her, not even when Penelope offered her a cup of the tea she had ordered, in the hopes that it might settle everyone's nerves.

"And you, Princess? Would you like some tea?" Penelope ventured.

"*Nyet!*" Princess Popkinova waggled a bony finger in the air. "First, ice. Then, fire. Someone is trying to kill us! We must go home, to Plinkst. Now!"

Madame Babushkinov stopped and turned. "For once we are in agreement. It is time to go home." She glanced at Penelope, and quickly looked away. "As soon as Ivan gets back . . . ," she muttered.

But it was another hour before Simon and Captain Babushkinov returned. Simon's teeth were chattering, and his hat had blown off along the way. "We lost the fiddler, on the roof, I think. He slipped through our fingers, like a shadow into the mist."

"Like a beet into the borscht," Captain Babushkinov said, shaking off his cloak.

Simon flopped into one of the lobby chairs and held his half-frozen hands toward the fire. "Beet into borscht! That's not bad, Ivan. Say, is there any more tea?"

Penelope was already up to ring for a fresh pot, for by now the first was cold. Madame Babushkinov strode to her husband. "Ivan Victorovich, this place will be the death of me! I beg you, let us announce our news now, so we may make our arrangements to leave."

Just as his invalid mother was more fierce than one might expect from a person so ancient and frail, Captain Babushkinov now looked more sheepish than one would have thought possible for a person so large and imposing.

"Natasha, no. Is late. All are tired. Will not go well. Also, the legalities . . ." Uneasily he glanced at Penelope. "Let us wait for morning, as we planned."

"If you cannot, I will tell her myself—"

"Ahwoo!"

"Ahwoo!"

Boris and Constantin skipped barefoot into the hotel lobby, dressed in their nightshirts and trading little childish howls of victory.

"Papa, look! We caught the emperor!" one of them boasted.

"And I gave him a black eye!" said the other. Once again there was no telling them apart, for they had taken off their name signs to go to sleep.

"No, *I* gave him a black eye!" the first twin said.

"Me!"

"No, me!"

Penelope looked past them, amazed. "Alexander . . . Beowulf . . . Cassiopeia—what have you done?"

The Incorrigible children grunted with effort as they pushed a luggage cart into the lobby. Veronika rode in front, dramatically posed like the figurehead of a ship. Upon the cart, his hands bound with toe-shoe ribbon and his ankles tied together with rope in an impressive array of sailor knots, was a man dressed all in black. A pair of thick-lensed eyeglasses lay broken on the cart beside him.

"He snuck in while we were sleeping," Alexander explained.

"He was very, very quiet," said Beowulf.

"But not quiet enough!" Cassiopeia added with unmistakable glee.

Simon was on his feet, furious. "Up to no good, I'll wager! Did you mean to set another fire, you rogue? Hanging would be too good for you!"

The prisoner was helpless as a turtle flipped on its back, but even so, Penelope instinctively pulled the Incorrigibles away from him. "But what happened when you caught him in your room?" she asked, her heart aching with concern, though they did not seem harmed.

"Papa, look! We caught the emperor!"

The Incorrigibles hung their heads. "I pounced, sorry," said Alexander.

"I growled, so sorry," Beowulf confessed.

"Very hard biting by Cassawoof! Sorry, I guess." Cassiopeia did not sound particularly remorseful.

Now, Penelope had sternly reminded the children many times not to pounce, growl, or bite; hence the apologies. But these were hardly ordinary circumstances! Privately she resolved to give each of them an extra biscuit as a reward for their bravery.

"And *we* challenged him to a duel," one of the twins said. "But he laughed at us!"

The other struck a fierce dueling pose. "No one laughs at a Babushkinov! I lost my temper."

"No, I lost *my* temper."

They balled their hands into fists. "And then," they cried in unison, "we punched him!"

They each took a mighty swing to demonstrate. If not for the swift intervention of their father, who seized them by the backs of their nightshirts and lifted them off the ground, they would have blacked each other's good eyes and ended up looking like twin raccoons.

"Well fought, my sons," the captain said. "But where was your tutor, Gogolev, during all this?"

Madame Babushkinov wrung her hands; she was

quite beside herself. "Yes, where is Master Gogolev? He was supposed to be minding you all!"

No one could answer this question. Julia began to whimper, until the princess hissed at her to stop.

Simon spun the luggage cart 'round until the man faced them. "Time to confess, you scoundrel!"

It was Edward Ashton. There were scratches on his face, and one of his eyes was swollen shut. Despite his predicament, he spoke with the cool authority of a judge.

"Good evening. Forgive me for remaining seated; I am somewhat hobbled at the moment." To Simon, he said, "As for confessions, I suggest you ask these ferocious children to explain their actions."

Simon took a step toward him. "You sneaked into their room. Isn't that explanation enough? And you set fire to the Left Foot Inn!"

Edward Ashton's dark eyes glowed like the polished onyx in one of the princess's many jeweled rings. "Why on earth would I set fire to a hotel full of innocent people? What do you take me for, Mr. Harley-Dickinson? Some kind of monster?"

It was then that Master Gogolev rushed in, holding a violin in one hand and dragging a man in a toga with the other. "I caught him!" the tutor cried. "I caught a

glimpse of his toga through the window, and ran outside in pursuit. Here is your Emperor Nero."

Gogolev handed the violin to Alexander. When he
let go of his captive, the man tottered for a moment,
then slowly crumpled to the floor.

"The Fall of Rome?" the Incorrigibles guessed, as if
the toga'd man was simply playing charades.

"Why, it is the clerk from the Left Foot Inn!" Penel-
ope exclaimed. "Wait—so *you* were Emperor Nero?"
With a terrible feeling of dread, she glanced at Edward
Ashton. His face was unreadable.

Captain Babushkinov's neck swelled with rage.
"Napoleon!" he roared, and lunged for the man's
throat. Dr. Martell and Simon struggled to hold him
back.

The clerk cowered and tried to hide himself
beneath the carpet. "You madman! I'm not Napoleon
Bonaparte! How many times must I tell you?"

"To set fire to a hotel full of guests is a terrible
crime. Perhaps you ought to explain yourself, sir," Dr.
Martell said sternly.

The man sniveled. "I just . . . couldn't stand it anymore. The hotel was full of guests! The Babushkinovs
had returned! All I wanted was to close my eyes till
my headache went away. Then some crazed wolfman

came and barked in my face about borrowing a cloak. 'Take what you want, wolfman, just bring me a headache lozenge!' I told him. Imagine my surprise when he reached into his pocket and handed me one. But I dropped the lozenge, and watched, helplessly, as it rolled and fell through a crack in the floorboards, never to be seen again."

"Nevermore!" the Incorrigibles crooned, in support of his sad tale.

"That was the last straw. There was never any fire; I just wanted you all to go home! I sneaked behind the scenery and set out some smudge pots, like they use in the theaters to create the effect of smoke and mist. I had some left over from my thespian days. When the ghost of Hamlet's father made his entrance, and the stage swirled with fog—talk about spooky! This toga was from a production of *Julius Caesar*, in which I performed the title role. '*Et tu, Brute?*'" he declaimed. "The fiddle is mine. I used to play at country dances for extra cash, between my theatrical engagements."

"Do you know the schottische?" Beowulf asked eagerly. He demonstrated a few steps.

The strange man was about to reply, but Simon interjected. "Say, I know you! You're Napoleon Smith! I saw your Hamlet in Chepstow, years ago. You were terrible, if you don't mind me saying so. All your iambic pentameter got off on the wrong foot. *TA-tum, TA-tum, TA-tum!* It was painful to listen to."

"Not as painful as my reviews. The critics carved me up like a Christmas goose. I gave up the stage and became a hotel clerk. But I still know a trick or two of stagecraft. 'Alas, poor Yorick!'" the man intoned, awkwardly misaccenting the words. " 'To be, or not to be!' Alas! To wit! Forsooth!"

On and on he babbled, and a pitiable figure he was. The police were summoned, and shortly thereafter the unfortunate thespian-turned-clerk was handed over to the authorities.

"Don't forget your violin," Alexander said, and handed the fiddle back to him. The man named Napoleon Smith plucked a sad refrain as he was hauled away.

"He was a terrible actor, true, but no one should be reduced to this. Theater critics!" Simon said, and shook his head.

MASTER GOGOLEV SEEMED TO BE waiting for someone to acknowledge his heroic single-handed capture of the arsonist, but now that Napoleon Smith was gone, all eyes turned to Edward Ashton on the luggage cart, still patiently waiting to be untied.

He addressed the Babushkinovs. "Captain, and my dear madame, it was you I came to speak with, to discuss our plans for the morning. But since the relevant parties are here now, I see no reason to wait. Shall we proceed?"

Simon held up a hand. "Not so fast! I'm still waiting to hear why you sneaked into the children's room in the middle of the night."

"Yes; identify yourself, please," Dr. Martell demanded, just as suspicious. "It seems you are known to the Babushkinovs, but that does not explain your actions."

"He is Edward Ashton," Penelope said quietly. "He is Lord Fredrick's father, long presumed to be dead."

"An absurd accusation," Ashton retorted. "Why not find Lord Fredrick and ask him? I don't see him here."

"It is absurd, but it is also true. And Lord Fredrick is indisposed this evening, as you well know," she replied, willing her voice to be firm. Whatever Edward Ashton and the Babushkinovs had planned was about to be revealed, and the feeling in her heart was not optimistic at all, but something far more frozen and doomed.

Captain Babushkinov pulled on his whiskers. "I don't know what you mean about dead Ashtons. This is my legal adviser. Judge Quinzy."

The hint of a mocking smile crept across Edward Ashton's face. "Judge Quinzy is precisely who I am. And I suggest you release me at once. Otherwise, I shall be forced to call the police and have these violent wolf children taken into custody."

"Violent wolf children!" Simon was livid. "Don't make me laugh! You may not be an arsonist, but you're a fake, and a schemer—"

"Mind your words, or I shall charge you with slander!" Ashton threatened. "I came to the hotel to see my clients, the Babushkinovs, and deliver a signed copy of the contract they engaged me to prepare. I walked down the wrong hallway by mistake—the east wing, instead of the west—and was attacked! By the wolf children," he added, in response to Madame Babushkinov's anxious look. "These untamed creatures misled Boris and Constantin into thinking I was a dangerous intruder, and naturally they defended themselves. Your two fine sons were not at fault, I assure you, madame."

The Incorrigibles looked bewildered. "Excuse me, but that is not what happened, Judgawoo," Alexander said politely.

"Wolf children should be seen and not heard," he

replied coldly. "Captain, the contract is in my coat pocket. Please, see for yourself."

Captain Babushkinov stepped forward, reached into Ashton's pocket, and pulled out a sheaf of papers, which his wife snatched out of his hands.

"The contract, at last!" She hugged the papers to her. "Judge Quinzy, I cannot thank you enough. You have been a good friend to us."

"In the first place, he's not really a judge," Simon said, indignant. "In the second place, he's no friend to anyone but himself."

"Enough talk!" Madame Babushkinov snapped. "This place sickens me. Now that the papers are final, there is no need to wait any longer. We leave tomorrow. Miss Lumley, you will come with us. From now on you work for the Babushkinovs."

"I—I beg your pardon?" She was sure she must have misheard.

Madame Babushkinov held up the document like a torch. "That is what this contract says. You shall be governess to our children. Pack your things. Tomorrow we leave for Plinkst."

"But that cannot be—that is to say, it must be an unfortunate misunderstanding. . . ." The look of triumph on Edward Ashton's face turned her heart to lead. "But this is England!" she protested. "No one can enter me into an agreement without my consent. We do not have serfs, as you have in your country. People are free to come and go as they wish. Why, it has been almost ten years since slavery was outlawed here!"

Captain Babushkinov chuckled. "Ah. Ha. Hah! Yes, you are free, unless you sign a contract that says you are not. Perhaps next time you might read what you sign, eh? Show her, Natasha."

Madame Babushkinov held out the contract. Penelope took it with shaking hands. She recognized the first page at once: it was the letter of terms she had signed on her first day at Ashton Place, when she accepted the position as governess to the as-yet-unnamed Incorrigible children. The contract was a "charming formality," or so Penelope had been assured at the time.

There was no denying that it was her signature affixed to the bottom. The terms she had agreed to swam before her eyes. ". . . right to transfer to another party . . . legally binding in all nations and sovereign states, without exception . . . failure to adhere to the terms of this contract punishable by imprisonment . . ."

She turned to the pages that followed. It seemed that a large sum of money had already changed hands in order for the Babushkinovs to purchase her contract.

"And Lord Fredrick Ashton has already agreed to this 'transfer to another party'?" she asked, though she could already see the answer, in the form of Lord Fredrick's signature, featuring a distinctive, swirling capital A.

The captain folded his arms. "I refer all questions to legal adviser," he said.

"Yes, he has agreed," Edward Ashton replied. "It is a pity he cannot tell you himself, but as you already observed, he is 'indisposed' this evening. I hope that does not hurt your feelings, Miss Lumley. But business is business."

It was as if she had fallen through a sheet of ice into the dark waters below. The contract threatened to slip from her numb fingers. Gently Simon took the papers from her and handed them to Dr. Martell, who put on his glasses and began to read.

The Incorrigibles had been trying hard to follow all this, but like most grown-up conversations about contracts and business and money, to them it was a train of words about uninteresting topics that simply went around in circles. However, whatever was being said was clearly making their governess unhappy, and Simon looked madder than both Babushkinov twins put together.

Cassiopeia tugged on Penelope's sleeve. "Lumawoo, what does it mean?"

"It means your governess is coming home with us," Madame Babushkinov said. "To Plinkst."

"To Plinkst, hurrah!" cheered the twins, and Veronika twirled.

"To Plinkst?" Cassiopeia's eyes were wide.

"Plinkst?" Beowulf echoed.

One look at Penelope's face confirmed that it was true.

"Very well," said Alexander, speaking for them all. "If Lumawoo is going to Plinkst, then we will go, too. We will be Incorrigible Babushkawoos." The three siblings stood tall and fearless. Variously they imagined how their lives might now unspool. They would become ballet dancers and army captains, dig for dinosaur bones in Siberia, train wolfhounds, learn to fence. They would be gloomy poets and failed beet farmers. It was hardly the future they had been expecting, but what future is? The Incorrigibles did not lack in the spirit of adventure. They had been raised by a Swanburne girl, after all.

"Hurrah! You shall live with us!" the twins crowed. "Our vows of eternal friendship shall last—eternally!"

Madame Babushkinov shook her head. "No, it is out of the question. We have four children of our own;

there is no room for more. We need a governess; that is all."

"Mama, please!" The Babushkawoos wrapped themselves around her legs. "We love them! We have sworn eternal friendship!"

"Out of the question!" Impatiently she tried to peel them off. "They are Lord Ashton's wards, not ours. If they came to Plinkst, they would have to work and earn their own keep. They would end up as serfs on our estate. Serfs!" she repeated, and gave a shiver of disgust, followed by a meaningful look at her children.

Veronika was the first to recoil. She let go of her mother and gazed at Alexander like a tragic fawn. "What a shame, that our eternal friendship should have to end so soon. But dear Alexander, I swear, when I gaze through the window of my carriage as I travel to the dress shop, or to my dancing lessons, or the shoe shop or the jewelry shop or the furrier, and I see you in the distance, toiling in the beet fields, I promise I shall think of our time together fondly, and also with shame, for how was I to know to what depths you would someday sink? And I will weep for that distant time—meaning, now—when we were social equals. Alas, that time is already past." Veronika bowed her head, and rose high onto her tiptoes, and took tiny fluttering steps away from the Incorrigibles.

"My daughter, you may have some brains after all," her mother said approvingly. The twins also looked repulsed, and mumbled some words of regret. Then they backed away to hide behind their father.

"Then we shall be serfs!" Beowulf declared with passion. "We will learn to grow beets!" His siblings nodded. The Incorrigible children hardly knew what beets were, and if they had they might have thought twice about this offer, but they would do anything to stay with their beloved Lumawoo. If the Babushkinovs had owned a pea plantation, the Incorrigibles would have gone to Plinkst to become pea farmers and eaten nothing but peas at every meal. That is how deeply they wished to stay with Penelope.

"*Nyet*," said the Captain firmly. "My wife is too proud to say it, but I am not. The beet farm is failing. The serfs are hungry. Soon they will starve. Is not easy being a peasant."

Madame Babushkinov rolled her eyes. "A hundred times I told him! We never should have gotten out of the hat business."

"As always, you are right, but what use is regret? The truth is, we cannot afford more mouths to feed, in the house or in the fields." He clicked his heels together. "Tsar Alexander, Boy, and Girl! I salute you and bid you farewell. We will always be grateful to you for saving Baby Max from the ice. But you are for England. Not for Plinkst. The teacher comes with us."

The children stood mute with shock and heartbreak, and clung to their governess like barnacles. Penelope longed to say something to comfort them, but she, too, was in shock. This was all Edward Ashton's doing, she knew that. But why?

"Bye-bye!" The Babushkawoos waved cheerfully at the Incorrigibles.

"We shall love your governess nearly as much as you do," Veronika promised. "About half as much, I would say."

"Unless she makes us do math," said one twin.

"Or read," said the other.

"Or think," said the first.

"So much for vows of eternal friendship," Simon muttered. He turned to Dr. Martell, who had spent this entire exchange examining the contract. "Any luck? Surely there's a loophole?"

He shook his head. "I am sorry to say this document is legally binding in every respect. Miss Lumley has no choice but to go with the Babushkinovs, or else she will face prison. Whoever wrote this contract knew the law very well."

All eyes turned to the captive. "Thank you for your kind compliments," Edward Ashton said. "Now, since my business here is done, I should like to leave." He lifted his bound hands in calm expectation, as if waiting for a servant to take off his cloak.

"Not so fast, dead Edward!" Simon was full of rage and bluster. "If you've schemed to have Miss Lumley sent away, it can only mean one thing—you've planned for some harm to come to her in a far-off land, where you can escape detection. But I'll not have it!"

"Do you propose to hold me here against my will, pirate? Try it, I dare you!" Even seated and bound, Edward Ashton's ice-cold voice could inspire terror. "Need I remind you? Piracy is a hanging crime, Mr. Harley-Dickinson." He turned to Penelope. "Breach of contract, Miss Lumley!" To the children, he barked, "Assault! Attempted murder! Kidnapping! One is enough to get you a whipping; two will send you to the gallows. Or perhaps you would rather live out your days locked in a zoo?"

The children stood proudly, but their lips trembled.

"Let him go," Penelope said.

Simon turned to her in disbelief. "What?"

"I am sure we do not know the half of his wrong-doings, but we lack proof—and we cannot take the law into our own hands." She kept her gaze upon him. "Release him. Dr. Martell, the gentleman is injured; would you be so kind as to examine his eye? I will go fetch some ice from the kitchen."

She turned and quickly walked away. After a moment, Captain Babushkinov did the honors; he pulled a knife from a hidden sheath within his boot and cut Edward Ashton free. Veronika gave a pained yelp to see her toe-shoe ribbons sliced to pieces. Otherwise, no one dared make a sound.

With catlike poise, Edward Ashton slowly rose to his feet. He flexed his ankles and wrists, pocketed the broken eyeglasses, and brushed off his black coat.

"I hope your friend is not so foolish as to think she can simply run away," he said sternly to Simon. "You ought to know me better than that, by now."

"Here's what I know, Edward Ashton: If I had the power to lay a curse on you myself, I would," Simon retorted, clenching his fists. But Penelope had already reappeared with the ice. Flustered, Dr. Martell offered to examine Ashton's swollen eye.

"That is not necessary, Doctor, but I thank you for your concern." He turned to Penelope. "A great adventure awaits you, Miss Lumley. May I be the first to say . . . bon voyage."

Penelope stepped toward him and extended her hand. With a curious expression, Ashton took it. They locked eyes.

"Do svidaniya," she said quietly. "It means, 'See you later.'"

The Fourteenth and Final Chapter

On a bridge to nowhere.

"SEE YOU LATER," INDEED—FOR while shaking Edward Ashton's hand, Penelope had slipped him a note, written hurriedly in the kitchen as she waited for one of the scullery maids to chop a piece of ice off the ice block in the cellar.

Meet me on the chain pier at midnight, she had scribbled on the torn-off piece of butcher paper. *We both want the same thing.*

Thank goodness for her excellent penmanship!

Even a note scrawled in haste with a sliver of coal from a cold hearth could be clearly read. But would he come?

She wrapped her cloak tight around her and shivered. There was no darker and colder and windier spot in all of Brighton than the far end of the chain pier at midnight. Here, with water everywhere around her, there was no place to run, or to hide.

It would take an ocean drum the size of a steam engine to re-create the slow-motion crash of the waves against the distant shore. The air was wet with ocean spray, and her mouth filled with the taste of salt. "If only I could see the stars," she thought, gazing up at the ink-black sky. "According to Simon, no sailor can navigate without them. Perhaps they would tell me something valuable about where I stand, and where I am headed."

As if in answer, the black velvet stage curtain that concealed the heavens drew open, parting just enough to reveal the immensity of the full moon. The cool blue light was a relief, but the man in the moon's familiar, kindly face looked fresh from a fight, with a blackened eye and a trickle of blood smeared across its lips.

Ahwoo!

Ahwoo!

Ahwoooo!

The skin on the back of Penelope's neck prickled, and not from the cold.

"Do you hear my son?" Edward Ashton stood quite close to her, unseen in the darkness. He pushed back the hood of his cloak until his face caught the moonlight. "What an odd meeting place. I would have preferred somewhere indoors, near a fire, with a fresh pot of tea close at hand. But there is not much open in the off-season, and the hour is late, so I suppose one must make do. Mind your step, Miss Lumley. It is dark out here, and the pier is narrow. A person could easily fall in."

Penelope felt strangely calm, now that he was here. "Edward Ashton. There is no need for us to pretend. I know who you are, and what you seek, and why."

"That makes two of us, then. But who are you, Miss Lumley? Can you tell me that?"

She took a deep breath. "Yes, I can. I believe—that is, I have come to suspect—that the Incorrigible children and I are all descendants of Agatha Ashton, just as you are a descendant of her twin brother, Pax."

He raised an eyebrow. "Well done. What else do you know?"

"I know you think the only way to end the curse

366

*"Mind your step, Miss Lumley. It is dark out here,
and the pier is narrow."*

upon the Ashtons is for your side of the family to . . . eliminate . . . mine." She spoke in a rush, for she did not want her courage to run out before she had said all that she had planned to say. "That is why I asked you here, so that we might speak frankly, and alone. For any family to turn against itself is not right. I am sure such a terrible act can never lead to a happy outcome."

His mouth twisted in anger. "It is not what I 'think.' It is what that blasted wolf decreed, on Ahwoo-Ahwoo, four generations ago!" He paused, and calmed himself. "The terms of the curse are clear. Only one side of the family can survive, or both will be destroyed."

"You wish to throw us to the wolves, in order to save yourselves," she said, without rancor. "I do understand. But surely there is another way—"

"There is no other way! And time is running out." His eyes flashed; his long fingers trembled. Penelope had always found him terrifying because of his cold intelligence, his fierce control, but now he looked half mad.

Ahwoo!

Ahwoo!

Ahwoooo!

Again came Fredrick's mournful cry. Ashton's temper flared red hot. "My son—my foolish son! For his own sake, I shielded him from all knowledge of the curse. I told him his full-moon 'condition' was an embarrassing but minor illness, shared by all the Ashton men in their youth. I counted on his own dimwittedness to prevent him from starting a family of his own. My mistake! He managed to find a wife even more dimwitted than himself. And now they have stupidly conceived a child." He paced the narrow width of the pier, a caged animal. "The curse can only be lifted in the fourth generation. Once their child is born, it will be too late. All of Ashton descent will be doomed. That includes you, Miss Lumley, and those wolf children, too. We will all be dead as the dodos. Extinct as the dinosaurs."

"I would rather take my chances with a long-dead wolf than become a murderer myself," she retorted. "And if you have been trying to kill us, so far you have not done a very good job." Instantly she regretted the remark.

"Four times I have tried to undo the curse!" he roared. "And four times I failed. The first plan was the best. What could be simpler? To have those three innocents stolen from their home and set loose in a forest where my son, an avid hunter with incredibly poor eyesight, roamed. One day Fredrick was bound to do them in. I was sure of it! One side of the family would have wiped out the other. It would be a tragic accident, but the curse would be over."

So it was Edward Ashton who had put the Incorrigible children in the woods! Penelope was full of questions, "Stolen from whom?" being chief among them, but Edward Ashton was lost in his own mad thoughts.

"Years passed. The children grew and thrived. Mortimer's spy, Old Timothy, made sure of that, expert sandwich maker that he is! And of course I let him, for I, too, needed the children to survive, at least long enough for Fredrick to find them. Yet he kept missing them, hunt after hunt, season after season! When the day came that he finally caught them, did he shoot? No! He decided to keep them as pets!"

Penelope thought of Nutsawoo, the rambunctious squirrel whom the Incorrigibles had also quite improbably taken in as a pet. "Unexpected things do sometimes happen," she said, with a mix of stubbornness and hope. "No one's fate is written in India ink."

"Written in the blood of wolves, you mean. In haste, I made a second attempt. You must remember it, Miss Lumley. You were there."

"It must have been the Christmas ball," she guessed. "You arranged the evening to set the children off, barking and howling and running back to the woods, so that you might stage another hunt. Is that it?"

"Correct. And this time I had a whole pack of hunters from our gentlemen's club in pursuit! They had been told the children were more animal than human, but even so, some were squeamish. It did not matter. Any of them would have stood aside and let me take the shot, for to have a judge owe you a favor is more valuable than money to a rich man. I would have preferred to let Fredrick do the honors, but as you may recall, my son was indisposed that evening."

"That Christmas fell on the full moon. I remember," Penelope said.

"We rode half the night, but the children were nowhere to be found. I thought the fates were mocking me. I feared the curse was a trick, a riddle with no answer. I thought the Ashtons were doomed. I confess, I lost hope. But by then you had arrived at Ashton Place, Miss Lumley. I began to take an interest in you. And my hope returned, for soon I saw what I had previously missed."

"Which was?"

His eyes flashed in the darkness. "For all those years I believed there were three 'cubs' to hunt. I was wrong. A fourth was delivered right to me, the day you came to work at Ashton Place, although it took some time and research for me to be sure. That hair color of yours. . . ." He smiled thinly. "It was clever of Mortimer to hide it. It threw me off the scent, for a while."

"You said there were four tries," she pressed. "What was the third?"

He covered one eye with a hand and hummed a few bars of a familiar tune.

"That is from *Pirates on Holiday*!" she exclaimed. "So it was you onstage, with the parrot on your shoulder!"

"Training that bird to howl took weeks. But it provoked mayhem, exactly as I had hoped. Once more I was in pursuit, with an angry mob at my command, and I had all four of you in my sights this time! But you escaped my clutches once more."

"Yes, for that time we had help." She had met Simon by then, and Madame Ionesco, too. Miss Mortimer had extended a warning, and even her parents—her own dear long-lost parents!—had sent a clue that led her and the children to a safe hiding place. "I know what the fourth attempt was," she said, realizing it. "It was when you arranged to set Bertha the ostrich loose in the woods of Ashton Place."

"A glorious chase! If those blasted wolves had not helped you and the Incorrigibles escape . . ." He swiveled his face away from her and briefly disappeared, like a new moon. When he turned back, his eyes gleamed yellow. "Another man would have given up. But I would not quit. Instead, I had to face facts—that despite all the soothsayers I had consulted, and all the spooky tomes I had read over the years, I did not understand this curse well enough. I must have missed some important clue. That is why I combed through Agatha Swanburne's letters and sought the old sailor's boyhood diary. That foolish, lilting poem!"

"But the curse was not in the poem," Penelope interjected.

"I know!" he bellowed. "Another cruel joke! Imagine my rage," though she did not have to imagine; it was on full display. "Page after page of useless, rhyming doggerel that told me nothing I did not already know. And then, when the news of the pregnancy reached my ears . . ."

He paced the width of the pier so quickly and so carelessly that Penelope thought he would surely fall in the water. "A baby!" he seethed. "There was no time to waste. I felt sure the old sailor must know more than what he had written in that awful poem. In a panic, with no clear plan, I came to Brighton. I gained entry to the HAM by getting a job there. I disguised myself, of course." At Penelope's puzzled look, he began to sing in a deep alto voice.

"What do you do with a drunken sailor
Earl-eye in the morning?"

"It was you who treated us to the punch!"

He nodded. "I thought it would be simple to pry the tale out of him, for all sailors like to spin yarns, especially when there is punch involved. Still, he refused to talk about the curse. His loyalty to the admiral was firm. And with each passing day, the birth of the fifth generation grew closer! I became anxious, and my impersonation took a toll on me: The padding and petticoats and long hours at the punch bowl made my joints ache. I began taking long, early morning walks on the beach to stretch my legs and breathe the fine sea air. The beach was empty in the off-season, which suited me—until the day I met Captain Babushkinov, taking his morning swim. His family had wanted a beach holiday, but he was short of cash. A trip to Brighton in the off-season was the only holiday they could afford.

"After that I saw him most mornings. At first we exchanged pleasantries, no more. But soon I began to formulate a plan." He stopped pacing and turned to her. "Have you heard of Siberia, Miss Lumley? A desert of snow and frozen earth. There, I thought—*there* is a place where a person could disappear, with no questions asked. Imagine how pleased I was to learn that the current caregivers for the Babushkinov children were so ludicrously incompetent! And although you and I are not friends, Miss Lumley, and can never be, I will be the first to say: You are a most excellent governess."

Her nod of thanks was nearly imperceptible.

"When the rich lose their wealth they fear one thing, far more than poverty. They fear they will lose their place in society, and they will go to any length to maintain it. My casual suggestion to the captain and his wife that a proper British governess would make them the envy of their wealthy friends fell on fertile ground—far more fertile than the rocky beet fields of their barren estate! I offered to draw up the contract at no charge, as an act of international friendship and cooperation. The funds to buy your contract from the Ashtons were conveniently provided by a private charity called—hmm, what did I call it? Ah yes! Leed's International Educator Swap."

"LIES," she said. "How fitting."

"I thought so as well. Now all I had to do was arrange an introduction."

"Between the Babushkinovs—and me?"

He nodded. "To secure them an invitation to Ashton Place seemed unlikely. However, it was surprisingly easy to get the Ashtons sent to Brighton."

This made her stop and think. "Dr. Veltschmerz!" she realized. "That awful man!"

"He is a terrible doctor, but what a cheerful fellow! Old Charlie was always the life of the party when we gathered at the club. He owed 'Judge Quinzy' a great deal of money from all the times I had beaten him at cards. He was only too happy to be forgiven those debts in exchange for one small favor."

The look on Penelope's face must have betrayed her disgust. Edward Ashton smiled. "Did it never occur to you that his instruction to take a January beach holiday was a rather . . . *unusual* prescription? Yet think of all the good it has done! My son and his wife are as happy as they have ever been. Constance is aglow with health. I daresay they are even looking forward to the child." A shadow crossed his face at the mention of his future grandchild, but it passed, and he went on.

"I gave Veltschmerz detailed instructions about what to tell Fredrick, but a comical mix-up over the hotel names threatened to foil my plan! The fool sent them to the Right Foot Inn instead of the Left, where the Babushkinovs were staying. Happily, it proved a simple matter to get the Russian family thrown out of the Left Foot Inn. Posing as a busboy, I merely let it be known to the captain that the front desk clerk's name was Napoleon. It sent him into a frenzy. He challenged the terrified fellow to a duel, and those spoiled, belligerent children of his did the rest. No disrespect to your future students, of course," he added wryly.

"Now," he went on, "with the Ashtons and Babushkinovs under the same roof, and the Babushkinovs craving an English governess the way a jewel thief craves diamonds, all that was needed was a catastrophe. A chance for you, Miss Lumley, to show your mettle."

"First, ice. Then, fire." The dark words of Princess Popkinova came to her mind. "You set us loose on thin ice," she said. "You were the man from the BIP."

He smirked. "Brighton Ice Patrol, at your service! There was no way to predict who would fall in, but it did not matter. I knew your heroic tendencies would be put on display. It is your nature, although I suppose that school of yours had something to do with it. You see, Miss Lumley, in my own peculiar way, I hold a very high opinion of you."

"I fear I cannot return the compliment," she said sharply. "And if the Babushkinovs knew how you endangered their children merely to get what you want, they might change their opinion of you as well."

"I will do *anything* to get what I want, Miss Lumley. Never forget that!" He seemed overwrought, and muttered to calm himself. "But no. There is no point in saving the family at the expense of its good name. There will be no murders at Ashton Place! No clumsy acts of violence while my son is nearby! Nothing that can cause a scandal. Time is running out, but still, I must have patience. Siberia would be ideal, but Plinkst is a start." He looked at her, a madman in the dark. "And without your watchful eye over them, I will have an easy time dispensing with the wolf children as well. If only those horrible Babushkinov children had not been with them in their room tonight! Don't glare at me like that, Miss Lumley! I would not have harmed them so blatantly. However, I would have persuaded them—oh, yes, I have no doubt that I would have!—to stow away aboard the ship that carries you to Plinkst. I would have prevailed upon their affection for you in the most tender way. Then I would have had all four of you in my clutches, far from England, where your gruesome fates would forever remain unknown. . . ."

"You are a monster," she said simply.

His eyes flashed yellow. "If I have become one, blame that crazed mother wolf. Would that the admiral had killed her, too, when he shot her flea-bitten litter! Think of the trouble it would have saved. Instead we find ourselves here, in the freezing dark, standing on a bridge to nowhere."

He turned around slowly, as if to take in their surroundings. "Dear old Brighton! Once more, Miss Lumley, you and that callow, swaggering playwright friend of yours led me to my prize. To pose as the admiral was a brilliant stroke, and so obvious I was shocked to not have thought of it myself. But no matter. The old fool, Pudge, told me precisely what I needed to learn. Finally, I know what happened that long-ago day on Ahwoo-Ahwoo." He tipped his head back and let his eyes half close. "There were five cubs killed by the admiral. Five cubs to be avenged. Now I understand. To end the curse, I will have to extinguish all five of you. . . ."

"Five?" Penelope's brow furrowed. If she and the Incorrigibles were the four descendants of Agatha Swanburne, as she suspected—then who was the fifth?

He must have seen the confusion on her face. "You still do not know, do you? You do not know the truth of how you and Agatha Ashton—pardon me, Agatha Swanburne—and those howling pupils of yours are related?"

There was no point in lying. She shook her head.

"Would you like me to draw your family tree? I could do it tonight, in the sand of the beach. How fitting it would be, to draw it all by moonlight—names, dates, places, all of it!—and then watch the tides wash your side of it away."

"There is no need," she said. Of course there was nothing Penelope would rather have seen than a glimpse of her own family tree—but no. She would not hear it from Edward Ashton. If anyone owed her an explanation, it was Miss Charlotte Mortimer, and that was a conversation that would simply have to wait until—when? The reality of her predicament hit her like a blow. When *would* she see Miss Mortimer again? Or anyone she knew, or loved? Surely not in Plinkst!

"No need?" he repeated, his voice smooth with contempt. "As you wish. Still, it would be terrible to meet your gruesome end without ever knowing the truth. Fear not, Miss Lumley. I promise I will tell you, someday. Someday quite soon. In Plinkst, perhaps, or someplace even colder. It may be the last thing you ever hear."

The clouds knitted together then, and swept them both into darkness. His voice continued, softer now, everywhere and nowhere. "In the meanwhile, it seems I shall have to pay another visit to your parents."

"My parents!" she cried. "But what—I mean, where— I mean, why on earth—?"

But when the soft light of the moon reappeared, Edward Ashton was gone.

PENELOPE COULD NOT SLEEP THAT night, of course. Through the wee hours of the morning, she sat up by the porthole window in room fourteen and waited for the dawn to come. When there was enough light to see by, she packed the few things she had brought with her.

Ought she take her book of melancholy German poetry in translation, or leave it with the Incorrigibles? She was torn, for the book had come with her everywhere since the day Miss Mortimer had given it to her. It was her most treasured possession. She tucked it into Alexander's sock drawer, where he could not miss it. "Better for the children to have it," she thought. "It may comfort them, when I am gone. Besides, I know all the poems by heart."

The children, being children, could not stay awake,

no matter what sort of dramatic events swirled around them, and they slept well into the morning hours. In one bed, Alexander curled on his left side, Beowulf on his right, their foreheads nearly touching. Together they made the shape of a heart. In the other bed, Cassiopeia lay flat on her back. Her tiny snores fluttered the strands of shining auburn hair that lay tangled across that sweet elfin face.

There was a part of Penelope that wished she might sneak out right then, and not have to say good-bye, but the boat did not leave until one o'clock, or so it said on the voucher of passage that had been slipped under her door during the night. But she would never do that, of course. Soon she would wake them, as she always did, and they would rise, and bathe, and dress, and have breakfast, and perhaps do a final lesson or two, for who knew how long it would be before she saw these three precious children again?

There was a soft tap at the door. A somber Mrs. Clarke stood there, holding a tea tray.

"Lord and Lady Ashton have asked that you stop by their table during breakfast. I thought you'd do well to have a cup of tea first," she whispered, so as not to wake the children. "I surely could use one myself. Might I join you, my dear?"

Penelope nodded and gestured for her to enter. They sat together wordlessly, drinking the soothing, restorative beverage, and Penelope was grateful for it all: the tea, the companionship, and the silence.

THE CHILDREN WOKE HAPPILY, AS they always did, but when they remembered what had happened the previous evening they immediately fell into despair. The march to breakfast was like a march to the gallows. It would be their last breakfast together for a long time. Each of them knew it, and there was no need to say it, but it was impossible to think of anything else, and so they walked in silence.

The Ashtons were already in the dining room, seated near the Babushkinovs. The Babushkinov children made a great show of not noticing the Incorrigibles walk by; if Penelope had not been so sad, she would have scolded them for their rudeness. "Yet I suppose there will be plenty of time to teach them manners," she thought, and let the matter drop, for now.

Lady Constance was plump and pink as a piglet and more radiant than ever. Lord Fredrick looked pale and fatigued as he tended to be the day after a full moon, but other than a few scratches and a throbbing headache, he seemed none the worse for wear.

(Unbeknownst to anyone, he had spent the rest of the night in the laundry room of the hotel, with his head buried among the clean linens. It had done little to muffle his howls, but it had proven a quite comfortable wolf den, and now he smelled pleasantly of soap.)

Lady Constance saw them come in; with a wave she bid them approach. "What glorious clear cold weather we have here in England! None of that awful smoke and burning smell that seems so characteristic of Italy. I suppose it has to do with Mount Vesuvius, and all those pesky eruptions. And speaking of volcanoes, you have a rather smoldering look about you this morning, Miss Lumley. I hope you are not unhappy about your new circumstances. Remember, travel broadens the mind! I myself feel quite a changed woman, since visiting Rome."

She placed a small box wrapped in pink paper on the edge of the table. "I will not pretend it has always been pleasant having you and the wolf children running about my house, for it has not. But I would not like it said that I am ungrateful! Therefore, I have a gift for you, in appreciation for your many months of service in our household."

Nothing could have surprised Penelope more than to receive a gift from Lady Constance; in fact, the idea made her nervous. Hesitantly she picked up the box.

"It is a seashell!" Lady Constance blurted proudly, before Penelope had even finished taking off the lid. This was not quite true, for it was one of the prop shells that the Incorrigible children had fashioned out of papier-mâché and paint, and that Lady Constance had gathered during their escape. Still, Penelope was overjoyed to have this keepsake made by the children.

"Thank you so much," she said. "I have been happy at Ashton Place. I am sorry to have to leave so abruptly." Somewhat against her better judgment, she added, "I hope I have done nothing to offend you during my employment."

Lady Constance trilled a careless laugh. "Oh, it would have happened soon enough, now that Fredrick and I are starting a *real* family," she said, with the emphasis on "real." "Really, Miss Lumley, you ought to be grateful to have found a new position with so little effort! As soon as we return to Ashton Place, a suitable home must be found for these three." She gave a dismissive wave at the Incorrigibles.

"A suitable home?" Penelope repeated, stunned.

"Surely you did not imagine that we would keep them on at Ashton Place, now that we will soon have a child of our own? But never fear. I imagine some orphanage or workhouse will be glad to take them, especially if Fredrick offers a charitable contribution to sweeten the tea, so to speak! Money can be very persuasive, you know. I am sure he would pay any price to get these awful wolf children away from our baby."

Orphanage . . . workhouse . . . Penelope felt she might be physically ill. Ironically, it was the words of Edward Ashton that gave her comfort. "There will be no murders at Ashton Place," she thought. "That is what he said." The Incorrigibles would not be wholly safe anywhere, of course, not as long as Edward Ashton remained set on their destruction—but nowhere would they be safer than at Ashton Place.

Her voice shook with emotion. "Lady Constance, please reconsider! Ashton Place is their home. The children have known no other. Please—I beg you—let them stay—"

Lady Constance flinched. "Calm yourself, Miss Lumley! It is unseemly to beg, and I should not like to remember you that way." She turned to her husband. During this entire conversation, he had been slumped in his chair, holding an ice pack to his head while waiting for someone to bring him a headache lozenge, as his last one seemed to have disappeared. (Clearly, he did not recall giving it to Napoleon Smith, but he had not been wholly himself on that occasion, either.)

"You agree with me, don't you, Fredrick?" she said brightly. "It is absolutely essential that we send these Incorrigible creatures far, far away before the baby comes. Who knows what dreadful habits our child might pick up from them? Barking and howling and baying at the moon!"

As she spoke, a look of bliss spread over Lord Fredrick's worn features.

"Dreadful habits, you say? Barking, howling, baying at the moon?" Suddenly energized, he leaped to his feet. "Miss Lumley is going away, of course, that's all settled. It seems I signed an agreement, though I don't remember a thing about it. A perfectly shocking amount of money was paid for your contract, too. And here I thought only Ashtons had money like that!" He chuckled uneasily, then grew serious once more. "But the Incorrigible children must stay at Ashton Place. Finders keepers, what? I'm their guardian, I found them, I'm keeping them, and that's that."

Lady Constance spluttered in disbelief. "But . . . but . . . Fredrick, what about our child?"

"Yes, what about our child? Good question! In fact, I would like our child to be raised alongside these three. Like brothers and sisters." He turned to the Incorrigibles. "Don't think this changes things, of course. You're not Ashtons, and never will be. But the baby will need company." He peered at the three of them until he could tell them apart. "You'll be . . . a—a junior governess," he said to Cassiopeia, and then, to her brothers, "and you two will be like junior tutors."

Unsure how to respond, the children turned to Penelope. Lord Fredrick's offer pleased them greatly, of course, for who would not like to help take care of a baby? Yet it was so unexpected, and so bittersweet, too, to come just as they were losing their own dear Lumawoo!

Penelope looked at Lord Fredrick with newfound respect. "I think it is a marvelous idea. Thank you," she added meaningfully, for now she understood. As long as the Incorrigible children were close at hand, every *yap* and *woof* and *ahwoo* that came out of the Barking Baby Ashton's mouth would simply be blamed on their influence. People would find it charming and funny, not freakish. There would be no shame at all attached to the baby's "condition," and that, she knew, was what Lord Fredrick wanted for his child above all.

Of course, Lord Fredrick did not know what she and Edward Ashton did—that the curse threatened them all with gruesome ends if a solution was not found before the baby was born in the first place.

"But in the words of Agatha Swanburne, formerly Agatha Ashton, we shall catch that omnibus when it arrives, and not one moment before," she thought, trying to cheer herself. She took the children aside and spoke to them with all the reassurance she could muster. "My dear Incorrigibles, you must obey Lord Fredrick. If he wants you to help care for his child, then that is what you will do. He is your legal guardian; that means it is up to him where you live. If he says Ashton Place is your home"—she felt a sob rising in her throat, and fought it back—"why then, that is where your home is."

"It is your home, too!" they cried, and hurled themselves at her.

She shook her head. "Not anymore." She looked up at Lord Fredrick, who grinned from ear to ear. "My lord, may I ask—who will be in charge of the children's education? They have very nearly mastered the multiplication tables. I would hate to see all that effort go to waste."

Captain Babushkinov must have been eavesdropping from his table. He put down his fork. "Take Gogolev!" he said. "I am tired of watching him mope around the estate. My wife will have to find another man to flirt with."

Madame Babushkinov turned a color that could only be described as beet red, but in front of everyone she had no choice but to play along. "My husband is joking, of course. Master Gogolev is incompetent and prone to unpleasant moods, but please, take him if you like. We will not need him anymore, now that we have Miss Lumley."

Gogolev stood and wiped his lips with his napkin. "Madame, I accept your insults as my due," he said, with a curt bow. Then he turned to Lord Fredrick. "Lord Ashton, I will humbly accept a position in your household, if you will have me." Overcome, he clasped his hands to his chest. "In fact, I beg you to have me! It is worse than being a hundred serfs, to be the slave of a mad passion like the one I hold for Julia, the baby nurse, who thinks less of me than if I were an insect under her foot! I plead with you, sir, as one man to another—put an ocean between us! If you do, I might have a chance for happiness, at last!" He fell to his knees, weeping. "Please, Lord Ashton . . . let me stay with you! Help turn these tears of grief and humiliation into tears of—if not joy, at least, something like contentment."

No one wanted this spectacle to continue, so it was quickly arranged. Gogolev would be the new tutor at Ashton Place.

Alas, his reprieve was brief, for Madame Babush-kinov was now angry. She sidled over to Julia and hissed, "Just as my husband longed to be rid of Gogolev, ten times that much do I long to be rid of you! You have more faults and shortcomings than a saint could bear, and I know you have designs on my husband!"

Julia trembled and stooped, and her eyes darted every which way.

"Fire both of them!" yelled the princess, waving her cane. "No great loss, either one."

"The Ashtons will soon need a baby nurse," Madame Babushkinov loudly declared. "My dear Lady Constance, I insist you keep Julia as well. You must! Consider it a gift from me to you. I will not take no for an answer."

Lady Constance was indifferent to the matter, and left it up to Mrs. Clarke. The housekeeper shrugged and agreed, for not even a matador accustomed to actual bullfighting would choose to argue with Madame Babushkinov in high dudgeon.

Julia stopped whimpering long enough to make a rare show of spirit. "Fine! I will stay in England! I am sick of Plinkst. I am sick of beets and borscht and my foolish love for the captain! I am sick of being abused by his wife! I would be baby nurse to a hyena to get away from this family! I would marry anyone who asks me, to escape these dreadful people!"

Gogolev fell to one knee before her. "Do you mean that, Julia?" he gasped.

"Yes! Anyone! Anyone but you, Gogolev. You are much too ridiculous, with your gloom and your bad poetry and your refusal to wear a hat."

"Ah!" Gogolev cried, tearing at his hair. "My purgatory of love is eternal! The pain! The torment! But on the bright side, at least I, too, will be far away from those horrible, dreadful Babushkinovs."

He and Julia both looked at Penelope with pity. Miserable as they were, clearly they thought she had gotten the worse part of the bargain.

EPILOGUE

A SUDDEN VIOLENT STORM POSTPONED the ship's departure until two o'clock, but it was one of those storms that leaves the softest, brightest sunshine in its wake. Like an apology from above, the sky cleared, and the seas grew calm. The extra hour for gossip and rumor ensured that the servants from Ashton Place knew all about Penelope's sudden change of employment. They gathered at the foot of the chain pier to bid her farewell. Margaret was there, already crying, and Jasper held her hand for comfort.

Mrs. Clarke alone had planned to remain at the

hotel, for she had already said her good-byes and did not think she could "bear it again," as she had told Margaret. Yet when the time came, there she was at the pier, standing solidly behind the Incorrigible children. Master Gogolev stood next to them, for he was in charge of them now.

The captain and his wife had already boarded the ship with their children and the princess. Julia was back at the hotel, being run ragged by Lady Constance. Her new mistress was as demanding as ten babies, as Julia would soon discover, but at least she did not need to be pushed in a carriage.

Penelope stood at the foot of the chain pier, with her few possessions in her carpet bag and a heart made of heaviest iron. Still, she resolved to be brave and brisk.

"Children, come close," she said, gathering them near her. "There is no need for tears, for we will see one another soon again."

They nodded.

"I will expect many picture postcards," she said. "And I will send many to you as well. Master Gogolev will teach you some Russian words, and doubtless I shall learn some, too. The verbs will be a challenge, of course. . . ." But then she trailed off, for Cassiopeia had begun to cry.

"But what will we tell Nutsawoo?" she said, sniffling.

Penelope took a deep breath. "Why, I shall send the little scamp a picture postcard of his own. Perhaps one from the Russian Imperial Ballet! It will all be a grand adventure. Keep at your lessons faithfully, my dears. I shall look forward to a good report from your tutor."

Now the boys had grown wobbly lipped.

Penelope could stand no more of this. "Mrs. Clarke, I think the children have had enough of this brisk ocean air. Is it not time for tea and biscuits at the hotel?"

Mrs. Clarke gave her a raw look but understood it was time to take the children away. "Come along, dearies. You, too, Master Gogolev; why, you look like you could use a few biscuits yourself! Poets have to eat, too, you know," she said, and took him by the arm.

Before the children left, Penelope kissed them, one, two, three. "Loveawoo, loveawoo, loveawoo," she murmured, which was all that needed to be said. They smiled bravely and waved and followed Mrs. Clarke down the boardwalk. Penelope watched them go. She could have stood there forever, watching them. If ever there was a moment to wish that time might actually slow to a stop, this would have been it.

"Fair winds to you," came the voice she hoped never to hear again, though she knew it was a vain hope. "I hope you enjoy your time in Plinkst. The bad news is that it is an unpleasant place; the good news is, your days there are numbered." Edward Ashton bowed. "When the gruesome end comes, I hope you will think of it as a sacrifice. A noble sacrifice, for the sake of your own flesh and blood. We are enemies, Miss Lumley. But we are family, too."

Simon insisted on walking her onto the ship. Down the length of the chain pier they walked, across the gangplank and onto the deck. He looked at home aboard ship, she noticed. He knew how to stand and sway in time with the movement of it. He poked around and examined every square inch of the vessel, as if he were thinking of buying it. He rapped on the mast and tugged at all the knots in the ropes.

"It's a fine square-rigger," he said, gazing up at the fluttering sails. "It's a good ship. It'll carry you across the sea safely, don't you worry." His eyes dropped to his shoes, and he cleared his throat, suddenly shy. "Say, Dr. Martell told me that my letters in bottles all washed up in Brighton. Fancy that! I was wondering, did you happen to read them?"

"Every word," she said.

He looked embarrassed. "Penelope, I want you to know . . . what I said in those letters . . . it's not quite like it sounds. . . ."

It did not matter, she realized, for her heart was already broken. "There is no need to explain," she said evenly. "I realize that you were lonely at sea. I would not hold you to sentiments written under such . . . unusual . . . circumstances."

"No, that's not what I mean! You *can* hold me to them. I mean, I want you to hold me to them. Especially now, that you have to leave. What I mean to say is . . ."

He rubbed at his hair and scuffed his feet like a schoolboy.

Penelope felt light-headed, but also impatient—they did not have much time! "Simon, are you trying to say that you still feel the same as you did when you wrote those letters?"

"No! I don't feel the same as what I said in those letters. What I mean is, I feel much more than that. I fancy myself a bard, of course, and believe me, I tried to put a few words together, but I never was able to say it big enough. What I said in those letters is no more than a puddle. What I feel in my heart . . . is like the sea." He spread his arms wide. "Like the seven seas, and seven times seven!" He paused. "Seven times seven is—wait . . ."

She smiled through tears. "Forty-nine seas is the answer. Which would be a great many seas," she said.

"Well, that's my point." He took a deep breath, and exhaled slowly. "Boy, it's good to be on the deck of a ship! That smell of the salt air gives a man hope." He had that faraway look in his eye. "I wouldn't mind setting sail with you, through all forty-nine seas and then some," he said, coming back to the subject at hand. "But even better would be staying on dry land. If you'd have me, that is."

Penelope was truly at a loss for words, but her shining eyes spoke sonnets.

Clang clang! Clang clang! It was the warning bell that meant the ship was about to sail. Urgently Penelope took him by both arms.

"Simon, you must speak to Madame Ionesco. Tell her about the wolves of Ahwoo-Ahwoo, and the exact wording of the curse, and the fifth cub! Ask her if there might be another way to end this curse—one that does not involve any of us getting thrown to the wolves."

"I will tell her. If anyone can help us, she can. She's a proper expert on curses and spookiness."

"I am afraid, Simon," she admitted. "This curse threatens to be the end of us."

"Madame Ionesco will know what to do," he insisted.

Penelope wished she could be as sure. "And promise me you will keep an eye on the Incorrigibles!" she said, her eyes welling up. "They are so clever and brave, but Edward Ashton will be lying in wait for them."

"I will, Penelope! I will! And I promise, if there's any trouble at Ashton Place, I'll take the children to live with me. They can be theater apprentices in London."

She was crying now, but still found strength to object. "But—but they would have such late bedtimes!"

"I'll make sure they don't. I promise."

Clang clang! Clang clang!

There was nothing more to say. They wrapped their arms around each other, tightly and for dear life, as if each of them was the mast to which the other one was lashed, in the midst of a swirling storm.

"Write to me, Simon," she said with a sob. "Care of the Babushkinovs' failing beet plantation in Plinkst!"

"I will, Penelope! I promise!"

Clang clang! Clang clang!

"All ashore that's going ashore!" the first mate cried.

They had to let go.

"I'll wave till I can't see you anymore," he said. "And

then for a few minutes after, just to be sure."

Her heart too full to speak, she nodded.

He walked away from her, just a few steps. Then he turned back. "If they have sauerkraut on board, make sure you eat it. You don't want to get scurvy."

"Aye aye," she managed to say, and gave a small, sad salute.

This time he walked away and did not turn 'round. The next time she saw that familiar, well-loved face, he was standing on the shore, waving, while she waved back from the deck of the square-rigger. Before long the ship set sail, and the faces on the shore turned to mere specks. Soon enough, they could not see each other anymore.

Still, she waved.

Day after day, day after day,
We stuck, nor breath nor motion;
As idle as a painted ship
Upon a painted ocean.

Water, water, everywhere,
And all the boards did shrink;
Water, water, everywhere,
Nor any drop to drink.

The lines were from that strange and unsettling poem by Mr. Samuel Coleridge, about the ancient mariner and the albatross. The poetic meter (it was all rhyming quatrains, more or less) tolled in Penelope's head, in time to the rhythmic slosh of water against the hull.

"Curses and prophecies are all very well, but nobody knows what the future truly holds. As sure and ruthless as he is, not everything may go according to Edward Ashton's plan, in the end," she thought stubbornly.

She looked over the bow at the tossing seas. The crests of the waves were streaked with foam, like the mouths of rabid dogs. She wanted to press her hands over her ears against the din of the howling wind, the mournful sound of the balalaika playing belowdeck, the gruff barks of the sailors and the moans and tantrums of the weeping, seasick Babushkinov children.

But she did not cover her ears. Instead, she listened, until the sounds of the voyage filled her down to the soles of both feet. Freely she felt the pain in her own heart, the loss of the Incorrigibles, of Simon, the helplessness of being in a vast ocean with nowhere to run to, a prisoner of time and tide.

How long would it be before she had news of them all? Would the Russian postal service prove as swift and efficient as the one in London? Or would it be more like the Tidal Post, an unpredictable maelstrom of currents and wind?

"If Simon's messages in bottles could get to me, anything is possible. I must not lose hope," she said, and then, as if to convince herself, "After all, no hopeless case is truly without hope."

But never in her life could Penelope recall feeling more hopeless than she did now. Not even the words of Agatha Swanburne offered any comfort; she felt she could not remember a single saying if her life depended on it.

"I am reminded of when I was a girl at school in music appreciation class," she thought. "All that Russian music, with its passionate outbursts, clamor, and noise. It was one storm at sea after another—oh, how it used to give me a headache! But now I am beginning to understand."

She lifted her face to the cold, wet wind, and sighed from a place so deep and sad within her she had not previously known it existed. She did not weep, for there was no point. She did not even protest. This was simply how things were at present, and she would have to endure what came next as best she could. She was a Swanburne girl, after all, and even the rising tide of *weltschmerz* in her heart could not keep her spirit submerged for long. "All voyages come to an end," she thought. "They must, for even the vastest sea is rimmed by a welcoming shore."

But at that very moment the horizon shifted, and the faint outline of the shore at Brighton could no longer be seen. The beach was gone; the chain pier was gone, too. She squinted and rubbed at her eyes, as though that might clear away the mist, but to no avail.

"Water, water, everywhere," she whispered, though there was no one to hear her but the sea. She looked up, half expecting to see an albatross. Luckily, there did not seem to be any supernatural birds of that spooky ilk anywhere near, only the chalk-white gulls—or were they terns?—swooping and cawing overhead.

"Be brave, my dear Incorrigibles. I shall return, though I do not know when, or how. And when I do . . ." She stopped. For surely her own parents had said these same words to her when they left her in the care of Miss Charlotte Mortimer at the Swanburne Academy for Poor Bright Females, so many years ago.

And where were her parents now? Edward Ashton claimed to know. Was he really intending to pay them a visit? Could they too be in danger? That thought alone was enough to fill her with a determination so deep no anchor could ever touch the bottom of it.

"I *will* return," she said aloud, blinking the mist from her eyes. "And I will put things right—but my way, not his. Somehow, I promise, I will. . . ."

To Be Continued . . .

Mysteries that leave you howling for more.

BOOK 1

BOOK 2

BOOK 3

BOOK 4

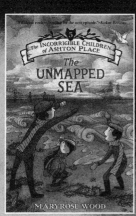

BOOK 5